I0552058

The Cornish Christmas Book Club

ALSO BY ANGELA BRITNELL

THE CORNISH ROMANCES BOOK CLUB
Book 1: The Back of Beyond Book Club
Book 2: The Cornish Christmas Book Club

LITTLE PENHAVEN
Book 1: One Summer in Little Penhaven
Book 2: Christmas in Little Penhaven

PEAR TREE FARM
Book 1: A Cornish Summer at Pear Tree Farm
Book 2: A Cornish Christmas at Pear Tree Farm

CORNISH CONNECTIONS
Book 1: A Cornish Summer at Cliff House
Book 2: A Cornish Escape to St Agnes
Book 3: A Cornish Wedding Retreat
Book 4: A Cornish Getaway to Herring Bay
Book 5: A Cornish Summer at Seaspray Cottage

NASHVILLE CONNECTIONS
Book 1: What Happens in Nashville
Book 2: Love Me for a Reason
Book 3: Here Comes the Best Man

STANDALONE
A Little Christmas Panto
Spring on Rendezvous Lane
Christmas at Moonshine Hollow
New Year, New Guy
Christmas at Black Cherry Retreat
Summer in Paradise Valley

The
Cornish
Christmas
Book Club

Angela Britnell

Choc Lit
A JOFFE BOOKS COMPANY

Choc Lit, London
A Joffe Books company
www.choc-lit.com

First published in Great Britain in 2025

© Angela Britnell 2025

Cover art by Alexandra Allden

ISBN: 978-1781899250

To Margaret Dyer Brown, good friend and long-time librarian, who has the Dewey Decimal system running through her veins, and cleverly thought up the brilliant name 'The Mighty Pen' for the new village bookshop.

CHAPTER ONE

'I could see it hurt my sweet-hearted Pixie to think of telling you this, so I offered to break the news for her. We decided it was best to wait until the lunches were out of the way, so here we are, I'm afraid,' Christos said to Tamara apologetically and draped his arm around her friend's shoulder. 'She's been in bits since we had the confirmation from the brewery yesterday. The poor thing couldn't sleep last night because she was so worried. I told her you would find something else and be fine, but she wouldn't listen.'

'You're giving up the pub and I'll be out of a job?' Tamara bit back tears as she glanced around The Rusty Anchor's pristine kitchen.

They had finished cleaning up after the Sunday-lunch crowd and had sent Rocky, the young chef, home. Usually this was when she and Pixie reheated their plates of leftovers and treated themselves to a glass of wine while old Jimmy Trevail worked the bar for a few hours. Not today.

This was devastating. Her income was precarious enough as it was, cobbled together from the part-time bar work, making the puddings they served in the pub and reselling bits and pieces online that she picked up at car-boot sales and flea

1

markets. The effort to stretch her available money grew harder every month. If she was forced to dip into the savings she'd gradually squirrelled away over the last few years, her dream of one day opening her own café would surely be over.

'Oh, lovey, that's not what Christos said.' Colour flared in Pixie's cheeks. 'Not really.' Although she'd moved to the village about twelve years ago when she'd taken over the pub, her Welsh accent remained strong, and broadened even further when she was agitated.

The two women had worked together all that time and had become the best of friends, although physically they couldn't be more different. Pixie was aptly named, and Tamara was her complete opposite.

Pixie was a little younger than Tamara so she still had another couple of years to go before she turned forty, but the long hours and commitment involved in running the pub had started to tell on her. Tamara certainly wouldn't want to take it on herself.

Once, she'd asked Pixie if she might be interested in joining the fabulous Back of Beyond Book Club with six of their other friends. Pixie had laughed aloud at the idea that she might have time for such a thing.

Despite the fact they'd often idly discussed what Pixie might like to do instead of running a pub, this sudden announcement still came as a shock.

'Why don't we sit down a minute?' Tamara pulled out a stool to perch on and Pixie followed suit. Christos remained by the door, silently watching them both.

'I was dying to tell you when Christos asked me to marry him a few weeks ago, but he thought it was better to wait until we firmed up our plans. He wants us to move back to Santorini near his family. We're thinking of opening a restaurant on the beach together,' Pixie said.

'Oh, wow.' *Wasn't Christos an estate agent with no experience in the hospitality business?*

'I know we've not been together long, but when you know, you know, right?'

2

It had only been about three months ago that Pixie had gone on a blind date with the movie-star-handsome Christos. In no time at all they'd become a bona fide couple, and Pixie had moved him into the small house she rented a little further along Church Street.

Next thing they'd known, Christos had whisked her off on holiday to Santorini to meet his family, and when Pixie had returned she'd talked non-stop about the beautiful island and its warm, friendly people. There was something about Christos that was a little too obviously handsome and charming for Tamara's taste.

'There's still a couple of weeks left in October and I'm not giving up the lease until the new year. We've a busy Christmas to get through first. Our favourite time of year, right?' Pixie's voice wobbled.

Tamara gave a sad smile. They did indeed both love the festive season. 'One last Spirit of Christmas dinner?'

'Absolutely.' Tears shimmered in Pixie's eyes before she blinked them away. This would be the tenth year for that particular tradition. It had started when one of their recently widowed older customers was set to be alone on Christmas Day, and they'd realised there were others in the village who would be struggling too. Serving a full Christmas dinner at noon, free to anyone who wanted to come along, seemed to be just what was needed. Delaying their own Christmas celebrations until later in the day didn't bother either of them — the reward was always worth it.

Tamara considered pointing out that falling in love with a place she'd visited on holiday for a fortnight was totally different to living there, just as dating a man for five minutes had no bearing on what sort of husband he'd make. But Pixie might — justifiably — ask what did she know? After all, Tamara hadn't had a serious relationship with a man since her brief disastrous marriage, and still lived less than a quarter of a mile from where she was born.

To Tamara, the idea of chucking everything in to start over in a place where she didn't even speak the language was

3

terrifying. That's perhaps what happened to a person who'd experienced the curveball of single motherhood at the vulnerable age of eighteen.

Not that it stopped Tamara from soaking up travel programmes on the telly and reading about the myriads of places she'd love to visit. But exploring the wider world outside Cornwall was simply part of a long list of unfulfilled dreams.

'The brewery already has a couple lined up from upcountry somewhere. Liverpool, I think.' Pixie touched Tamara's hand. 'The two of them plan to work the pub full time—'

'So they won't need me.' Tamara didn't believe in beating around the bush.

'I don't know . . .' Pixie heaved a sigh. 'But I'm guessing they might not.'

'Don't tell me, the new landlady is an expert cook, so they won't need Rocky or my puddings either.'

'The brewery said they'd run pubs before and won awards for their food. Doesn't mean they did it themselves, though, of course. We'll break the news to Rocky tomorrow. I couldn't face telling him today as well as you.' Pixie's voice cracked and Tamara could see her friend was barely holding it together.

'He'll be gutted. Especially with the new baby.' The hard-working young chef and his partner had recently had a little boy, and Tamara knew every penny was tight for them too. 'Sorry,' she said. 'I shouldn't make you feel worse. I'm happy for you both and haven't even said congratulations.' She made herself smile at Christos. 'I wish you both every happiness and I'm sure Santorini will be a damn sight warmer than Cornwall. I bet you won't need to pack your wellies.'

'Maybe now Toby's settled, it'll be a chance for you to do your own thing.' Tamara could tell Pixie was desperate to turn this into something positive for them both. 'You could open the café you've talked about for years. You're a great baker and the locals all love the puds you make here, so I'm sure they'd give you plenty of business. Then there's all these

4

new people moving in.' She screwed up her face. 'Drives up the house prices for the youngsters who want to stay, I know that, so there's mixed feelings in the village, but it's good for business. I've heard that new development up the road by the surgery is about finished. What've they called it?'

'Trelawney Court.'

'That's the one. There'll be a dozen fancy homes with owners who aren't short of money.' Pixie's face brightened.

'Yeah, I'll think it over. Silver linings and all that.'

She'd learned to put on a brave face when her useless ex-husband, Fred, had left her to raise their newborn baby alone. As a naive seventeen-year-old she'd been swept off her feet by the handsome older man with his rumbling Bristol accent, whom she'd met in a nightclub in Newquay. He hadn't been living in Cornwall long and had told her he'd had no family left in Bristol apart from a couple of distant cousins. Tamara had fallen pregnant the first time they'd had sex. Fred had only asked her to marry him under pressure from Tamara's father, and, swallowing her doubts, she'd agreed for the sake of their baby. Any hope that they might have become a proper family had faded when Fred had left her while she'd still been in the hospital after giving birth to Toby. Tamara could never stand the thought of people feeling sorry for her, so worked hard to appear cheerful and positive.

'Talk it over with Toby,' Pixie suggested. 'He's a sensible boy. You did an awesome job with him.'

'I think so too.' Despite never going far with her own education or career, she'd pushed Toby to excel and make the most of every opportunity. It'd been one of her proudest moments when Toby had received his nursing degree last year. 'He loves working with Josie. She's tough, but he's learning so much from her.' One of her best friends in the village, and a fellow member of the Back of Beyond Book Club, Josie was a senior staff nurse at the nearby hospital. 'Josie reckons, despite only being twenty-two, he's incredible with the older patients and should consider specialising in geriatric care.'

5

'I could see him doing that. I think he and Chloe make such a great couple.'

'Yeah, they are. Chloe's getting on well at Plymouth uni. They're a bit like ships that pass in the night sometimes, but they make it work.'

It'd been a surprise when her quiet, self-effacing son had fallen for the supremely confident, strikingly beautiful Chloe. The circumstances of her arrival in Penworthal were interesting to say the least, but, after a few setbacks, the young couple had fallen in love and moved in together. They were renting Gwartha-an-Dre, a beautiful old farmhouse on the outskirts of Penworthal that belonged to Melissa, another of Tamara's book-club friends. Melissa had married Nathan Kellow, Chloe's uncle, a little over a year ago and had moved into his gorgeous Victorian house in the centre of the village.

'Do you still want a bite of lunch?' Pixie stood up.

'No, thanks.' She'd choke if she tried to force any food down.

'I'll go and take over from Jimmy. See you tomorrow.'

Tamara nodded and jumped up. She shoved the stool back under the counter and hurried out of the kitchen, taking a moment to steady herself. It was inevitable she'd meet someone she knew on the way home and it'd be intolerable to break down when casually asked how she was. She pushed away the depressing statistics about Cornwall's ever-diminishing job opportunities and low wages, and focused on the fact she had plenty of time to get her ducks in a row.

Having a bloody good cry would have to wait.

* * *

A frisson of excitement and trepidation took hold of Gage as he drew up and parked outside the building. He was only a couple of days away from signing the deeds on the shop and then the sign in its now-dingy front window would have a bright-red sold sticker plastered across it.

6

He wound down his window and leaned out for a closer look. This was Church Street, the only road going through the village, and, sure enough, he could see the tall steeple from here. It was supposedly one of the highest in Cornwall. On the opposite side of the road was a pub, and a few doors away from that looked to be a small convenience store.

Gage turned his attention back to what would soon be his own premises. The local firm he'd hired to help with the renovations was scheduled to arrive on Wednesday. The old building was structurally sound and had been used as various business premises up until a couple of years ago. So, it was only a matter of giving everything a good clean, getting the electrics and plumbing checked, installing a new front door to replace the rotten one and then applying a fresh coat of paint inside and out. If all that went to plan, he could then start ordering stock and finally open his bookshop. The flat above the shop was in good enough shape for him to move into soon, and he would get around to doing it up sometime later.

His best mate, Taff Morgan, thought he was out of his mind. They'd joined the Royal Marines together as raw, naive sixteen-year-olds a couple of decades ago, and no one had ever called Hal Morgan, a Welshman from Glamorgan, anything but Taff. Gage soon acquired his own nickname, the Prof, for always carrying a book around whether he was in a foxhole in Iraq or a ship in the middle of the Atlantic Ocean.

'I know you've got a decent pension so can afford to eat the losses for a while, but when I looked at a map Penworthal was hardly even on it!' Taff said. 'I get you haven't settled since you got out, but there are plenty of steady jobs for ex-forces types with your background. I've told you before, the security firm I'm with would snap you up, dodgy leg or no dodgy leg. There's plenty of background investigation work available, stuff you can do sitting at a desk. You could do it in your sleep.'

Taff couldn't wrap his head around Gage's determination to cut himself off from his old life. During a twenty-year

7

career, Gage had seen action all over the world, but physically — and mentally — he'd paid a high price. At one point he'd tried marriage, but that had soon crumbled into dust. Now all he wanted was peace and to be surrounded by his beloved books.

Well, that wasn't strictly true, because there was another thing he craved and it was the reason he'd paid over the odds to secure this particular shop. The tiny Cornish village of Penworthal, just three miles from the coast, had grabbed hold of his heart when he'd visited as a young boy. Gage hoped it would work the same magic now and provide the chance to re-establish a connection with Becky, the only family he had left.

He took one last look at the shop window before starting his car engine back up and driving away. He took a right turn past the hairdresser's shop onto Wesley Lane. Gage slowed to a stop outside number nineteen. He could see it was well-cared for, from the freshly cut grass to the immaculate flower beds still boasting an impressive display of colourful blossoms. A short, stocky man with thinning fair hair ambled out of the house. He clambered into a small white van with *P. Johns Plumbing* on the side and then drove off down the road.

That must be Paul, Becky's husband.

He'd been able to discover from the electoral roll that Becky still lived at the same house, but Gage had no idea whether the couple had any children. If they did, were any of his half-nieces and nephews even aware of his existence?

His heart thudded in his chest and he felt clammy all over. Perhaps he should have rung Becky first to test the waters. It'd been thirty years. Thirty bloody years, which basically made them strangers. Would she really want him here now, dragging up old wounds and stirring up family stories she might prefer to forget?

She might not even remember him because the last time they'd met, Gage had been only seven and Becky would've been about nine. He hadn't been old enough to ask questions

8

when his father, Wally Harris, had casually introduced the little girl with big brown eyes and a kind smile as Gage's half-sister. It had been much later that he'd discovered the full story.

Gage eased out of the car and limped across the road. He pushed open the gate and made his way up the gravel path. The sight of the gleaming brass knocker, shaped like a Cornish chough, made him smile. Years ago, he hadn't been tall enough to reach it, so his dad would hoist him up to lift the brass bird and drop it with a loud clatter. Today the door opened almost immediately.

'I know you've got a living to make, but I'm not buying anything so don't waste your breath trying to sell me new windows or insurance.'

He would've known Becky anywhere. The woman standing in front of him was simply a taller, comfortingly plump and more mature version of that little girl. The long dark hair that used to reach halfway down her back was cut short and he spotted a few greys. They shared the same slightly long nose as their father, although Gage's was a little more prominent. Faint lines feathered the edges of her mouth and eyes, but he suspected they were caused by frequent laughter, unlike his own.

'Oh, my lord.' Her hand flew up to cover her mouth. 'Gage? Gage, is it really you?' She grabbed his arm. 'Come in, do.' Becky half dragged him over the step and next thing he knew, she was hugging him so hard he could barely breathe. After loosening her grip, she held him at arm's length. 'Where've you been all this time, my love?'

Tears stung his eyes and blurred his vision.

'I'll put the kettle on, then you can tell me everything.'

'It's a long story.' His gaze swept cautiously around. 'Are your family home?' Gage hoped she'd cotton on that he wasn't up for unburdening himself in front of strangers.

'No. For once I've got the place to myself.' Becky's warm chuckle filled the air. 'Miracles will never cease. My hubby, Paul, got called out on a job and the kiddies are scattered to the winds this afternoon.'

9

'How many do you have?'

'Four,' she said proudly. 'Two girls and two boys. Emily's the oldest — she's just turned eighteen. Danny is sixteen. Ollie's fourteen and little Lily is thirteen. They keep me busy!' A curious look came his way. 'You got any family of your own?'

Gage shook his head. He nervously ran a hand over his closely cropped hair. After twenty years of regulation haircuts, he hadn't adjusted to the idea that the sky wouldn't fall in if he failed to stick to his fortnightly trim.

Another perceptive stare landed his way. 'Are you hungry? My vultures left enough from our Sunday roast that I could easily make you up a plate.'

'I'm fine, thanks.'

Memories flooded back as he trailed behind Becky and noticed how few changes she'd made to the house. The patterned carpet was a little more faded, but the plain cream walls, while the same colour, appeared to have recently been treated to a fresh coat of paint. The old-fashioned brown furniture, once of decent quality, couldn't be given away these days. Scattered around was the detritus of family life. Trainers kicked off and left where they fell, and video-game controllers strewn over a scratched coffee table.

'Sit down and I'll stick that kettle on.'

Gage suppressed a smile when she opened an old biscuit tin and dumped a pile of scones on a plate, before opening the fridge to pull out a tub of clotted cream and a jar of jam.

'Help yourself.' It was an order, not an offer. This didn't count as making him proper food, this was Cornish hospitality, and if he didn't eat she'd be offended. 'You'd better start talking. I don't know how long we'll have without being bothered.' Worry lines furrowed her brow. Her unadulterated pleasure at seeing him again was starting to fray as the possible repercussions of Gage's arrival sank in.

10

CHAPTER TWO

Tamara let the heated discussion swirl around her. Tonight, her mind wasn't on *Wuthering Heights* but her own troubles. She had hoped to keep her job crisis to herself for a while yet, especially as Pixie had sworn her to secrecy until the official brewery announcement was made next month. But they hadn't accounted for Vernon Bull and his network of informants. It irritated the curmudgeonly village shopkeeper no end that his premises were considered the gossip hub of Penworthal, but that didn't stop him eavesdropping with admirable efficiency. Added to this, he was a member of the parish council, another source of gossip disguised as conscientious service to the local community.

The upcoming changes to The Rusty Anchor were apparently public knowledge. Tamara's phone had started ringing non-stop once the news had travelled around her friends, until she'd been forced to turn it off to save her sanity.

But she'd had no choice about facing them all tonight. They usually held their book-club meeting on the first Tuesday of every month, but when half the group had been laid low by a nasty bug that had swept through the village, they'd been forced to postpone it for a fortnight. So far tonight, she'd

11

managed to stay brisk and cheerful when anyone raised the subject, but her resolve would melt away if anyone was too sympathetic.

'If Evelyn catches you daydreaming, you'll get a rap on the knuckles.' Laura nudged her elbow.

Their leader (although she bristled when they called her that), Evelyn Taylor, was still every inch the teacher. Both the village primary school and Evelyn were now retired, but the former headteacher's steely gaze could still put the fear of God in her former pupils.

Melissa, the sole American among them, was the only one who hadn't grown up in Penworthal, but it didn't make her any less vulnerable to Evelyn's expectations. Their seven-strong group had started about two years ago as a way to ease Melissa back into socialising after the death of her first husband. Its tongue-in-cheek name, Back of Beyond, referred to Cornwall's geographical remoteness, and the group had become even tighter after going through a lot together. Now there was nothing they wouldn't do for each other.

'How's Josephine?' Tamara asked her friend.

'She's walking now and getting into everything. Mum's already warned me we'll have to watch her at Christmas or she'll have the decorations off the tree in no time.' Laura's mild exasperation was totally put on. She worshipped her little girl, the miracle baby she'd never thought she'd have. 'Barry's ever so good with her. Got the patience of a saint, he has. He's working all hours so I can stay home with her until she's a bit older. Hopefully then I'll get my old job at the nursery school back and things will be easier.' She yawned. 'This sofa's so comfortable I'll fall asleep in a minute. What're you going to do when Pixie—'

'Tamara. Laura. Are the two of you "yeses" or "nos"?' Evelyn's piercing stare fixed on them.

A prickle of heat raced up Tamara's neck and she didn't need a mirror to know she was bright red. Laura looked equally flustered.

Each year the club picked a theme, and this year it was books that'd been adapted for film or TV but hadn't been read by many club members. They were discussing the adaptations too, to see how faithful, or not, they were to the book.

'We didn't quite catch the question.'

'You do surprise me. I'm doing a poll to find out who is glad they've now read *Wuthering Heights*, or re-read in some cases, and who prefers what I would describe as the more sanitised versions beloved of cinema and television.' The neatly phrased question made it clear where her sympathies lay. 'It's a mystery to me how they've managed to turn Heathcliff, who was a deeply disturbed man, into a romantic hero. An absolute abomination in my opinion.'

'I thought the book was proper creepy,' Laura said decisively. 'I saw it once on the telly and had nightmares for a week. Didn't make me want to go to those bleak Yorkshire moors either. Kate Bush's song was good though.'

Evelyn's neatly plucked brows shot up.

'Well, I loved it, Evelyn.' Tamara decided to go for it. 'I hadn't read it before, but I can see it must've been such a shocker when it was written. The book doesn't flinch away from exposing the darkness that's in all of us. We tend to see love as selfless, but this story shows it can be the most selfish of emotions. That's part of what makes it a hard read. I've always been a fan of Gothic literature and this is the pinnacle for me.' Several people stared as though she'd grown two heads. 'I think the fact it was written by a woman who lived a very isolated life makes it even more pertinent.'

'Those are very perceptive comments.' It stung her to hear Evelyn sound so surprised. 'I'll put you down as a yes, you're glad you read it, and Laura as a no?'

They both nodded. Melissa was the only other one siding with Evelyn and Tamara. That was no great surprise because as a book editor she read a wide range of genres.

Josie, an intensely practical nurse, said she had better things to do with her limited spare time than read about a

13

bunch of dysfunctional people, several of whom needed mental-health evaluations in her opinion.

Tamara had wrongly assumed that Amy might appreciate *Wuthering Heights* because the paralegal tended to favour more serious books, but not this time.

Good, sensible, motherly Becky said it wasn't her sort of thing, but she could see why some liked it. That was her polite way of saying it was a load of rubbish. Ever the peacemaker.

'If anyone is interested, a new film adaptation is coming out next year.' Evelyn's dismissive tone implied she wouldn't be watching it. 'Has anyone any further insights to share?'

Josie spoke up. 'I think we're ready for whatever treats Melissa has in store.' It was a given that the host for the month laid on drinks and snacks, any sort of cake being a perennial favourite of the group. 'Then I, for one, want to see the fancy new bathroom Nathan says would make his father turn in his grave.'

They all knew about the deal Melissa had made when she'd married Nathan. He'd been her late husband's best friend, and a rather traditional dyed-in-the-wool bachelor when they'd got together. She'd agreed to move into his beautiful old Victorian house if she could make some changes. Old Mr Kellow, Nathan's dad, had been a stickler for treating the place like a museum exhibit to be preserved at all costs, whereas in Melissa's view there was a huge difference between respecting tradition and being a slave to it.

Tamara didn't consider herself an envious woman, but would happily give her soul for this house. Melissa's updates were already making it shine and she had more planned. Sympathetic double glazing had been fitted to the original sash windows. Boldly painted walls showed off the ornate white ceiling mouldings. A colourful piece of striking modern art hung above the black cast-iron fireplace instead of a dingy fox-hunting scene. Tamara's absolute favourite space was the kitchen and she dreamily imagined herself baking there. Modern appliances were interspersed with free-standing

14

cabinets painted in a soft duck-egg blue and gleaming copper pans hung from the ceiling. The newly installed open-shelving showed off charming pieces of china and glass, authentic to the period, that Tamara had helped to track down. It'd been sheer bliss to indulge her love of poking around car-boot sales and flea markets with someone else's money.

'A bit different from our cramped terraces, isn't it?' Laura glanced around the spacious living room. She and Tamara lived in two of the village's many former council houses.

'You could say that.' Tamara playfully rolled her eyes. 'Come on, it's time to get down to the serious business of the night. I'm starved. I gave up dinner because I heard there'd be brownies. Not that brownies are very *Wuthering Heights*.' She grinned. 'Heathcliff seems more like a "crust of mouldy bread and hunk of cheese" sort of guy. Ripped apart with his sharp teeth.'

The noise level rose as everyone swarmed into the kitchen. There was a lot of chatter about Christmas, along with a little good-natured competition as to who'd started their festive shopping and who hadn't given it a thought. Tamara belonged to the latter group, as opposed to the super-organised Amy who fanatically raided the post-Christmas sales for bargains to gift people the following year.

'Are our cakes homemade again, Tamara?' Laura asked.

'Of course they are.'

At least she didn't have to puzzle over what to buy her book-club friends. A couple of years ago, Josie was complaining that a decent Christmas cake was wickedly expensive to buy these days and she certainly didn't have time to make her own. Tamara had offered to make one for her and before she knew it, everyone wanted one.

'You know I always bake them the first week of October. They get a dousing with brandy every week until early December. Then they have to dry out a bit before the marzipan goes on and they're iced.'

Icing them was the fun part, because she personalised the decorations. Sometimes they'd be linked to a hobby or

15

interest, and on other occasions they reflected a significant event that had happened to that person during the year.

'You're so awesome to do that for us. It's my favourite gift.'

Tamara noticed Becky and Evelyn huddled off in one corner, deep in conversation. Evelyn was grimacing and Becky looked far from her usual happy-go-lucky self. Suddenly, without saying goodbye, Becky disappeared out the back door.

So much for being more open with each other. It seemed Tamara wasn't the only one who'd been putting on a brave front tonight.

* * *

Gage set down the scrubbing brush and stretched his back until it gave a satisfying pop. After the signing late yesterday he'd been too antsy to go back to his bed-and-breakfast accommodation, so he'd come straight here and spent the night cleaning the flat. Over the years it had mostly served as storage space for the shop, but minimal improvements under the last owners had made it suitable for residential let. It wasn't fancy, but would certainly do him for now.

He dumped the dirty water down the sink and tidied everything away before heading back downstairs. It was almost nine o'clock in the morning now and the pale autumn sun was doing its best to break through the grey, cloudy sky.

He gazed out the large bay window that faced Church Street and stared across to The Rusty Anchor pub. It was definitely on his list of places to check out soon.

When he'd been stuck in grim situations around the world, conversations with his fellow marines had frequently turned to reminiscences of home. Escapism in its simplest form. It helped when you were coping with sand sneaking into every crevice of the body and fighting to keep clean with wet wipes, to dream of sitting around a roaring fire in an old pub with real ale on tap.

16

Gage chuckled. Knowing his luck, Penworthal's hostelry would be all fake-oak beams, noisy, jangling fruit machines and blaring music.

To the left of the pub was the Penworthal Stores, which would be useful to have on the doorstep.

The young postman pushing his delivery trolley came to an abrupt stop outside and peered in, as if surprised to see signs of life. From Gage's understanding, this property had been various things in its time including a barber's and a short-lived nail salon, but had stood vacant for a couple of years after the café it had most lately housed had gone out of business. The postman gave a cheery wave and ambled on.

An elderly man with a walking stick went into the shop, probably to buy his daily paper — he didn't look like someone who'd get his news online. Gage found himself sizing everyone up as potential customers.

He yawned and was debating whether to finish up, get a shower and snatch a few hours of sleep when a woman strode into view. From here she looked positively Amazonian. Despite the dull, chilly morning, she wore short sleeves that showed off impressively toned arms. While all this was running through his mind, the woman marched across the road to stand in front of the window and glower at Gage.

Never a man to back down, he limped over to the door and flung it open. 'Good morning.'

'You've bought this shop?' It sounded more like an accusation than a question.

'Yep. I'm Gage Bennet.' He stuck out his hand and after a brief moment of hesitation, she shook it. The strength in her grip took him by surprise and when she let go, he rubbed his fingers together. What did she do for fun? Bend iron bars?

'Tamara Pascoe. So, what're you going to do with the place?'

It seemed easiest to simply tell her, so he did.

'A bookshop?' Her ruddy, tanned skin bore no traces of make-up and the natural, tousled blonde hair brushing her

17

shoulders would scare any stylist to death. Despite that — or because of it — she drew the eye. His eye. 'You'll be bankrupt in a year.'

'I take it you're not a reader.'

The sharp comeback threw her, and pinpricks of heat flared in her cheeks. 'I certainly am! And I love bookshops. But—'

'You think I'm crazy,' he said bluntly. 'It's a little quiet here, I admit. But you must've heard the famous quote from that Kevin Costner film, *Field of Dreams*, that goes a bit like "If you build something, people will come"?'

The challenge made her big blue eyes narrow on him. 'Good luck is all I can say.'

Her scathing comment put his back up.

'It's none of my business, but why pick Penworthal?'

Gage weighed up how honest to be. He couldn't mention his connection to Becky, because his half-sister had been taken aback by his plan to open a shop and settle in the village. Unless she'd told them by now, her husband and children knew nothing about Gage. Wally's long, secret affair with Gage's mother had been firmly swept under the carpet by Becky's mother. She'd replaced it with a lie that the Harrises' marriage had ended by mutual agreement because they'd drifted apart.

'I'm sorry, Gage, my love, but you've properly caught me on the hop. Give me a bit of time and we'll sort things out.'

That hadn't been the open-hearted welcome he'd foolishly hoped for, but, in Becky's defence, he could see she'd hated sending him away with nothing more than a vague promise.

'I visited a few times as a kid and loved it,' he told Tamara. That was true enough. 'I was looking for somewhere to settle after I got out of the Royal Marines, so it seemed a good choice. I'm also a huge book nerd.' It irked Gage that he was forced to defend his choice of location when it was frankly nobody else's business.

'Me too.' The confession came reluctantly. 'I'm in a book club with six of my best friends, so I'm sure we'll all be customers.'

He reined in his urge to say, 'Don't force yourself.' Making himself agreeable to people didn't come naturally to Gage. If he wanted the business to succeed, he'd have to grit his teeth and learn to like it. He hadn't paid much attention to all the warnings about the difficulties of adjusting to civilian life, but they'd been right.

'Great. I need all the booklovers I can find.'

'I'd better get on. The scones and sticky toffee puddings won't cook themselves.'

'You're a cook?'

Tamara pointed across the road. 'I make the cakes and puddings at the pub, and I'm a part-time barmaid too. But the landlady's giving up the tenancy in the new year and there's a good chance I'll be out on my ear when the new people arrive.' She straightened her broad, muscular shoulders. 'No point in whingeing, is there?'

He sensed there was something else she wanted to say, but she clamped her lips tight on whatever it was.

'I might pop over later for a pint.'

'Feel free.'

Gage wasn't sure why his gaze dropped to her left hand. Ringless. That didn't mean too much these days, though. As he glanced back up, their eyes met and he felt himself redden. Tamara tossed her head and turned away.

19

CHAPTER THREE

'So, dish all the dirt. Who's the hunky hottie and what's he up to over there?' Pixie cornered Tamara in the kitchen where she was elbow-deep in scone mixture.

'His name's Gage Bennet and he's opening a bookshop of all things.'

She ignored the 'hunky hottie' reference. That part of the equation she was still struggling to process. The tug of attraction he'd set off was merely a natural reaction to Gage being the first decent-looking, intelligent man she'd met in ages. Nothing to do with the way his dark-blue eyes had turned pitch-black as he'd studied her. Or how his fit, muscular body had filled out the old grey T-shirt and worn jeans. Even before he'd mentioned his military service, she'd noticed his close-cropped black hair and the confident way he'd held himself.

Over the years she'd had a few dates, but calling them relationships was a stretch and Tamara had never been tempted to share her house or life again. When her friends asked if she was lonely or missed sex, she laughed and assured them she was too busy to be lonely and that battery-operated substitutes were far less trouble than a living, breathing man. But now Toby had grown up and was out on his own, was that still true?

'I told him I can't see him lasting long. Where is he going to find enough customers here?' Being negative about Gage and his plans put her on safer ground.

'What about all the new people moving in? And there's no other decent bookshop in a twenty-mile radius.'

'I s'pose.'

'So is he even hotter close up?'

'I didn't pay much attention.' The skin on the back of her neck prickled.

'I'll believe you, thousands wouldn't. You sly thing. The other single women around here will claw your eyes out for getting in there first.'

'I didn't *get in* anywhere and for all we know he could be married, gay or whatever.'

'Yeah, right, if you say so.' Pixie nudged her. 'Bet you wish you'd tidied your hair a bit and slapped on some make-up before going over?'

'Absolutely not.'

The lie brought out her friend's filthiest laugh.

'Anyway, his looks won't matter if he's as brisk and no-nonsense with potential customers as he was with me.'

'Handsome, brooding and full of mystery. Yummy.'

'I need to get these scones in the oven,' Tamara said firmly.

'Hey, it just struck me. This Gage person could solve all your problems.'

'I don't need you or anyone else matchmaking, and I'm sure it's the last thing Mr Bennet needs.'

'Matchmaking? That never occurred to me.' Pixie's affronted huff might've worked if she hadn't fidgeted and stared at the wall behind Tamara's head. 'What I was *trying* to say is that lots of bookshops have in-house cafés to lure customers. You could suggest that to him and offer to run it.'

'I spoke to the man for all of two minutes and most of that we were at odds. I'm hardly going to breeze over there and tell him how to run his business so I can wangle a new job.' Her exasperation broke through. 'I get you're trying to help, but—'

21

'I feel guilty. Okay?' Pixie turned pink. 'We're mates. I hate that I'm dropping you in the shit and swanning off to sunny Greece.'

'Don't say that again. Ever. You'll make me cry and it'll be ugly.' A feeble smile accompanied the warning. 'I'm happy for you. Right. End of story. Now, let me do these scones. I've still got the rest of the puddings to see to.'

'In a minute.' Pixie folded her arms and pulled out the glare she normally reserved for belligerent drunks on a Saturday night. 'You're the first to step up when other people have problems and always there when your book-club mates need you. You were ace when I lost my mum and I poured my heart out to you when I wasn't sure how Christos felt about me, and vice versa. Now you need help and that pisses you off. True?'

Tamara tried to swallow the lump in her throat, but it wouldn't go away.

'You don't always have to be strong.'

Yes, yes, I do. Because if I don't, I'll fall apart.

Her determination to keep her emotions under control stemmed from the day Fred had blithely announced he didn't have what it took to be a husband and father, and they'd be better off without him. It had only been a week after she'd given birth, so her stitches had still itched and her boobs had been so sore she'd had to bite back tears when Toby had latched onto her cracked nipples. Every inch of her poor stretched-out body had hurt. Fred had known her parents wouldn't have been able to help much because they'd still had her sister, Tracy, at home, who'd only been eight at the time. But Fred had walked out anyway.

That was the last they'd ever seen of him. His child-maintenance payment appeared in the bank on time every month until Toby had turned eighteen, but Fred had never once got in touch to ask about the son he'd abandoned.

She'd been forced to call on the same strength when her parents had both died while Toby was still young. At the time,

22

Tracy hadn't been old enough to be independent, so she'd lived with them for several years before moving into the flat over the hairdresser's shop and managing it for the absentee owner. A few months ago, Tracy had shocked everyone by emigrating to Australia to live with a man she'd met online.

Pixie shook her head and walked away.

Tamara sagged against the counter and took a few deep breaths before straightening her back. She would cope, because that's what she did. By herself.

* * *

'Bye, lads, and thanks. See you in the morning. It's looking great.'

Gage waved the painters off with a sigh of relief. The electrician and plumber had been and gone first thing this morning and thankfully had found no additional work that needed doing.

It was half five, so he hoped the pub was open. Wednesday had been a long day, but now it was time for a well-earned pint.

Not looking like this, it's not.

No one would need to ask what colour he'd chosen for the interior of the new shop because his clothes were splattered Jackson Pollock style in splashes of pale green and soft white. He'd persuaded the supervisor to give him a paintbrush so he could lend a hand.

A few months ago, Gage had joined an online forum of independent booksellers, which was a goldmine of useful advice. But he'd chosen to go against the general consensus that shops needed to be bright and cheerful to draw customers in. Some of the pictures that other bookshop owners proudly posted made his eyeballs hurt. When *he* entered a bookstore, it was in search of a sense of peace. A haven from everyday life. Somewhere he could lose himself and potter around, for hours if he felt inclined, without being pressured by desperate sales assistants. That might not sound like a moneymaker, but Gage was convinced he could make it work. Time would tell if his USP — Unique Selling Point — would pay off.

Even after the first coat of paint, the shop's main area had already been transformed from a dark and dingy space. Tomorrow's weather forecast was good, so the supervisor had told him they'd paint the outside first thing. Gage couldn't resist having another look at the sign that had arrived that afternoon and was ready to hang over the door. The dark-green background and simple gold lettering were exactly as he'd envisaged.

The Mighty Pen
New and Used Books

Despite spending over half his life living by the sword, as it were, he had a strong belief in the power of the written word so this seemed appropriate for the next stage of Gage's life.

Gage had moved his things over from the guesthouse yesterday, so it'd be simple to go up to the flat and strip off to have a wash and put on clean clothes.

Ten minutes later he locked up the shop and crossed the road. He hesitated before deciding to turn left, instead of right towards the pub. He hadn't bargained on how swiftly his tea-making supplies would disappear and if they weren't restocked, he could have a strike on his hands in the morning. Buying what he needed in the village shop would kill two birds with one stone by giving him the chance to meet his business neighbour.

The Penworthal Stores weren't the enemy, or even a direct competitor, but it was ingrained in him to find out as much as he could about the people and places around him. Instead of being dusty and outdated as he'd half expected, the shop boasted sparkling clean windows, behind which an eye-catching display of items was highlighted with big red arrows announcing this week's sale prices.

24

An easel set up on the pavement tempted customers with the promise of fresh sandwiches, hot pasties and pizza. Gage stepped around a galvanised bucket jammed with plastic-wrapped bouquets of colourful flowers, and an old-fashioned bell jangled as he pushed the door open. That was an addition he'd be wise to buy before opening his shop. He'd be working alone until he could afford to hire an assistant, so it could function as low-tech security.

A low wooden beam almost caught him out, but he ducked just in time.

'I wondered when you'd show your face.' A gruff man's voice came from somewhere at the back of the shop.

'Me?' He navigated down the narrow main aisle to the long wooden counter. A short, stout, older man with unnaturally ink-black hair peered at him from behind round wire-rimmed glasses.

'No one else here, so I must be talking to you.' The man huffed. 'You've bought Gummow's old place across the road. Must need your head tested. No one's made a go of that place for donkey's years. I'll give you till Easter.'

His officious manner reminded Gage of Captain Mainwaring in *Dad's Army*. Although Gage hadn't been born when the show first came out, he had fond memories of watching the repeats with his father on a Saturday evening.

'Georgie tells me you're selling books of all things.' The man's cackling laughter filled the shop.

'Georgie?'

'Georgie Rowe. My cousin. He and his lads are doing up your place.'

The penny dropped. 'They're good workers. I'm Gage Bennet, by the way.'

'I know that.' The shopkeeper scoffed. 'Vernon Bull.'

He shook the man's outstretched hand.

'Where'd you get your gammy leg?'

Gage didn't mind the intrusive question. It was better than people sneaking furtive looks, too polite to satisfy their curiosity. 'Sudan. Royal Marines.'

25

'I s'pose it could've been worse. I expect a lot of your mates weren't as lucky,' Vernon said matter-of-factly.

'True. I need tea supplies.'

'I'll bet. Eat and drink you out of house and home, they will.'

He bustled off and started picking things off the shelves. It seemed fruitless to point out that Georgie and his men should be done in a couple of days, so he didn't need an industrial-sized box of cheap teabags, a huge bag of sugar and two litres of milk.

Vernon stopped at a display by the door and selected three packets of biscuits to add to the stack. 'They're on sale. Three for the price of two. Georgie likes his custard creams, and you can't go wrong with digestives and ginger nuts.' Back at the counter, he wedged everything into a large blue plastic bag. 'Next time I'll have to charge you five pence if you don't bring your own, but you can have it for free today.'

Gage stifled a smile. At a wild guess, he'd say very few customers got something for nothing out of Mr Bull. Gage certainly hadn't. Now the shopkeeper could boast about their meeting and send the abridged story of his injuries around Penworthal. If Vernon found out the main reason why *this* particular village, rather than any other location, would soon have a bookshop, he'd rub his hands with glee. Gage's sympathy for Becky increased. When he'd made his plans, he'd had no real concept of what the fallout could be.

'Cheers.'

'If there's anything you want to know about the village, you ask me. The Bulls have been around these parts since Methuselah was a baby.' Vernon cackled at his own joke.

Before he could be pinned down any longer, the shop bell rang again and Gage took that as his signal to beat a swift retreat. If a certain barmaid was working, she'd probably inflict another barrage of intrusive questions on him and he wasn't in the mood. Instead, he'd call it quits for the day and get some much-needed sleep.

26

CHAPTER FOUR

Toby cornered Tamara near the freezer in The Rusty Anchor's kitchen. 'So when were you going to tell me, Mum?'

She squirmed. She'd been mean, cowardly — or both — in ignoring her son's calls. It'd been inevitable that he would hear eventually, but later rather than sooner suited her.

'I was waiting until I knew for sure.' A feeble excuse, even to her ears. 'No point worrying you over nothing.'

'I'm your son. I'm *supposed* to worry about you.'

'No, you're not. That's my job.' Tamara crossed her arms and glared. He glared back. The new steeliness he'd acquired during his nursing training caught her out. 'Look, I'm sorry, all right?'

'Have you started looking for another job?'

'I won't be sponging off you and Chloe, don't worry.'

Toby went eerily still, as if he couldn't believe what he was hearing.

'Sorry. Again. I shouldn't have said that.'

'No. You shouldn't.' He shook his head. 'You've given me *everything* all these years.' Toby held up a hand to stop her interrupting. 'Willingly, I know, but don't you think if I could help you for a change, I'd want to?'

27

'Yes.'

That admission brought back her son's impish smile. 'There, didn't kill you, did it?'

She managed a wan smile. 'I can't stand here nattering any longer. It's opening time in a few minutes. Rocky's off because his baby's sick and you know Fridays are always jammed. Are you working tonight?'

'No, thank heaven. Chloe's on the way back from Plymouth. She's meeting me here for our first date night in ages.' He stifled a yawn. 'I'm on the back end of four nightshifts and not at my sparkling best, but once I see Chloe it'll all be good.'

How awful was it to envy her own son? It wasn't that she resented his happiness. Far from it. But seeing the young couple so in love and shaping their futures together reminded her she'd never had that for herself. Oh, she was well aware that people the world over had it far worse, but that was little consolation on lonely evenings.

'It'll work out, Mum.' He clasped her shoulder and the comforting touch brought a prickle of tears to her eyes.

'I know. Now, off with you.' Tamara shooed him away. It took a few moments before she was composed enough to join Pixie in the bar.

She heard Gage's rich, deep voice before she saw him. Despite herself, Tamara couldn't resist checking him out from a safe distance. He'd smartened up tonight. A dark-blue open-necked shirt. Snug-fitting jeans. His nose might be a little long, his mouth on the narrow side and eyes too deep-set to fit the brief for conventional good looks, but she'd never been much for those anyway.

Tamara had learned the hard way to take her own looks, and those of other people, with a pinch of salt. At school, the same boys who'd been her friends since they were five had changed into alien beings and started leering when her breasts had sprouted almost overnight at the age of twelve. Around the same time, she'd started shooting up too and had eventually towered over most of them.

28

'This gentleman is looking for you.' Pixie's innuendo-laden voice made Tamara wince.

'I didn't . . . exactly . . .'

Gage's ruddy cheeks shouldn't amuse her, but they did.

'I was telling Pixie we'd met and she said you were working tonight and . . .' His voice trailed off, as if he'd decided the hole he'd dug was halfway to China already.

'Pixie, Jimmy Trevail's waiting to be served,' said Tamara. The wizened old man propping up the far end of the bar was gesturing with his empty beer glass. 'Why don't you see to him and I'll deal with things here?'

Her boss reluctantly scurried off, but only after throwing them both a triumphant look.

'Liking village life so far, are you? I'm sure you got the full interrogation Pixie reserves for new customers?'

'She tried her hardest, I'll give her that.' A smile tweaked the corners of his mouth before spreading upwards to his eyes.

Tamara foolishly met his gaze and was floored by the unmistakable flare of interest mirrored back at her.

'Tamara, love, can we get the usual when you're free?'

She stared at Nathan Kellow as if she'd never seen him before.

Melissa wriggled in beside her husband and grinned at Gage. 'You must be the new guy. We want to hear all about your awesome bookshop. Bring your drink over and join us. We've snagged our favourite table by the fire. Another friend from our book club is there too, so it'll give you a chance to practise your sales technique.'

'Uh, great. Thanks.'

Gage looked like Peter Rabbit when Mr McGregor cornered him in the vegetable garden. That had been Toby's favourite book as a child, although her soft-hearted son would cry at the part when Peter's mother sent him to bed without any supper. She always had to reassure him that Peter's siblings would sneak him some food so he wouldn't go hungry.

Tamara tried to give Gage a surreptitious encouraging smile, but it wasn't sly enough because Melissa immediately intercepted it. Her friend's eyes flared and became greener, overriding their usual predominantly grey colour. If she cottoned on to any sort of mutual attraction, they were in deep trouble.

These days Melissa tended to think of herself as Penworthal's answer to Jane Austen's *Emma*. Admittedly with some justification. Last year she'd scored a hat-trick.

She'd prodded Josie, her old neighbour and best friend, into a relationship with the dishy Harry Bishop, a police inspector, so now they were happily married.

Melissa had also had a hand in Chloe and Toby coming together. But her pièce de resistance had come when she'd convinced Evelyn to give Quinten Moore a chance. Their book-club leader's marriage had been anything but blissful, and her widowhood had come as a relief, so she had always been adamant that life on her own suited her. Melissa had cleverly introduced Evelyn to Quinten, Nathan's old literature professor, which had proved a stroke of genius. The couple spent more time in each other's company these days than they did apart, and Melissa's next mission was to convince them to give up one of their homes and move in together. His bright yellow VW Beetle had been spotted outside Evelyn's overnight so many times it hardly made a ripple in the Penworthal gossip machine these days.

Tamara didn't intend on being her friend's next matchmaking victim. She didn't need a man in her life, hot or not, and particularly not a grouchy one like Gage Bennet.

* * *

Gage sank into the nearest chair and took a long, refreshing swallow of beer. One and All, a solid hoppy local ale, was just how he liked it. The Rusty Anchor seemed to fit all of his criteria for a decent local. Cosy, but not dark and gloomy.

30

Unobtrusive piped music. No fruit machines. Even the motley collection of old anchors and other nautical décor dotted around was quirky rather than tacky.

In fact, if it wasn't for this friendly ambush, he'd say it was close to perfect. He'd made good mates in the forces, but that had come from living and working together in close quarters and a shared focus on the mission. But now he was floundering and frequently unsure how to behave around so-called 'normal' people.

'They don't bite, if that's what's worrying you.' The laconic comment came from the tall, auburn-haired man who'd introduced himself as Nathan Kellow. Literature professor at a nearby college and husband to Melissa, the take-charge American who'd initiated this impromptu get-to-know-Gage session. 'Talk books and they'll be putty in your hands. That includes me.' He gave a self-deprecating smile. 'You're doing something I've dreamed of for years. Perhaps it's every booklover's dream?'

'Possibly. Might be stupid, though.' He shrugged. 'Most seem to think so.'

'No, not stupid.' Nathan regarded him thoughtfully. 'You strike me as someone who would do their homework and think things through before acting.'

'But?' He sensed one hovered around the positive affirmation.

'Don't get me wrong — I love Penworthal. My family has lived here for generations, so it's in my bones. Although considerably more people have moved in from other places recently, it's retained a great sense of community. But if I were opening a bookshop—'

'You wouldn't locate it here.' Gage's less generous side cursed Becky for forcing him to lie. He gritted his teeth and trotted out the same less-than-honest story about visiting as a kid.

'Fair enough. I hope you can make a go of it.' Nathan didn't sound convinced. 'Are you planning to specialise?'

'He's asking because he's nutty about Cornish authors, especially Daphne du Maurier. Aren't you, darling?' Melissa

31

snuggled into her husband's shoulder and playfully fluttered her eyelashes. From a distance people might be fooled by her feathered cap of silvery white hair, but, close up, Gage could see they were about the same age. Books and covers. The comparison appealed.

'I'll be selling a small but wide selection of new books in all genres. When I'm more established, I'd love to dip my toes into Cornish literature and history, so I'll be picking your brains then, Nathan.'

'Anytime.'

'About two-thirds of my stock will be used books, a lot of which I've collected over the years. Since I was a kid, really.' The tips of his ears burned. The storage shed he'd rented in St. Austell was crammed with over fifty boxes of books, everything from *Thomas the Tank Engine* to the complete six-volume set of *The Second World War* by Winston Churchill. 'There's a heavy bias towards military history, because that's my particular fascination. That will hopefully bring in customers from all over, too. We're a persistent lot and always searching for that elusive title.' As usual, talking to fellow booklovers helped him to loosen up.

'Yeah, Nathan would sell the house — and probably offer me along with it — for a first-edition du Maurier.' Melissa gave a throaty laugh. 'Until then he has to make do with sighing over Evelyn's collection.' She pointed to the elegant older lady with snowy-white hair falling flatteringly to her shoulders, who perched on a stool by the fire.

'They're exaggerating, Mr Bennet.' Her lips were painted the same arresting bright pink as her polo-neck jumper. 'I happen to have a few volumes because my mother worked for Lady Browning at Menabilly and Daphne rather took me under her wing.' Evelyn's piercing stare bored into Gage. 'And before you ask, they're not for sale.'

'I wouldn't—'

'Maybe not, but it's best to be clear about these things.' Her clipped tones were uncompromising. 'You are most

32

welcome to come and see them anytime you like. I'd be more than happy to introduce you to the delights of her incomparable writing if you're not familiar with it.'

'That's very kind and I'll definitely take you up on the offer. I've never read any of her work.' Gage met her sharp eyes, and something passed between them. It was as if she sensed he was struggling and wanted to offer a lifebelt.

'In case you hadn't guessed, Evelyn taught at the village school and was its headteacher for many years.' Melissa's eyes shone. She leaned across and touched Evelyn's knee. 'She's intimidating to all, right?'

'Stuff and nonsense. You're perfectly capable of standing up for yourself. You've proved that. Don't pay any attention to them, Mr Bennet.'

'Call me Gage, please.'

'And deprive myself of imagining you as father to the five Bennet girls in *Pride and Prejudice*? Absolutely not!'

Evelyn's throaty laugh took him by surprise. There was a huge sense of fun under the somewhat austere facade.

'As young Melissa hasn't thought to introduce him yet, this is Professor Quinten Moore, my companion.'

The silver-haired man sitting by her stuck out his hand and Gage leaned over to shake it.

'Companion makes me sound like a lapdog, or a gigolo.' Two dimples appeared in Quinten's plump, pink cheeks. 'Rather flattering at my age.'

'What am I supposed to call you? "Boyfriend" is ridiculous. You're seventy-five and I'm seventy-four, for heaven's sake. "Partner" implies we live together, which we don't and—'

'Why don't we?'

'What are you asking?' Evelyn sounded puzzled.

'You know how much I care for you, so—'

A slow swelling ringtone, Beethoven's Fifth if Gage wasn't mistaken, started playing, and Evelyn fumbled in the black leather bag by her feet to pull out her mobile.

33

'My goodness, it's my sister ringing from France.' All the colour left Evelyn's face. 'Sorry, but I'd better answer in case something's wrong.'

Gage sensed someone standing behind him and turned as Tamara rested her hand on the back of his chair and bent down to whisper in his ear.

'Did I miss something?'

'I might be wrong, but I think Professor Moore almost proposed to your friend.'

Tamara squealed.

'Of course, Ophelia. You're welcome for as long as you like.' Evelyn threw a despairing look Quinten's way. 'When are you coming? Tomorrow! I'll be at the station to meet you.'

After the call ended, no one spoke for a while.

'That was a surprise. My younger sister, Ophelia, is moving back to the village.' Evelyn's bright, positive vibe was at odds with her blank expression. 'None of you are old enough to remember her because she's lived in Saint-Malo for about forty-five years. I'm not sure why yet, but she needs a home so she'll be living with me for the foreseeable future.' Her wistful look rested on Quinten.

'Is that good news?' Tamara asked.

'We shall see.' Evelyn's tart response made it clear she wasn't discussing the subject any further. As she eased off the stool, Quinten sprang up too. He picked up a deep purple cashmere shawl from the table and wrapped it around her shoulders. 'Quinten, I believe I'd better go home alone tonight.'

The poor man looked as though he'd been slapped, but did his best to collect himself and hurriedly expressed his complete understanding. He jammed a jaunty black fedora on his head, said his goodbyes and left.

Once Evelyn left too, another silence fell. An awkward one. They didn't need Gage, a stranger, hanging around while they dissected this piece of news. He made his own excuses and headed for the door.

'Don't judge Evelyn too harshly.' Tamara caught up with him, grasping his arm. 'It must've knocked her for six. I didn't even know she *had* a sister.' A wry smile wreathed her face. 'Every time you think you know someone well, this sort of thing happens.'

'We all keep secrets. Even from those we're closest to.'

'Sad, isn't it?'

For a few fleeting seconds, Gage felt a complete affinity with this woman he barely knew, and who he'd been swift to decide was as uncompromising as himself.

'Yeah.' His voice came out in a croak. 'I'd better be going. Lots to do at the shop.' If he stayed any longer, he'd be tempted to do something stupid. Like be honest with her.

CHAPTER FIVE

Tamara was at a loose end. After she'd finished making the puddings for Sunday lunch, Pixie had shooed her away.

'Don't worry, you'll still get your full pay, but Christos is coming in to help me,' her friend had said. 'We don't have a ton of bookings today, so it'll be a good chance for him to get some more experience.'

So far, Tamara wasn't impressed by Christos's idea of 'work'. It seemed to consist of chatting up the female customers, the youngest and most attractive ones, and being nowhere to be found when a barrel needed changing.

'You could work on some more recipes for our Decadent December Desserts specials?' Pixie suggested. The idea was to tempt customers with something new for each day of the month and prove there was more to festive treats than the ubiquitous mince pies.

'I'm not really in a baking mood.'

Now, Tamara had already speed-cleaned the house and the week's washing was out on the line, so what should she do with the rest of the day? She had no intention of turning up on Toby and Chloe's doorstep to intrude on their rare free Sunday together.

There was the usual flea market in Par, but she needed to tighten her belt even further now and not fritter away money she didn't have. It'd be fruitless to promise herself she'd only buy suitable items for reselling, because if she spotted a porcelain pig, all bets would be off.

Her obsession had started on her fifth birthday when her late Aunt Edith had given her a bright pink money bank, which squeaked a cheerful oink every time a coin was put in its slot. Even Toby didn't know the full extent of her collection because most of it was boxed up in the attic, ready to be displayed one day. Some people would call it sad, but she logged her porcelain pig purchases in a special pink notebook and gave them all names, recording when and where they'd been bought and how much she'd paid for them.

There was no milk in the fridge so she could take a wander down to Vernon Bull's shop, which opened on Sundays albeit for slightly shorter hours. The shop was a lot smarter these days, thanks to Chloe's success in persuading the stick-in-the-mud shopkeeper to make changes. Toby's partner had worked there full time for a while before starting her new university course and still picked up a few shifts whenever she could. Tamara might even treat herself to a pizza if there were any fresh out of the oven.

The weather was mild for late October, so she didn't stop to put anything on over her thin T-shirt. She'd learned to swim in the cold Cornish seas, long before it was labelled 'wild swimming', has been part of a gig-boat racing crew as a teenager and still surfed whenever she had the chance. A little cool air didn't bother her.

The sun warmed her shoulders and a straggle of puffy clouds dotted the almost Mediterranean-blue sky, making it hard to believe in only a couple of months it'd be Christmas. Tamara ordered herself to stop being such an ungrateful cow. She had her health, a roof over her head, a loving son and his partner, and great friends, and she lived in a beautiful part of the world.

37

Instead of heading straight to the shop, she impulsively turned onto Poltaire Road and strode past the doctor's house and surgery to see what the new development looked like now. The last time she'd checked, only two of the houses were finished, while the others were still in various stages of construction.

Despite lingering misgivings about whether places like this were an asset or a curse, it was clear that whoever had designed Trelawney Court had done an excellent job. With the sympathetic use of local granite, typical Cornish slate roofs and mellow paint shades in light pinks, soft blues and pale green, the new homes blended in better than she'd envisaged. Two sets of six houses, none of which were cookie-cutter identical, fanned out on either side of the entrance road.

'Not a bad spot, is it?' A well-built older man with iron-grey hair and a slight stoop strolled out from the nearest garden, or at least what would be a garden when it was more than a square of recently laid turf. 'This one's mine.'

'It's very nice.'

'But you're local and aren't sure about more incomers. That's understandable.'

Tamara shifted awkwardly under the strength of the man's piercing blue eyes. 'Villages that don't expand eventually die, but those that do often end up losing the sense of community that drew people there in the first place.' She shrugged. 'It's a conundrum.' Remembering her manners, she stuck out her hand and introduced herself.

He smiled. 'Wilf Buckingham. My family were from these parts originally before they moved to the London area, so maybe that makes me a little more acceptable?' His eyes twinkled.

'More than a little.'

'I've recently retired from the hotel business, but I'll need to find something to keep me out of trouble. My wife, Karen, is a great crafter, so she'll be looking for like-minded people and she'd love to find a local choir to join as well. Is

38

there anything like that going on in the village at Christmas, perhaps?'

'There's the Christmas Eve service at the church, and we have a free lunch on Christmas Day at the pub for anyone who's on their own or simply needs a meal.'

Wilf nodded in approval.

'A lot more people put up lights outside their homes these days, so the village looks really pretty at Christmas.'

'What about a Christmas tree?' Wilf asked and must've noticed her confusion. 'I mean a village one.'

'We've never had one. The parish council is always short of money, so I don't think they could afford it.'

'What about that tree?' Wilf pointed to a nearby dark-green fir. 'That's got to come out because the builder says it's too close to the house. If you could think of a good central spot, I could have him dig it up and replant it. We could put it in a large pot for the holidays and then plant it back in the soil somewhere afterwards.'

Tamara's brain raced. 'There's a patch of grass outside the church that would be perfect.' Her face fell. 'But lights are expensive and—'

'If it wouldn't be stepping on anyone's toes, I'm happy to pay for them.'

It struck her that maybe this was what Penworthal needed — a burst of new energy and ideas. Just like Gage with his bookshop. A lot of the dyed-in-the-wool locals wouldn't agree of course, but wasn't that often the way?

'That's a wonderful idea and very generous. If you like, I could have a word with Vernon Bull who owns the village shop and is on the council?'

'Great. Let me know what he says.'

'I think you and your wife will be huge assets to the community.'

'But don't barge in and act all big-headed and try to take over, right?'

'I didn't say that.'

39

Wilf chuckled. 'Hotel business, remember. Good at reading people.'

Too good. 'I'd better be off. You'll have to pop into The Rusty Anchor so I can buy you your first pint at the village pub. And your wife, of course. I work there sometimes, so I might be behind the bar.'

'We'd be delighted.'

With a cheery wave Tamara left, buoyed by the encounter, and headed back to Church Street. Another distraction kept her from Vernon's shop and she crossed the road, lured by the new sign fixed to the front of Gage's shop. She swallowed down a wave of regret at it not being the café of her dreams.

The Mighty Pen
New and Used Books

Talk about a transformation. The shabby building looked completely different already, with a fresh coat of white paint on the walls and a new, glossy, dark-green door. The glass in the large bay window shone, and plastered across it was a large sign announcing that the shop would be opening soon. It gave links, including a scannable QR code, to social media pages where people could check for updates.

'What do you think of it?'

She turned with a start and felt her face light up like a Christmas tree. Gage had pulled up next to her in a white van and was leaning out of the driver's window.

'Looks great.' Tamara tried not to sound too grudging.

'Fancy checking out the inside?'

'If you like.'

'I could do with a second opinion before I go any further.' He climbed out and pushed the van door closed.

'Then you shall have it, Mr Bennet.'

After he'd left the pub on Friday she'd unashamedly pumped Melissa for a word-by-word account of everything

40

that had been said, and Evelyn's play on his name had amused her.

'Very funny.' Gage's smile was tight and strained, as if from infrequent use.

As he walked over to join her, Tamara became aware for the first time of the pronounced limp in his left leg. Their eyes met, and her breath caught when his expression turned deadly serious.

* * *

'Come inside, I'd much prefer to talk there rather than in the street.' A tingle of resentment nagged at him. The last thing he needed was her pity. Gage stood back to let her go first.

'Oh, wow, it's going to be seriously gorgeous.' Her face lit up. 'The green-and-white colour scheme is perfect. Bookshops should be peaceful, welcoming places.'

'That's exactly how I feel.'

She wandered around and ran her fingers over the old wooden counter he'd retained from the shop's previous evolutions. Tamara swung back to face him. 'How've you done all this in such a short time?'

Her enthusiasm drew him in and Gage found himself telling her about the meticulous preparations he'd started about six months ago. Once he'd found the property, there'd been the purchase to complete, the business name to register and insurance to sort out. Then there'd been the research to do on the local demographic to determine who might be his potential customers. The steepest learning curves had been in designing the space, selecting and ordering books, and setting up the website and social media sites — crucial these days.

'I've loved having something to get my teeth into again.'

'I had no idea so much was involved and it makes my tin-pot idea of opening a café here sound totally unrealistic. I wouldn't have known where to start.'

41

'If it's any consolation, I didn't either. But you strike me as smart, so you'd have figured it out.' Gage hesitated. 'Did I tread on your toes buying this place?'

'Not at all. I didn't have the money. I dare not touch my measly savings now, not if I'm almost certainly going to be jobless in the new year.' The flat statement struck hard.

'I was fortunate that the money wasn't a big issue, partly because of this.' He tapped his left knee. 'It bumped up my pension significantly. I've lived pretty frugally too, one way or another.' Gage was anxious to get this next part out of the way. 'I was injured a couple of years ago in Khartoum. 40 Commando were on a humanitarian mission to evacuate British nationals from Sudan and we ran into a spot of bother.'

'A spot of bother?' Her eyebrows shot up. 'Is that a classic example of British understatement?'

He managed the ghost of a smile. 'I guess. It's not that I won't share all the details, but I can't for security reasons. Let's just say, our intelligence wasn't what it should've been and we were pinned down. I was shot trying to escape and it shattered my kneecap. This one's a fake. After some heavy-duty reconstructive surgery and intense physio it does a pretty good job, but I'll never run marathons again.'

'Did you before?'

'No, but I played a lot of rugby and basketball. I was huge on keeping fit. It's more of a challenge now.' It'd been a struggle to reach the point where he could sound nonchalant about it all, but nothing changed the fact he was no longer fit, strong and close to invincible.

'That's a bummer.'

'Yeah, well, that's life.' Which was a lot more than his old mate, Angus McDonald, could say.

Known as Farmer, for obvious reasons, the soft-spoken Scotsman came home in a flag-draped coffin to be buried with full military honours in front of his heartbroken wife and three dazed children.

42

'I should get back to work,' he said reluctantly. 'I've got the van to unload. It's full of all the used books I had in storage.'

'Would you like a hand?' Colour suffused Tamara's face. 'I didn't mean to imply—'

'Don't bloody tiptoe around me! I've had enough of other people's pity to last a fucking lifetime.' The words burst out before he put his brain in gear. 'Hell, I'm sorry. I don't know what came over me. Just go,' Gage whispered.

'No.'

'What do you mean, no?'

Tamara smirked. 'I had you down as a fairly intelligent man, so I didn't think simple English was beyond your understanding. I said no, because I'm still happy to stay and help.'

'Even though I'm a rude, ungrateful bugger?' He might as well say it himself.

'Go figure.'

Her unrestrained laughter sent a surge of warmth racing through him.

'Come on, I'll help.'

Outside, he opened the van's back doors. 'There's at least fifty boxes, I'm afraid.' His gaze drifted to her muscular arms. 'Not that they'll be a challenge to you. The first time we met I wondered if you bent iron bars for fun. You must be at the gym all the time. I was going to ask you for a recommendation so I can get back to regular workouts.'

'The gym? Sorry, but I've never darkened the doors of one in my life unless you count PE lessons at school. I'm sure St Austell must have a gym, but there's nothing closer.' She playfully flexed like a bodybuilder. 'Hauling beer barrels up from the cellar. Digging my garden. Surfing. That's where these come from. I'm a pretty serious coastal walker too.'

'I used to love a good hard hike, but these days I have to pace myself and uneven ground can be tricky.' He swallowed a wave of bitterness. Some days it felt like he'd lost a lot more than a kneecap.

43

'I'll take you sometime if you like? Show you the best spots and those it's probably best you avoid. A lot of people use mountaineering sticks, so that might be worth a try.'

'Thanks.' Gage appreciated her unsympathetic practicality. 'It'll be hard to fit regular gym sessions around running the shop anyway. I'm not sure why I'm admitting this to you, but I about knackered myself shifting these boxes earlier.'

'I'm not surprised. So where are we putting them?'

'In the old kitchen for now, out of the way. They're all numbered, so I want to keep them in order to match my spreadsheet when I'm ready to unpack and start shelving.'

'Right, you go inside. I'll haul the boxes in. You stack.' She smiled and waved him away.

Gage could hear his old mates laughing to hear anyone ordering him around this way, but he worked hard to keep a straight face in case he offended her again.

* * *

'So, what made you join the marines?' Tamara picked up her steaming mug. As soon as they'd finished, he'd offered to put the kettle on.

'I was living in Bristol. I'd just turned sixteen and hated school. Me and my mates were always bunking off. We were aimlessly wandering around the city centre one day and passed a recruiting office. Someone dared me to go in and so I did. It didn't take much for the chap to talk me into applying.'

'That's very young. What did your parents think? Did they support you?'

He was slow to answer. 'By that time, it was only me and my mum. We weren't hitting it off. Usual teenage stuff.' Gage's smile didn't reach his dark, moody eyes. 'The training was tough, but I relished the discipline. The camaraderie. All the travel. Later on, I went to night classes and retook my exams, and eventually got a degree in history. That's when they sent me to officer training. Not much more to say, really.'

44

At a shrewd guess, she'd say it was nowhere close to the full story.

'What about you?'

'Born and bred in Penworthal. My parents both passed away within a couple of months of each other – cancer – when I was only twenty-three.'

'I'm sorry, that must've been tough for you.'

'It was awful.' Tamara didn't know him well enough to say any more. 'I've one sister, Tracy, who used to manage the hairdresser's shop but now lives in Australia with her partner. My childhood was nothing out of the ordinary, but, like you, it all changed when I was just a teenager.'

Shock flickered over his face when she told him succinctly about Toby.

'I don't need you feeling sorry for me, thank you very much.'

'Sorry for you? Who says I am? I can't believe you're old enough to have a twenty-two-year-old son, that's all.'

'You haven't seen me first thing in the morning.' Tamara realised what she'd said and covered her face with her hands. When she peeked through her fingers, his face was redder than hers. 'Forget I said that. Please.' She studied him some more. 'You should grow your hair longer,' she blurted out. What was it with her and her big mouth around this man?

'My hair?' Gage ran a hand self-consciously over his close-cropped head.

'Then you'd resemble Hugh Grant and pull the female customers in droves.'

The puzzlement on his face said he didn't have a clue what she was talking about. Why would he? Macho Royal Marines probably didn't watch romcoms. Unless they had wives or girlfriends who forced them to, something else she had absolutely no business touching upon. 'You've never heard of *Notting Hill*, have you?'

'The neighbourhood in London?'

45

'No, well, yes, but . . .' Talk about tying herself in knots. 'It's the name of one of my favourite films.' By the time she finished explaining the plot, Gage's smile was positively impish.

'So if I'm to be the floppy-haired, shy bookshop owner, who's playing Julia Roberts' part? I can't quite see any stunning A-list Hollywood actresses stumbling across The Mighty Pen and swooning over me.'

Like Hugh Grant in the film, Gage genuinely had no idea how interesting and outright sexy a lot of women might find him. Not that she did herself of course.

'I bet she'd be high-maintenance, though, and that's not my style.' He shuddered, as though it had struck a nerve.

'Oi, all right to come in, mate?' Georgie Rowe threw open the kitchen door and ambled in, grinning at them both. 'Sitting down on the job? Won't get no work done that way. The wife wanted me out from under her feet, so I thought I'd finish putting your shelves together.' His beady eyes registered Tamara's presence. 'Didn't interrupt nothing, did I?' A coarse laugh burst out of him.

'Tamara's been kind enough to help me shift all these boxes.'

'I'd better be off.' She exhaled with relief and was glad to be saved from herself. 'Things to do. See you around.'

46

CHAPTER SIX

'Here we go, girls.' Tamara strode out from the pub kitchen carrying two loaded plates. 'You're my guinea pigs today. These are two of the recipes I'm trying out for our Decadent December Desserts specials. The first is a spiced Victoria Sandwich cake. I brushed the cooked and cooled cake with a lightly spiced sugar syrup, added a touch of the same spices to the cream and used a tart blackcurrant jam to change it up. There are also mincemeat, fresh lemon and clotted cream shortbread fingers.' Tamara set the plates on the table before flopping into the nearest vacant chair between Melissa and Josie. 'I need your honest opinions so don't be shy.'

Josie snorted. 'As if.'

Evelyn had sent a group message asking anyone free this morning to join her and her sister for coffee. If curiosity killed the cat, there would be an awful lot of dead moggies around Penworthal. Tamara knew for a fact that Josie had switched shifts and Melissa had postponed a Zoom meeting with one of her authors by claiming a fictitious cold, all so they wouldn't miss out. Amy was furious she couldn't get out of being in court today. Laura was all set to come and bring the baby with her, but Josephine had been poorly in the night so

47

they were stuck at home. Becky wasn't here yet and no one knew if she was on her way or not.

'OMG, this sponge is awesome.' Melissa exhaled a happy sigh and licked a blob of cream off her fingers.

'It passes your dry-cake test, I hope?' Tamara asked. It was something of a standing joke that her American friend didn't have a high opinion of most British cakes.

'Oh, it sure does. Nathan would wolf this down too.'

'You know what you're doing all right.' Josie chimed in. 'I'm not a huge mincemeat fan, but you haven't put too much in the shortbread and the lemon makes all the difference.' She snatched another off the plate.

'Tell us quick, before they arrive,' Melissa said. 'You said you had something on our mystery guest — so dish the dirt.'

Tamara leaned in closer. 'Chloe was home from uni and working in the shop on Saturday. Vernon had heard the gossip about Evelyn's sister coming and knew Chloe was in here on Friday evening, so he asked for all the details of what she'd heard. Apparently, Vernon is the same age as Ophelia and they went to school together. He reckons there was some sort of family row and Ophelia left. Hasn't been back since.'

'What was it about?' Melissa asked.

'He either wouldn't say, or didn't know.'

'I didn't expect such a wonderful turnout on a Monday morning.' Evelyn's brisk voice put a stop to their speculations. 'I'd like you all to meet my sister, Ophelia.'

The woman, who took a dainty step forward, made Tamara feel like a huge, ungainly lump. Her birdlike figure, expertly cut dark hair, subtle make-up and beautifully cut black wool trousers and grey silk blouse all screamed French chic. And money. Ophelia obviously subscribed to Wallis Simpson's mantra that a woman could never be too rich or too thin. Tamara couldn't help wondering why she'd made the sudden move from France. Judging by the sisters' awkward body language, it seemed unlikely that loving and missing each other topped the list of reasons.

48

'*Bonjour, mes amis.*' Ophelia's piercing gaze swept around them all. 'Evelyn's told me so much about your little group. I had no idea book clubs were still a thing, but I suppose in out-of-the-way places where there's nothing else to do, you have to make your own entertainment.' The implication was that the group's name was more than appropriate. 'I believe I shall find it amusing to join you next month.'

The silence was deafening until Melissa tactfully jumped in and assured the acid-tongued stranger that she'd be very welcome.

'Help yourself to cake and I'll fetch the coffees.' Tamara jumped back up.

'I'll have a *café au lait*,' Ophelia said peremptorily.

'Sorry, but we only do Americano, latte or cappuccino.' She resented the need to apologise. 'I think a latte is the closest to what you're used to.'

'Perhaps, but the proportion of milk in a latte is much higher. Unappealingly so. A *café au lait* is far more coffee-forward. I will have an Americano instead. Black.' The Gallic shrug made her disdain clear and Tamara's hackles rose. Ophelia was as Cornish as her sister, so who did she think she was fooling with the sophisticated French act?

Ophelia's brittle voice followed her to the bar as she sharply turned down Evelyn's offer of cake with the dismissive statement that she *never* ate between meals.

'Who's the snooty cow?' Pixie whispered. 'Has she got a poker up her bum?'

'If she doesn't, then it won't be long before Evelyn shoves one there.' Tamara's prediction made her friend snort. 'That's her sister, Ophelia. She's been living in France.' She passed on their orders and Pixie soon had them ready for her to carry back.

The usual chatter started up again.

'A little birdie tells me you were seen helping the hunky Mr Bennet out on Sunday. Stocking his shelves, were you?' Melissa's innuendo-laden comments set off a round of raucous laughter.

49

'I only gave him a hand carrying a few boxes in.' Tamara took a swig of hot coffee to cover the flush creeping across her cheeks.

'If you say so.' Josie smirked.

'Has anyone else had a sneak peek at the new houses?' By the time Tamara had told them about meeting Wilf Buckingham and everything he'd said, the conversation changed tack. Melissa was all for welcoming the newcomers and making the most of their new ideas. Anything that made the village livelier and more of a community was good in her opinion. Evelyn, as expected, was a little more reserved in her judgement, needing proof that the new arrivals had staying power. And Josie said she didn't have time for knitting groups and choirs, but if that's what people wanted then it was fine by her. The response to Wilf's idea of a village Christmas tree, though, was overwhelmingly positive.

Only Ophelia remained aloof, languidly sipping her coffee as though wondering how much longer she had to keep up the pretence of being interested.

'How's Quinten?' Josie asked Evelyn, with a pointed stare. 'I thought you were off to Lynmouth this weekend for that ballroom dancing thing?'

'It was a possibility at some point, but now Ophelia's here I'm far too busy. Quinten understands. We've spoken on the phone a few times.' Underneath the brisk tone lurked a clear air of disappointment. 'We should be going.' Evelyn slipped her coat back on.

It saddened Tamara to see her friend's hair fixed back in its old, severe style and the more flattering colours she'd started wearing nowhere to be seen. 'We're off to Truro so Ophelia can shop for a few things.'

'I doubt I'll find anything stylish, but sometimes one has to make do.' The dismissive comment came with another of Ophelia's sweeping glances that encompassed them all, and their surroundings. '*Au revoir*.'

50

There was a round of muted goodbyes, followed by stony silence until the sisters were out of earshot.

'So, who else around here might know what the story is with Evelyn and Madame Prissy?'

She had to smile. Melissa would get to the bottom of this if she died trying. 'No idea. Some of us have to get back to work. Pixie needs milk from the shop and I need a word with Mr Cheerful himself about the possible Christmas tree. See you later, girls.'

* * *

Through the shop window, Gage spotted the woman who'd filled his thoughts since yesterday rushing out of the pub and racing off down the road. He dithered for a minute, then grabbed his keys and hurried out of the door, remembering just in time to lock it behind him. Before he could call out to her, Tamara dived into Vernon Bull's shop. Without stopping to wonder why he was so intent on chasing after her, Gage set off in a loping half-jog, half-walk.

The bell jangled when he threw open the door and the next thing he knew, his forehead cracked on the low oak beam. The wood won. He stumbled, tripped over a display of toilet rolls and crashed to the floor in a crumpled heap.

'Oh, my God — are you all right?'

It was almost worth the pain shooting through his bad knee when Tamara tore herself away from talking to Vernon and raced across to bend over him. She was close enough that her subtle spicy perfume overrode the pungent smell of disinfectant from the nearby shelf of cleaning supplies. He worked on breathing through the shock so he could assess whether getting back on his feet was a possibility.

'Should we fetch the doctor? Hopefully Judy's in the surgery.' Worry seeped the colour from her skin.

'Hang on a minute.' Gage managed to roll up to sitting.

51

'Let me take a look.' The shopkeeper muscled in. 'I'm St John's Ambulance Brigade. I've done the course.'

It wouldn't be tactful to point out that his own battlefield first-aid training trumped the shopkeeper's any day. He'd learned the hard way that there weren't always qualified medics around when you needed them.

Tamara crouched beside him. 'If you feel it's the right thing to do, we'll help you up. Vernon, could you bring a chair?' She threw the man a pointed look, and he huffed but disappeared towards the back of the shop.

Gage rubbed his sore head and decided it wasn't too bad, although he'd probably have a knot in it later. He cautiously stretched out his left leg and massaged the knee. The pain had settled to a nagging ache. 'I'm pretty sure it's only twisted.' Not that 'only twisted' was good, but in comparison to the alternatives he'd take it.

'Here you go, son.' Vernon set an old wooden chair next to them. His brow was knotted with worry. No doubt he was afraid Gage would sue him. 'Think you're up to it?'

Gage opened his mouth to warn them he wasn't a light-weight, but shut it equally fast when Tamara pinned him with a stern glare. It said if he didn't believe she was capable of lifting him with one hand tied behind her back, he was a bigger idiot than she'd thought.

'I think so. Thanks.' It didn't escape his notice that she swiftly positioned herself on his left side to take the majority of the strain. Halfway up, Vernon lurched so Tamara slid her arm around Gage's waist to steady him and relieve the pressure on his leg.

'Tea, I think, Mr Bull. Plenty of sugar.'

There was no medical proof that the common remedy beloved by all British people worked, but in houses all over the country, and on innumerable television shows, they used it for everything. Tea was accepted as the universal cure. Actually, Gage detested sweet drinks. In fact, he rarely touched sweet things of any sort. Another of Tamara's quelling looks came his way, so he didn't say a word.

52

'When you've had your drink, we'll either take you to the surgery or call Judy to come here. Your choice.'

Before he had a chance to decide which was the lesser of the two evils, Georgie Rowe came in.

'Oi, what's up with you, mate?' The builder simultaneously peered at Gage and selected a tin of peas.

By the time Vernon had pompously run through an inordinately detailed explanation, several more customers had trickled in. The whole rigmarole was gone through again until Gage felt like a zoo exhibit. The shopkeeper would start selling tickets soon.

'I'll fetch my car to run you up to the surgery,' Tamara said firmly. 'Don't you dare move until I get back. I've still got Toby's crutches in my garage from when he broke his ankle. You can use those.'

'Thanks.'

'No probs.'

The door bell tinkled again and Gage glanced up to see who else had arrived to join the festivities.

'Oh, my love, what on earth have you done to yourself?'

The sight of Becky's white face pained him worse than the knee. Amazingly, in a village this small, they hadn't bumped into each other since his misguided visit just over a week ago. Probably by design on her part. He couldn't speak for the lump in his throat. Her over-the-top reaction wouldn't go unnoticed and could bring trouble in its wake.

'He fell and hurt his knee, but we knew what to do to help,' Vernon said boastfully.

'I'm getting my car, Becky, and taking him to see the doc.'

He couldn't help thinking that Tamara would've made a good soldier. She'd assessed the situation and taken action. Questions could wait until later.

'Tea, Mr Bull?' Tamara's sharp question presented as more of an order, and the man turned puce. Being told what to do in his own domain didn't sit well.

He scuttled off and Tamara followed suit. By some sort of osmosis, the few customers scattered around the place and

53

pretended to get on with their shopping. Whispered conversations drifted his way and Gage could only imagine the wild speculations being dreamed up.

'If you're being looked after, I'll get on home,' Becky muttered, still clutching her handbag to her chest.

'I'm fine. Don't worry about me. Honest.'

She blinked back tears and ducked her head in a brief nod, then couldn't get out of there fast enough. Whatever shopping she'd come in for clearly wasn't as important as making her escape without being plagued by questions.

'Here you go.' Vernon reappeared and thrust a mug in his hand. 'If you're all right, I need to get back to serving.'

'Of course. Thanks.' Heaven forbid an injured customer should hold up the wheels of commerce.

Gage winced as the sickly-sweet tea hit his tastebuds, but dutifully gulped it down. He'd caused enough trouble one way or another today.

* * *

Tamara stared unseeingly at the dog-eared magazine, a spring issue touting how to attain a beach-worthy body in four weeks. Calling someone 'my love' was a common expression in Cornwall, so it hadn't been strange to hear Becky spontaneously call Gage that at the shop. But what did niggle her was Becky's pale, frightened expression. It went far above the more normal level of concern everyone else had shown for Gage, considering he was basically a stranger. In the car he didn't say a single word. Of course he was in pain, so might not have felt up to talking, but she strongly suspected he'd taken refuge in that excuse to avoid answering any questions.

'Good news.' Judy appeared, smiling broadly.

Behind her, Gage limped stoically along, leaning heavily on the crutches.

'He was lucky. He hasn't wrecked the artificial knee or broken any bones around it. Some of the ligaments are

54

sprained and there's significant bruising. Painkillers. Rest.' She nodded at him. 'Use the crutches for a couple of weeks to keep weight-bearing to a minimum. No stairs, unless it's unavoidable, and then only if someone is around to help. You're generally a fit man, so I'd say within a month you'll be back to normal.'

Frustration pulsed off him. The timing couldn't be worse.

'I'll look out for him, Judy, and thanks for fitting us in.'

'You're welcome. Who needs a lunch break anyway?' The doctor laughed.

Tamara liked Judy. They were about the same age and she got the impression the other woman was lonely too. Her position as the village doctor was isolating because it wasn't easy to make friends with people who were also your patients. Once, she tentatively suggested that Judy might consider joining the book club, but the offer was turned down on the basis that her long, often unpredictable hours wouldn't allow for it.

'Come on, let's get you home.' Tamara was struck by the realisation that it wasn't that simple. 'You've moved your stuff into the shop flat, haven't you?'

'Yeah.' Gage sounded wary, as if it were a trick question.

Out in the car, she planted her hands on the steering wheel and turned to him. 'You won't be able to manage the stairs. My sofa opens out to a double bed and I've got a downstairs loo, so you'd better come and stay with me.'

'I couldn't possibly—'

'Do you have a better idea?'

His silence answered for him.

'Didn't think so.'

Gage glowered. 'Did anyone ever tell you that you're pushy?'

'I bet you wouldn't say that to another man.' She turned on him with a vengeance. 'You'd call him take-charge and capable.'

'Sorry. All I really meant was that you didn't need to—'

'Worry about you? It's what friends do. I hope we're that.'

55

'Yeah. Yeah, we are.' His head drooped and the tips of his ears turned pink. 'About what happened at the shop — with Becky — it's tricky.' A sigh puffed out of him.

'It would be. You don't do simple. I've worked that out already.'

That brought out a semblance of a smile.

'So, are you going to accept my offer or keep on being stubborn?'

She could tell it was on the tip of his tongue to argue. It certainly would be on hers if things had been the other way around. Neither of them liked the idea of accepting help unless they were absolutely forced to. Recognising the similarity between them made her uneasy.

'I'll accept your offer for tonight, and then we'll see.'

She could tease him about sounding so grudging, but put herself in his shoes and let him keep the rest of his pride intact.

'Okay. Number eight, Chapel Street, next stop.'

Now she could smile, but the terror that had consumed her when she'd seen him sprawled over the floor in Vernon Bull's shop would linger a very long time.

CHAPTER SEVEN

'Shall I pop over to the flat and pick up anything you might need?' Tamara asked. 'If you don't mind me looking around—'

'I'm hardly in a position to mind, am I?' Gage regretted his sharp retort when Tamara coloured. 'Sorry. Again. I could blame it on the leg, but—'

'Natural grumpiness is more accurate?'

'Afraid so.' He wriggled his keys out and passed them over.

'Fair enough. Are you happy sitting there until I get back?'

After they'd manoeuvred him out of the car and into her small semi-detached house, she had settled him in a comfortable chair by the window. Gage was knackered. His knee throbbed and all he longed to do was take another dose of pills and crash.

'Or at least tolerate it for the time it'll take me to run down to the village and back again?' Tamara smirked.

Having his mind read this way didn't sit well. 'No problem.'

After the door closed behind her, Gage slumped down in the chair and closed his eyes. What a position he'd landed himself in. Being dragooned into sharing a house with the woman who frustrated and fascinated him in equal measure was a recipe for disaster.

57

'I'm back.'

He jerked awake. It was disconcerting that his highly trained instincts appeared to have deserted him because he hadn't heard Tamara return.

She flashed a smile and started taking the seat cushions off the sofa. 'I'm afraid the mattress is thin and probably not very comfortable.' She pulled out the metal frame and set the legs on the carpet.

'This is luxury compared to some of the places I've bedded down over the years.' That didn't come across as the compliment he'd intended.

'I'll get some sheets and make up the bed. After I've shown you where to find the loo, I can unpack your things if you want and then leave you in peace.'

He drew on his last reserves of strength to thank her.

'I've got to go back to work and help with the lunches, but I'll be home about half two. I'll be doing a bit of baking then, but I'll try not to make too much noise. I'm working on another recipe to use in the pub over Christmas. Today it's my take on a German strudel, but with dried cherries, marzipan and pistachios. You can try it out later. I'm working this evening, but I'll be sure to leave something for your tea when I head out.'

His throat constricted. It'd been forever since anyone fussed over him and he didn't know how to handle it.

Ten minutes later he was alone again. Gage hobbled to the bathroom and got a glass of water to swallow another pill. Something snaked into his brain as he waited for the pain relief to kick in. His shop. In all the chaos, it hadn't crossed his mind. Only this morning he'd blasted all over social media that The Mighty Pen would open in a fortnight. Fat chance of that happening now. He could hear his friend Taff saying, 'Good move, Prof. Get out of this one, you silly bugger.'

* * *

58

A timid knock stopped Tamara in the middle of pouring custard into a small white jug. The only people who usually came to the kitchen's back door were bringing deliveries, and that was during the day.

'Hang on!' she shouted. 'Be there in a minute.' She filled up the jug, wiped off a couple of drips and set it on the serving plate alongside a generous bowl of warm apple-and-blackberry crumble. Crumbles might be old-fashioned, but they were always a bestseller in the winter.

Tamara flung open the door and was astonished to see Becky standing there. Her friend looked pale and drawn, and kept giving furtive glances around as if afraid someone might see her.

'Come in. I've got to take this through, but I'll be right back.'

Harry Bishop looked surprised when she almost flung the plate in front of him, barely stopping long enough to say hello. Normally she enjoyed a chat with Josie's husband, but not tonight.

Back in the kitchen, she found Becky slumped on a chair in the corner. Instead of suggesting a quick coffee, she whipped the brandy bottle from the cupboard. This was the cheap stuff they used in cooking, so she didn't think her friend would complain. She sloshed a generous measure into a glass and pushed it into Becky's shaking hands before pouring a more modest amount for herself.

'Sip that and then tell me what's got you flustered.'

'First off, you've got to tell me how that poor man is.' Becky gulped the brandy down and held out her glass for a top-up.

Playing along for a minute, she trotted out an update on Gage's visit to the doctor.

'That's a relief. I was some worried.'

Rocky was off tonight, which meant she was doing all the cooking. Any minute now Pixie would either come in with another order or need her behind the bar. If she didn't hurry up and get her friend talking, the opportunity would be gone.

59

'Why?'

'What do you mean, why?' Becky's flushed cheeks gave her away.

'You're the kindest person I know, so, yeah, I'd expect you to be concerned. We all were. But you freaked out in the shop. You couldn't have been more upset if it'd been your Paul or one of the kids who'd got hurt. What's Gage Bennet to you?'

'You can't tell anyone else.' Becky's deep brown eyes filled with tears. 'Promise me.'

'I promise.'

'Leastways not until I say so.' She wrung her hands so hard they turned white. 'He's my half-brother.'

Tamara's mouth gaped open. 'Oh, wow!' She'd known Becky all her life and remembered her mum well, but only had a few vague memories of Mr Harris because the couple had divorced early on. 'Your dad married again? I didn't realise.'

'Later on he did, but . . .' Becky flushed to the roots of her hair. 'Gage was born before Mum and Dad split up.'

'Oh, right.' Her head spun. 'Who else knows? Your family must, surely?'

'No. No one. At least not as far as I know.' Becky plucked at a ragged fingernail.

'Don't feel you've got to tell me anything else you'll regret later.'

'I've got to or I'll go round the bend. I hadn't clapped eyes on Gage for nearly thirty years, see. Not till he turned up on my doorstep about a week ago.' Distress flooded Becky's voice. 'We only met a few times as kiddies when Dad brought him over, but I recognised him straight off.' Her gaze turned misty. 'He was a lovely little chap and I was so excited about having a brother, but when I was daft enough to say so Mum turned on me something awful. Told me I wasn't to mention Gage's name again. Ever. The story she told everyone here is that they got divorced because they weren't getting on, so it was all friendly-like.' She snorted. 'Pack of lies. He'd been

60

carrying on with Gage's mother for years and got her in the club, so for a while he had two families on the go.'

'You'll have to tell Paul and the kids.'

'I know.' An anguished wail burst out of her. 'My man's honest as the day is long. What's he going to think when he finds out I never mentioned having a brother these last twenty-odd years?' Becky sagged like a punctured balloon. 'But I've got no choice, have I? Gage never said he wanted to keep it secret, but he's not a villager, is he? He doesn't know how places like this work.'

'It'll be okay. You know what Penworthal's like. It'll only be the juiciest piece of gossip until something more interesting comes along.'

Becky didn't look convinced.

'We'll all have your back. No one messes with the Back of Beyond Book Club and lives to tell the tale.'

That brought a wan smile to her friend's troubled face.

'Do you want me to update the girls, and Gage?'

'Not Gage. I'll see him first thing in the morning. But if you'd tell the club, that'd be great.' Becky heaved herself off the chair and ran a hand through her bedraggled hair. 'I must look a sight. I didn't even run a comb through it before I came out or put a bit of lipstick on. I'd better get on home or they'll be wondering where I'm at.'

'It'll be all right, you'll see.'

'I expect you're right.' There was no conviction in Becky's voice. 'I never thought to ask how he's going to manage. He won't be able to get up them stairs to the flat, surely?' Her brow knotted. 'I'd offer to have him at ours but—'

'He's staying with me. I've got a sofa bed in the living room and a downstairs loo.' She didn't go into the whole story of her and Gage's animated discussion — or argument — over the subject.

'You're a kind soul to do that.'

'Off you go and break the news.'

Tamara couldn't help wondering what other secrets Gage was keeping.

61

CHAPTER EIGHT

The box of books dropped from his hand and crashed to the floor. 'Fuck.'

Gage could weep with frustration. The last time he'd shed a tear had been at Farmer's funeral and before that it had been on the dismal night he'd lain wide awake in a hospital bed in Plymouth, waiting to find out if the doctors could save his leg. He'd had far less of an emotional reaction the year before all of that when his marriage had finally crossed the finish line, probably because it'd been creeping slowly in that direction for most of its short life.

Tamara burst through the shop door and her bright blue eyes blazed with fury. 'Did you seriously sneak out and hobble all the way down here from my house on crutches?'

'It's not far. I've done worse. Usually with a heavy pack on my back.' He'd avoided taking his pain medicine this morning to keep his head clear, but was regretting it now.

'Didn't you hear the magic word the doctor said? Rest.' She spelled it out in shouty capital letters.

Tossing back one of his usual clever sarcastic answers seemed unwise.

'What were you trying to do anyway?' She pointed to the box at his feet.

62

'Shelve books.' Gage ran his fingers through his spiky hair, which was edging past regulation length now. 'Epic failure.'

'I saw your Instagram and TikTok posts. November eighth is the big day?'

He grunted. 'It's supposed to be, but that's not happening, is it?'

'Why not?'

She seriously had to ask? Being bubbly and positive was one thing, but sometimes facing reality was the only way. That's what he'd been forced to do after the doctors had done their best to pin his knee back together using bolts and titanium plates, along with the caveat that no reconstructive surgery or intense physio would ever restore it to normal strength.

'I'm not being a Pollyanna and I'm not stupid,' she said fiercely.

'I never said you were!'

'You *could* push back the opening or you could accept help.'

'I suppose I—'

'You promised you'd let me tell him!' Becky burst in, eyes flashing with anger. For some reason it was focused on Tamara.

'And I've kept that promise.'

Gage backed off. He had no idea what was going on, but dealing with crutches was hard enough without the risk of being knocked off balance by two angry women.

Becky's cheeks turned ruddy. 'I saw the two of you having a good old chinwag and I thought . . .' Her shoulders sagged and her chin drooped.

'You were wrong. I'll go and leave you to talk.'

'No, stay.' Becky looked embarrassed. 'I shouldn't have snapped. I'm a bit on edge, that's all.'

'How about I put the kettle on?' Gage hoped that was a safe-enough offer.

'I'll do it,' Tamara said decisively. 'You two sit.' She dragged a couple of chairs out from behind the counter. 'Go on.'

63

If she'd somehow wriggled the story of their connection out of Becky, why hadn't she said something to him already?

Once he'd manoeuvred around and lowered himself gingerly into the chair, he dropped the crutches beside him on the floor. 'What's going on, Becky?' he asked. 'Do people know about us?' When she glanced at him, there were tears in her eyes and her brief nod sent his stomach plummeting. 'That's not down to me.'

'I know, my love.' A heartfelt sigh slipped out. 'I put my foot in it at the shop yesterday after I saw you looking so poorly. Couldn't help it.'

Gage covered her cold hand with his own. 'Don't apologise for caring.' His voice cracked. 'This is all my fault and I'm sorry. Really sorry.'

'You've nothing to be sorry for. I shouldn't be such a stubborn old fool. Lies always get found out.' Becky's brave smile touched him. 'Tamara's been a good friend since we were little girls in white knee-high socks together, so I dumped it all on her at the pub last night. She's a plain speaker and she told me what I needed to hear. Said if I didn't tell the truth now, people would speculate and that'd be worse.'

'Makes sense. How did your family take it?' he asked warily.

'Worried myself in a tizzy about nothing, didn't I? I'm a proper numpty sometimes. Paul wasn't that bothered. Said it were my dad's mistake, not mine.' Blobs of heat lit up her cheeks. 'Not that I'm calling you a mistake.'

It wasn't the first time he'd been called that, but she didn't need to feel any worse by him saying so. The number of conversations he'd overheard between his parents, blaming each other for his existence, was nobody's business.

'What about your children?'

'They think it's cool. That's youngsters for you. In their eyes, it makes me not so boring and they can't wait to meet their new uncle.'

Gage was speechless. He'd wanted this for so long that the effect of it being within reach was overwhelming.

64

'We all want you to come to Sunday lunch soon.'

'I'd love to.' He picked up Tamara's perfume before her soft footsteps.

'Is everything—'

'Everything's great,' Gage said to reassure Tamara.

'I'm glad.' She set the tray on the counter and passed each of them a mug before taking the last one for herself.

'Vernon Bull will think it's Christmas and Easter rolled into one when this spreads around,' Becky said with a wry smile.

'I've got to get off to work now, or Pixie will skin me, but I'll be done by three.' Tamara jumped up.

'She's the best baker around,' Becky said with a warm smile. 'Always gives everyone in our book club a Christmas cake, she does. And her mince pies put any of the so-called fancy ones you can buy to shame. Got a proper light hand with pastry, she has. Melt in the mouth, they do.'

Tamara's flushed face told Gage that she didn't accept compliments well. 'I should warn you that your sister is a great one for exaggerating. I'm off. We'll talk later about how you can get this place open in time.' She gave him an arch look. 'Unless you've had enough of my place after one night and think sleeping in a chair here is a better option?'

His cheeks heated. 'I'll be grateful if you can put up with me until I'm mobile again.'

'I'll probably survive.' A hint of amusement played around the edges of her mouth.

Once the door closed behind her, Becky threw him a puzzled look. There was no alternative but to explain the situation. He got the sinking feeling he knew which side his sister would come down on, and it wouldn't be his.

'It's obvious, isn't it, my love?'

'Is it?'

'You need an extra pair of hands. Offer Tamara a part-time job here. I'm sure she could fit it in around the pub because that Christos is working shifts now, supposedly trying to learn the business alongside Pixie.' Becky snorted.

65

'You don't think much of him?'

'I know a lazy, untrustworthy man when I see one. I'm afraid Pixie's going to find out the hard way. Anyway, back to Tamara. She's a hard worker and can do the physical stuff you can't manage for a while.'

There were a million reasons why this was a terrible idea, but he suspected his sister wouldn't want to hear them. Being thrown into Tamara's orbit at home and work? He doubted she'd be any more enthusiastic about Becky's idea than he was.

'Well?'

'I suppose I could ask her,' he said reluctantly.

'You do that. Anyway, let's get busy. We can chat while we work. I want to hear more about what you've been doing all these years.'

* * *

'Work for you?' Tamara heard her voice turn shrieky. While she'd been at the pub, she'd racked her brains thinking how to help Gage get the shop open and juggle all her other commitments. This hadn't made the list.

Gage shuffled awkwardly on his crutches and seemed inordinately interested in the newly sanded and polished wood floor. 'Becky came up with the idea. I told her it was daft.'

'Part-time for a fortnight to get the shop open, then probably a couple more weeks after that to get you back on your feet properly, right?'

'Yeah, then I can manage alone.' He surreptitiously crossed his fingers.

Tamara's raised eyebrows said what she thought of his optimistic plan. 'I'll ask Pixie this evening and let you know one way or the other when I come home.'

It would all depend on whether Christos could take time off his own job to work her daytime shift. She could still go in first thing to do the puddings and prepare those that could either be served cold or were easy to warm up. Rocky was

66

perfectly capable of taking the job over, but she was reluctant to give it up before she absolutely had to, if only because of the extra money it brought in. She would still be there in the evenings as usual. It should be easy to round up any more help they needed from her friends, too, but she'd keep that possibility to herself for now. They were awesome at supporting each other, and this was for the good of the village. No one wanted Penworthal going the way of so many others and turning into a Cornish ghost town with few viable businesses and no community spirit left.

A bigger problem was how Toby would react if she took up Gage's job offer. Her overprotective son had already had a go at her for inviting a strange man to stay. Toby hadn't softened when she'd appealed to his compassionate side as someone who spent his days helping sick people. She'd made a point of laying it on a bit by describing Gage as a sharp-tempered, somewhat unfriendly man who'd only moved in with her because he had no choice. There was an element of truth in that, but the more she got to know Gage, the more Tamara was inclined to feel her that like her, he'd been dealt a challenging hand in life.

'Wouldn't doing all this be too much for you?'

Every time she thought they were getting on better he came out with something like that.

'I didn't mean to imply—'

'I bet you were on duty around the clock many times and never gave it a thought. Being a mum's that way and I did that alone, so I don't think a few weeks' hard work is going to kill me. After all, I'm doing it to help a friend.'

The emphasis on the last word made him wince.

'Right, let's get you home now. You look exhausted.'

His grey skin and the tightness around his mouth and eyes were sure indicators, and she wasn't having him relapse on her watch, leaving her to face the doctor's wrath.

'I am. Thank you.' His quiet agreement took her by surprise. For a second their eyes met and Tamara couldn't breathe.

67

'No problem,' she said briskly. 'I've got a couple of steak-and-mushroom pies for our tea if that suits you? They're left over from lunchtime.'

'Anything will do. I'm not fussy.' Blobs of heat lit up his cheeks. 'I—

'Didn't mean to sound grouchy and ungrateful. I know. We're both straight talkers. I prefer that.' A shiver trickled down her spine. 'Let's go.'

CHAPTER NINE

'I'm sorry, I didn't know you'd be down this early. I hope my moving around didn't wake you?' Gage said apologetically.

He blinked at the sight of Tamara walking into the kitchen, clearly straight out of bed by the sight of her tousled hair. It was a struggle to fix his gaze on her face rather than the rest of her. A skimpy pink cami was stretched to its limits over her generous breasts and her loose, flowery shorts showed off long, toned legs.

'I was about to say the same.'

The colour in her cheeks was a sign she was equally embarrassed, and rightly so. At least he'd remembered to pull his boxer shorts back on before getting out of bed, but that was it.

'I usually shower before I come down for breakfast, but—'

'It's your house to do what you want in. I'll leave you in peace.' Gage shifted his crutches to turn around and retreat to the living room.

'Don't be silly. I'll make us a cup of tea.'

'Thanks, but at least let me put some more clothes on first.'

69

A smile played around her mouth. 'Okay.'

He made a swift escape and exhaled noisily when he reached the safety of his temporary bedroom. Since the disaster of his brief, unsatisfactory marriage and his accident, women and relationships had fallen off his radar. He'd never been good at either in the first place, so it hadn't bothered him. Apart from when he'd worked alongside his comrades, Gage's nature was suited to being solitary. Until five minutes ago. Was it simply the reaction of a celibate man to a gorgeous woman? He didn't think so.

Any thoughts he might've had of doing something about it went out the window as logic flooded back in. After a rocky start, they'd only now arrived at some level of friendship. She had generously opened her home to him and now they'd started working together. One wrong move could destroy all that. Gage knew from bitter experience that was how his life tended to go.

It didn't take long to tug on a shirt and a pair of sweatpants. He was back in control now.

* * *

'If you're ready, we'll go,' Tamara said, trying not to snap. Something had changed this morning between them, but then swung right around again to leave her confused and off-kilter.

When she'd strolled in to find him half-naked in her kitchen, she hadn't known where to look. Not strictly true, because she'd stared, maybe even ogled. He'd done the exact same thing to her and although she was out of practice with men, Tamara still recognised admiration when she saw it. Gage's tight black boxers left little to the imagination and she had an excellent one of those, which filled in the gaps far too well. The rest of him was pretty easy on the eye too. Muscles like his, honed from years of tough living, were far more of a turn-on to her than the kind acquired in the gym. But when he'd returned fully dressed, it had been as though someone had dropped him in an ice bath. He'd been polite but distant,

70

sharing breakfast with her and keeping conversation to his plans for the day.

'Sounds good. Sorry I couldn't manage to fold up the bed, but I've left everything as tidy as I could.'

'That's fine. I won't be doing an inspection later. You're out of the marines now.'

Gage looked shamefaced. 'Sorry. Again. I'm still adjusting. I should be better than this by now — it's been eighteen months, but—'

'Who says so? Everyone's different and we all cope with life challenges at our own pace.'

'You're a wise woman.' By his heightened colour, that admission hadn't been what he'd planned to say.

'You'll get there. But if we don't go now, I'll be late and then you won't get the benefit of my help as early as I'd hoped.' Usually she walked to work, but she'd offered to drop Gage off at the bookshop first. Tamara glanced at his crutches. 'Don't you dare hurry outside, though, or you'll be spreadeagled on my path and we'll be calling Dr Judy again.'

'And you'll be stuck with me even longer.'

'Oh, God, please don't say that.' The back-and-forth teasing was something they'd slipped into the last few days, and she bit back a smile when he didn't immediately shut down again.

Tamara gathered up her recipe book and handbag. Not saying another word on the subject struck her as smart.

* * *

Gage straightened his tie in the mirror and smoothed down his hair. He wouldn't have changed out of his jeans and warm jumper, but a summons to Evelyn's house seemed to demand a little more effort on his part, so he'd gone for a pair of dark-blue slacks and a crisp white shirt.

It'd been a confusing day and he'd been left in an awkward limbo where Tamara was concerned. He sensed her

71

relief when he kept things friendly but businesslike while they worked together, and could only suppose she was as mixed up as he was. A quiet evening to sort out his thoughts would have been very welcome.

Evelyn's invitation to dinner and to see her Daphne du Maurier collection had come during a brief phone call at lunchtime. He and Tamara had been taking a break to eat some sandwiches she'd brought home from the pub.

'I'll pick you up at six,' Evelyn had said. 'And take you home when you've had enough of our company.'

What could he say other than thank her and assure her he'd look forward to the evening? Tamara had joked that he could be their spy in the camp because she and her friends were intrigued to find out how things stood with the sisters.

The doorbell rang and he levered up from the chair to tuck his crutches under his arms. He made his way to the front door and smiled at Evelyn's opening salvo.

'I assume you don't need help out to the car?'

He assured her he'd be fine and carefully manoeuvred out of the house. It only took a few minutes to drive down to the village and along Church Street, where they stopped outside a neat white bungalow. Tamara told him it was a long-standing source of amusement that Evelyn named her home *Shangri-La* after an imaginary location in one of her favourite books, *Lost Horizon* by James Hilton. Supposedly a remote, peaceful, idyllic paradise, it seemed like a wildly inappropriate choice for the plain, unpretentious house built in the architecturally challenged 1960s.

'Oh, *mon Dieu*, you poor man.' A glossy, svelte woman with incredibly high cheekbones and a tight, immobile face stood in the front doorway, posed like a catwalk model. 'For heaven's sake, bring him in, Evelyn, dear.'

Evelyn snorted and turned back to Gage. 'In case you were wondering, this is my sister, Ophelia.' She shooed the woman out of the way and led their little procession inside. 'Do come through to the lounge. Ophelia can entertain you while I put the finishing touches to our meal.'

72

The long, narrow room was tastefully furnished, if slightly old-fashioned, but his eyes were drawn to the wall of glass-fronted bookcases at the far end, the dark wood gleaming from regular polishing.

'You shall have your fill after dinner, Mr Bennet,' Evelyn said with an amused lilt to her voice.

He dismissed the idea of sitting on the deviously soft-looking burgundy velvet sofa, with its multitude of plump cushions, and eased himself into a tan leather button-backed chair, which looked relatively easy to get out of again. Gage dropped the crutches beside him onto the carpet.

'Seats you sink into can be a nightmare. I had a hip replacement last year, so I do have some idea.' Ophelia's unexpected sympathy threw him.

'Yeah, that's true. You've recovered well, though.'

'I have from that, it's true.'

Gage studied her more closely and he realised that, underneath her very static features, Ophelia had the creamy-grey bruised look people acquired when they were swamped in pain and exhaustion. All the plastic surgery and make-up in the world couldn't hide that. Was her health the reason she'd returned to Cornwall so abruptly?

'Does Evelyn know?' He knew he shouldn't have asked when the shutters came down and she turned away. What had prompted him to say that out loud? It was a monstrous invasion of her privacy. 'I'm sorry, please forget I spoke.'

Ophelia's head drooped and her blood-red talons clutched the arm of the sofa. Before he could apologise again, she flung her head up. 'What I don't understand is how *you* caught on like that?' She snapped her fingers. 'But *she* hasn't.' Her anger was overlaid with frustration.

'I've seen a lot of suffering over the years, Ophelia, in all kinds of people. It's toughened me on the outside, but—'

'Scratch the surface and you're a marshmallow.'

'Pretty much.' His admission brought the faintest smile to her thin lips.

'Books are your painkillers, aren't they?'

73

Gage's jaw dropped. He'd never thought of it that way. Instead of self-medicating with drugs or alcohol, like so many others, he lost himself in words. 'You're smart.'

'Not the brainless, shallow, sharp-tongued bitch I pretend to be?'

A hot flush raced up his neck.

'I don't mind saying it for you. I know what people think and that's okay.' She puffed out a sigh. 'If they're thinking that, they aren't feeling sorry for me.' Ophelia's chin tilted. 'That's what I absolutely can't bear. Dislike. Hatred, even. I can cope with those.'

'I get it.' Gage touched his knee. 'When this happened, I shut people out. Doctors. Friends. Comrades in arms. In my mind I saw pity as the absolute worst word. Now I'm coming to see it's not. Indifference beats it every time.' Penworthal was starting to change him and hopefully for the better.

'Perhaps.' She gave a cat-like smile. 'Tell me about the mysterious Quinten. I've heard his name mentioned and accidentally interrupted a couple of surreptitious phone calls. I can't imagine my uptight sister having an illicit lover, but, if there's nothing dodgy about him, why's she keeping him out of sight now I'm here?'

He dithered over how to answer. For a start, he'd only met the man once and talking about the couple behind their backs felt wrong.

'Ophelia, did you not think to offer Mr Bennet a sherry?' Evelyn strode in, tutting.

'*Pardonnez moi*, I shall do it immediately.' Ophelia might as well have saluted her sister.

He realised that Ophelia's French accent had virtually disappeared when they'd been talking privately, but had returned full force when her sister had appeared. Another piece of armour used to hold people at bay?

'You'll find the new bottle in the kitchen.' That was a dismissal if ever he heard one. Evelyn's sharp gaze narrowed on him as Ophelia left them alone. It must be clear they'd

74

been discussing something important, but he took a guess she'd refuse to ask what it was about. 'The beef is taking a little longer to cook than I expected, so we could take a quick look at my books now if you like?' She picked up his crutches and held them out.

'Of course. I'd be delighted.' Gage levered out of the chair and steadied himself before following her. 'I'm afraid I've never read any du Maurier, so you'll have to guide me where to start.'

Evelyn opened one of the glass doors and studied the books on the top shelf before selecting one. She handed it to him with a reverent look on her face. 'Some might consider this an unusual choice because *Rebecca* and *My Cousin Rachel* are more well-known, but I think *The King's General* will suit you better for now. It's set in Cornwall during the English Civil War, and, for me, Honor Harris is her most independent and adventurous heroine. I suspect you admire that sort of woman.'

He felt his cheeks heat and saw a distinct twinkle in Evelyn's observant eyes. It wouldn't surprise him if this astute woman had an inkling of something that he was fighting against — the draw towards Tamara that simply wouldn't go away.

'I'll get a copy with the next order I place for the shop.'

'Not necessary. You can borrow this one.'

'I couldn't possibly.' Gage didn't have a clue how much the first edition was worth, but, from Melissa and Nathan's comments in the pub, he guessed it was extremely valuable.

'Of course you can.' She bristled. 'I recognise a fellow booklover when I see one and I'm sure you will take great care of it.' The spark returned to her piercing gaze. 'You wouldn't fold pages to mark your place, read it in the bath or bend the spine back to set it down.'

'I wouldn't dream of it.' He risked a smile, something that felt increasingly familiar these days. 'Hanging, drawing and quartering is too good for book desecrators.'

They were laughing when Ophelia returned and he received a sharp look that was eerily similar to her sister's.

Gage hoped she didn't think he'd been sharing what they'd spoken of earlier. He held up the book and gently explained what had amused them so heartily.

'My sister values her books above everything.' The tartness was unmistakable and Evelyn's previously warm expression tightened. Ophelia held a silver tray out to him. 'Sherry?'

'I hardly think he can manage to take a glass until he sits down, do you?'

'Silly me. Thoughtless as ever.'

Gage suppressed a sigh. This would be a long evening.

CHAPTER TEN

'I come bearing fresh scones.' Tamara pushed the shop door open and breezed in, swinging a white paper bag in her hand. 'They're my latest experiment for Christmas. Spiced cranberry walnut with a drizzle of cranberry icing.'

'Oh, God. Not more food.' Gage groaned. 'I don't mean to be unappreciative, but I'm still recovering from tackling the full roast beef dinner Evelyn plied me with last night. She piled my plate so high it would've fed a crew of navvies. After that came a gigantic bowl of apple crumble swimming in custard. I'm afraid Evelyn saw feeding me as part of my recovery process and as you know she takes things very seriously.'

'I want to hear every detail. You can at least drink a cup of tea, right?'

'Always.'

She breezed off to the kitchen and soon returned with two mugs. 'Sit down and spill the beans.'

He took the drink from her and perched on a stool.

'Was I right about Ophelia being stuck up and full of herself? I suppose they were polite around you? I don't expect you found out why she came back to Penworthal when it's obvious she and Evelyn don't have much time for each other?'

77

An odd expression crossed Gage's face.

'You're not going to tell me, are you?'

The tips of his ears turned pink, but he didn't blink. 'Let's leave it that I had a great meal and came away with a du Maurier first edition to read.'

'Wow! You are honoured. You've definitely won Evelyn over.' She angled a sly smile. 'Ophelia, too? Was she less acerbic with you?'

'We talked.' Gage cleared his throat. 'You might want to give her a second chance is all I'm saying.'

'Okay.' Tamara dragged out the word. She pulled a scone out of the bag and nibbled one end. 'A little less spice next time and the walnuts need to be chopped finer.'

'Have you always loved baking?'

'Absolutely.' Despite being mildly annoyed that he was determined to keep his counsel about Evelyn and Ophelia, she couldn't resist telling him about her passion. She started with her first inedible attempts, all the way through to creating her own recipes, and the dreams she had about making a living from them. She felt herself flush. Not prettily, because she wasn't made that way unfortunately, but the hot, mottled red sort of blush that took ages to fade away.

'Don't be embarrassed.' Gage placed his hand over hers. The sleeve of his jumper rode up a few inches to expose a dusting of fine dark hairs. It reminded her of yesterday morning and his broad, muscular chest, memories of which had kept her awake long into the night. Their eyes met and held. His sapphire-blue eyes bored into Tamara as he bent his head towards her. Within kissing distance. At the last second, he closed his eyes and took a couple of deep breaths. 'Tell me if I'm out of line.' The timbre of his voice deepened and turned husky.

'You're not.' Every negative thing she'd once believed about this man turned to dust.

Gage's hand lifted to her face and a throaty moan slipped out of her as his stroking fingers set her skin on fire. 'I thought I was more patient.'

78

'Are you going to kiss me anytime soon?' The breath left her body when his mouth pressed against hers, hot and needy.

The tip of Gage's tongue thrust its way in and she was on fire, imagining what it would be like when they made love. When. Not if.

A shrill wolf-whistle, loud claps and ragged cheers made them spring apart, and Tamara jerked her head around to see a small gaggle of people gawping at them, a grinning Melissa at the forefront. Why hadn't it occurred to either of them that they were in full view of the shop window? The sight of them in a clinch was a notch up from Penworthal's normal Friday morning entertainment of watching the bin men come around. Vernon Bull ambled over from the shop as well now, obviously afraid of missing out. When she'd reassured Becky that her connection to Gage would soon be old news, Tamara hadn't expected to be the one replacing it on the top-gossip spot.

'The sooner this knee heals, the better,' Gage murmured against her hot cheek. He lifted a hand and waved to their fan club. That spurred several people to move away, but now she spotted someone who hadn't been visible before. The very last person who needed to see her kissing someone he'd never even met, someone she'd assured him she didn't even much like. Toby's white face and bulging eyes said it all.

'Your son?' By Gage's flat voice, he sensed this was a disaster.

'Yeah. That's Toby.' It raced through her head whether to go out and drag Toby in here, do the introductions and get it over with. But he sprinted off and was soon out of sight. If she chased after him, it might make things worse.

'Hell, I'm sorry. I didn't think—'

'Neither did I.' She managed a feeble smile. 'I'll catch up with Toby later. It was a shock, that's all. Once I introduce you properly, he'll be fine.' Would he though? He'd become more protective recently, as though it was his turn to look out for her. Tamara pulled herself together. 'We'd better get to work. Show me how we're going to shelve these books according to your master spreadsheet.'

79

'I love it when you get all take-charge on me.' His brows knotted together. 'That's not me making fun of you either. Women weren't allowed to fight in the Royal Marines until 2018, and many blokes I served with were dead set against it. I never understood why they felt so threatened. To my mind, anyone who could pass the bloody hard training deserved to wear the green beret and play their full part. You'd have done great.'

'Me?'

'It would've suited you down to the ground.'

Tamara's face heated. 'I think that's the best compliment any man's ever given me. I'm not the red-roses-and-fancy-perfume type, but tell me you think I could do a route march with a heavy backpack and slog through mud, and I'm your girl.' She beamed. 'Now, Prof, let's get busy with those books.'

* * *

A sharp rap on the front door stirred Gage from his thoughts. He'd been brooding over where this morning's kiss had left him and Tamara. His determination to keep her at a safe, friendly distance had flown out the window. The last thing he wanted was to hurt her. His ex-wife had once called him emotionally closed-off. She claimed he hid behind the macho culture of the Royal Marines, where, in her view, his inadequacies were seen as a plus rather than a hindrance. But Ophelia's comment crept back into his brain. If she could see beneath his stoic surface, to what she'd called the 'marsh-mallow' underneath, perhaps Victoria was wrong? He really hoped so, because if not he'd probably screw up with Tamara too. That thought was unbearable.

He pushed out of the chair and tucked the crutches securely under his arms before hobbling out into the hall. Evelyn stood on the doorstep and gave him a tight smile.

'Are you checking up on me to make sure I haven't damaged your valuable book?'

80

'Hardly, Mr Bennet.' She held out a stout, ornately carved walking stick. 'I bought this on my hiking holiday in the Alps and thought you might find it useful.'

'Thank you. I appreciate it.'

'I would like a quick word if it's not inconvenient?'

'Uh, no, of course not. Come in.' Gage's heart sank as he stood back to let her step inside. It didn't take a genius to guess why she was here. He'd learned how to deal with hostile enemy interrogations in the marines, but had the feeling Evelyn might be a match for anything he threw at her. 'May I take your coat?'

'I shan't be staying long.' She propped the stick up by the coat stand in the hall and followed him into the living room.

Gage gestured for Evelyn to take a seat on the sofa and commandeered his usual chair.

'I'll get straight to the point because I believe it's far better to be honest. Not that it's always appreciated.' She shrugged. 'Ophelia doesn't care for it. She never did.' Evelyn fixed him with what Tamara referred to as her headteacher stare. 'Are you going to tell me what she's being so secretive about?'

'No.'

His swift response visibly took her aback.

'Even if I knew the full story — which I don't — it's not my place to share it. If you're such a proponent of honest conversation, why don't you try it with your sister?'

'You don't understand. The history between us is . . . difficult.' Her penetrating eyes studied him. 'I suspect you've heard speculation around the village. Mostly down to the oh-so-reliable Mr Bull, who knows Ophelia of old.'

He couldn't deny it without lying.

'Suffice to say, there's been no love lost between us for a very long time.' She looked wistful. 'There's the chance I've been wrong about something, but I don't think so. Ophelia has made it clear she's only here now because she has no choice, but why is that?'

Gage gave her credit for persistence. 'Ask her.'

81

Evelyn scoffed. 'You think I haven't?'

'Ophelia needs you right now, but the two of you are equally stubborn and she won't beg.' He spread his hands on his thighs. 'That's all I'm saying.'

She threw back her head and laughed. 'No wonder Tamara's losing her head over you.'

'I think you're jumping the gun there. We're . . .' His voice trailed away and he made do with a shrug. How could he explain when he didn't understand it himself yet?

Two pink circles blossomed on Evelyn's cheeks. 'If I were thirty years younger, or the reverse, you're the sort of man who'd catch my eye.'

'But think how jealous poor Quinten would be. You strike me as the sort of lady who could cope with both your sister's challenges and a lover without too much difficulty, so why are you shutting him out? Martyrdom isn't an attractive trait.'

For a second she looked stunned, before shaking her head and seeming to gather herself. 'Time I went home, I think, Mr Bennet. You've certainly given me food for thought.'

Mission accomplished.

* * *

Tamara crept into the house and latched the door quietly behind her. She kicked off her shoes and hung up her wet mac before shaking her hair out of the scrappy ponytail she'd pulled it back in for work. A sliver of light came into the hall from the living room, and she wondered if Gage was awake or had fallen asleep with the light on. Her routine after a long day on her feet was to make a cup of tea and take it up to bed. But wouldn't it be unfriendly not to offer him one too? She chuckled to herself. They'd gone past 'friendly' this morning. It bothered her to be alienated from Toby. She'd give him a ring tomorrow and try to smooth the troubled waters between them.

This was silly. Apart from anything else, Gage was a guest in her house and it was nothing more than a perfectly normal

82

gesture to see if he needed anything. She tapped on the door. 'I'm back. Would you like a cup of tea?'

'Come on in. I promise I'm decent.' His deep voice throbbed with amusement and she blushed, remembering their encounter in the kitchen yesterday. And their kiss earlier.

Tamara walked in and found him sitting in the chair, reading. They'd decided to leave the sofa-bed set-up during the day, so he didn't have to struggle doing it himself or wait for her to help. It made the room seem even smaller and after this morning's kiss, it was impossible not to picture him stretched out in the bed. 'Studying up on Daphne's writing?'

'Yeah, it's pretty good so far. I love discovering new authors and I'd probably have never tried her if it wasn't for her number-one fan.'

'Evelyn will expect a report when you're done. Just like at school.'

'That wouldn't surprise me. She was . . . quite vociferous when she trusted me with the book.'

She sensed him holding something back, but chose not to press.

'Busy night at the pub?'

A tired sigh slipped out. 'It always is and Christos isn't much help. He spends more time chatting up female customers than he does working.'

'You must be exhausted.'

'I'm used to long days,' Tamara said determinedly.

'Nathan rang me earlier. I'm not sure how he managed it, but he talked me into joining the Proper Choughed quiz team tonight.'

Tamara snorted. 'You might live to regret that. The Back of Beyond Brains are formidable. We've got a three-game lead this year over Proper Choughed and as it's Halloween night, we'll be out for blood.' She bared her teeth.

'I'll remember to bring garlic and a wooden stake.'

'You do know costumes are obligatory?'

'Yeah, no problem,' he said blithely.

She recognised a lie when she heard one. 'Really?' She smirked. 'You don't strike me as the dressing-up type.'

'I'll have you know my karaoke tribute to John Travolta's *Saturday Night Fever* routine was the hit of the 2008 Christmas show in Kabul.' As the words left his mouth, she guessed he wished them unsaid. 'But with this gammy knee, my dancing days are over.'

'A full performance won't be required, but you in a tight, white suit could throw us ladies off our game. Take one for the team, Gage.'

'I might consider it if you channel your inner Sandy from *Grease* — not when she's all sweet, but—'

'Tight black leather and attitude. And here was me thinking you weren't another predictable man.' She gave a playful sigh.

'What can I say?'

'I'll give it some thought.' Far too much probably. 'Right. How about that cup of tea? You've got to try a scone too and no excuses about being full from last night.' She disappeared into the kitchen and soon returned with a laden tray. 'There you go.'

'Thanks.' He gave the scone a wary look.

'Don't tell me. You're one of the rare men who doesn't like sweet things?'

'Okay, I won't.'

'Won't what?'

'Tell you you're spot on and therefore make you mad at me.' Gage shrugged, as though it was his lot in life to put people's backs up.

'Relax. I prefer honesty, remember?'

He picked up the scone and cautiously took a bite, then another. 'It's not bad. Not too sweet, although I'd probably—'

'Prefer it without the icing.'

'Well, yeah. Sorry.'

'Nothing to be sorry for. We're all different. At least I won't have to fight you for the thickly iced corners of

84

Christmas cake.' She licked her lips. 'They're my absolute favourite.'

Gage shuddered.

Next thing they were both laughing and Tamara felt back on safer ground.

CHAPTER ELEVEN

'Do you think he'll have the nerve?' Pixie pushed a strand of messy blonde hair out of her face. 'God, this wig is getting on my nerves.' Her Halloween costume was inspired by an old picture of her namesake, Pixie Geldof, wearing a skimpy black satin slip-dress, electric blue tights, black lace-up Doc Martens and a huge silver cross around her neck. They'd had a good laugh over the hairstyle because, instead of sexy and tousled, it looked like a bird was using it as a nest.

'He turned a funny colour when I prodded him about it.' Tamara snickered. 'A bit like gone-off milk? Sort of green around the edges.'

'He'll do it for you, lovey. Anything to get in your spandex trousers.' Pixie waggled her fake eyelashes. She'd grumbled about them too earlier and was deathly afraid they'd come unstuck and land in someone's pint.

It'd seemed a fun challenge when she considered playing off his half-promised John Travolta impersonation by channelling her own inner sexy Sandy. Now she simply felt exposed and uncomfortable.

'Don't be daft. Things aren't like that between us.'

'What about the famous kiss? We've all heard about that.'

86

Tamara's face flamed. 'One kiss. We got a bit carried away, that's all.'

Pixie sniggered. 'I'd say you did.'

'Anyway, Christos couldn't keep his eyes off you earlier in that outfit.' She firmly changed the subject.

'Only until Emily paraded in and then his eyes shot out on stalks,' Pixie said dryly. 'I'm surprised Paul let her out of the house in that Elizabeth Hurley look-alike safety-pin dress. She's only just turned eighteen for Christ's sake. Where she got her looks from, I don't know.'

'True.' Paul and Becky were lovely people, but regular looking. Somehow, their eldest daughter was a slender, doe-eyed, brunette knockout.

Tamara found Christos's interest disturbing too, on several levels.

'I've told him you'll stop work at half seven to join your quiz team, so he'll have to pull his finger out then.' Pixie's voice wobbled. 'I'm not sure he's cut out for this.'

'I suppose it's a huge learning curve and very different from what he's used to. For both your sakes, I hope he gets there and soon.' Deep down she wasn't convinced, but time would tell.

'Yeah, I need to cut him some slack, I suppose. It's early days.'

'I'll pick up the dirty glasses, okay?'

They'd spent ages this morning decorating the pub. Black silky cobwebs dotted with huge scary plastic spiders were draped from the rafters, and white, eerily realistic skeletons were tucked into the best spots to startle people. Rocky had done an awesome job carving pumpkins to dot around the place, all lit with safe LED candles so they didn't end up calling the fire brigade. While they'd been fixing it all, they'd joked that after they took it down again, it'd almost be time to decorate for Christmas. They wouldn't be the first in the village to get in the festive spirit because the Webb and Burt families who lived next door to each other in Wesley Lane had

87

put theirs up already. The quasi-friendly rivalry had started a while ago now and seemed to escalate annually as each tried to outdo the other. Oversized inflatables were the thing these days, and, this year, a giant Father Christmas in one garden looked scornfully across at the huge snowman next door, who topped its height by an annoyingly obvious degree.

'Wow, you don't look like anyone's mother-in-law tonight!' Chloe sidled up to her with a laugh. Her son's striking blonde partner *was* Taylor Swift in a gold tasselled mini-dress and thigh-high sequined boots that sparkled under the lights. 'It's just as well Toby's working — he'd be fretting about us both. He's such an old woman sometimes.' She said it lovingly, but turned pink when Tamara didn't answer. 'Has he been in touch? I've done my best to—'

'I've tried to contact him, but haven't had any luck so far.' She told herself that he'd come around when he was ready.

'I'm sorry. I've told him he's being an arse, but he refuses to talk about it.'

'It was a shock. I get that. I should've handled it better.' She tried to smile. 'Or not snogged Gage like a randy teenager in full view of half the village.'

Chloe spluttered. 'Looking at it that way, I suppose his point of view has some validity.'

'Yeah. He's used to me being Mum and not much else all these years.' Her cheeks burned. 'But it was one kiss. That's all. Yeah, Gage is staying with me, but there's nothing going on.' It was starting to sound like an empty declaration, although it was basically true.

'I'll have another go at Toby. Promise.' Chloe grasped her arm. 'Anyway, let's forget him for now and enjoy ourselves.' She checked Tamara out again. 'Gage is pretty gorgeous, though, and I predict he'll drop to the ground when he sees you — like Danny Zuko falling at Sandy's feet, absolutely slayed.'

'I hope not. He'll do his knee in again.'

'You didn't argue with the gorgeous part.'

88

Tamara's blush deepened. 'I've got work to do, then it's time to join the girls and get my brain in gear. You should rope some of your friends in and form a team.'

'We're all too scattered around, plus I'm not quite ready to concede this isn't a very middle-aged hobby — not yet. See ya.' Chloe breezed off.

For a second Tamara wished she was as carefree and sure of herself, then kicked herself for forgetting the girl's traumatic experience last year when she'd been stabbed during a robbery that had gone wrong. No one's life was perfect.

'There you go. That's the last for now.' She plonked a tray of dirty glasses on the bar and wiped a sheen of sweat from her face.

'Wine?' Pixie asked.

'No, thanks. I'm boiled alive. A pint of soda and lime, loaded with ice, please.'

'Coming up.'

Tamara pressed the drink to her forehead and closed her eyes in relief.

'Wow!' Pixie whistled under her breath. 'Now that's what I call a costume.'

'What . . .' The glass almost slipped from her hand when she followed her friend's gaze to see Gage had walked in. A quick look around told Tamara she wasn't the only woman with her tongue hanging out. The fact he was still on crutches didn't detract from the way the white three-piece suit hugged his fit body, and he'd unbuttoned the black shirt enough to show a tease of dark hair. His slicked-back hairdo wasn't quite up to John Travolta's, his hair being far too short, but it did the job.

'He's working that for all it's worth.' Pixie giggled.

Tamara heard the song 'You're the One That I Want' reverberating through her head. 'I'm going to join the girls.'

The Back of Beyond Brains' standard spot was near the fireplace, which meant walking right past Proper Choughed. Tamara's doubts resurfaced.

89

'Go for it.'

Tossing her head gently in case the long curly wig fell off, she grabbed her drink and set off. Sandy didn't *walk* in this outfit — she *strutted*.

* * *

Gage hadn't missed the surprised looks floating around, but focused on joining his team. Half an hour ago, he'd still been in his jeans and a thick jumper, but some reckless urge had made him change. It might've been the gleam in Tamara's eyes when she'd handed over the outfit she had fetched from the flat for him. Why he'd even kept it was a mystery.

'Hello, mate. I'm Paul. Becky's hubby. Sit yourself down. We got your first pint in.' Paul stood to shake his hand, using the other to hold on to a green feathered cap. 'Supposed to be bleddy Robin Hood. Becky fancied herself as Maid Marion. I told her I drew the line at wearing tights though.' He rolled his eyes. 'That's some get-up you're in. Anything to do with our friendly barmaid?'

'Maybe. Long story.' He dropped into the chair they'd saved for him.

'Nathan got screwed over worse than us.'

'I'm afraid Melissa's obsessed by the *Bridgerton* books and is mad about the show too, so she's got a thing about men in Regency dress. Enough said?' Nathan tugged at the high white pleated cravat forcing him to hold his head unnaturally high.

'Have you seen how tight his trousers are? Poor sod will have to use a crowbar if he needs a—'

'Shut it, Paul,' Nathan said good-naturedly. 'Gage gets the general idea. Anyway, it's a toss-up between me and Harry who looks the biggest plonker.'

'Hercule Poirot, right?' The centre-parted oily hair, toothbrush moustache, formal suit and shiny black patent shoes were instant giveaways.

'Yep.' Harry took a swig of beer. 'My only consolation is Josie's got a thing about the little man, so I should be in

90

luck later. Her prim Agatha Christie costume with the grey curly wig, frumpy dress and lace-up flat shoes will have to go though.' He guffawed.

'This here's Micky Broad.' Paul nodded at the thin-faced man to his right. 'He says he's a chimney sweep, but I reckon he's used that as an excuse not to wash for a few days, right, mate?'

'Sod you.' Micky gestured with his middle finger.

'You won't beat him when it comes to geography. And that's Ian Geach.'

A bulky, ruddy-faced giant of a man was the only one not in costume. He was hunched over his phone and briefly glanced up to nod.

'He don't say much, but he's ace at music and art, all the fancy stuff, aren't you?'

'Mebbe.'

'Gage here's a military-history nut,' Paul added. 'His mates in the forces called him Prof, so we've got two now, hey, Nathan?'

'More the merrier.'

'But his is the real thing,' Gage added. He almost spat out a mouthful of beer as he clocked Tamara, who stood in front of him dressed as his ultimate fantasy. With too many curious eyes watching, the only option available was to stare. So that's what he did, long and hard.

Tamara's lush, glossy red lips curved in a sultry smile. 'I'll get Pixie to play "Saturday Night Fever" later.'

'I'm no dancer, remember.'

'Spoilsport. Good luck with the quiz. You'll need it. The Back of Beyond Brains will be on fire tonight.' With that parting shot, Tamara sashayed away, giving him a heart-stopping view from the rear.

It was a struggle to focus when his mind was fixated on Tamara, and his eyes followed her all the way to her seat, but Pixie tugged the rope of a large brass ship's bell hanging at the bar several times. 'Take your seats and turn those mobiles off. Jimmy's coming with the first-round question papers — the

91

subject is Entertainment. You'll have fifteen minutes to write down your answers.'

'Oi, mate. We know where your brain is in those tight white trousers, but drag it back to the quiz for fuck's sake or those bloody women will beat us again.' Paul nudged his arm.

'Sorry.' He forced himself to refocus.

Initially he wasn't much help because he rarely watched television and was less interested in celebrity gossip than the Pope. But the next round was History, and Gage was irrationally pleased when he beat Micky to answering a tough one on the D-Day landings.

The ship's bell rang again. 'Half-time. Back in your seats ready to go in fifteen,' Pixie shouted.

'My round.' Gage stood up and tucked his crutches in place.

'I'll give you a hand to carry them back,' Nathan said. 'I know what these reprobates drink.'

'Should do by now, mate.' Paul chimed in. 'Brought you in as a sub, we did, last year, and now you're a regular fixture. Hope you will be too, Gage, if we don't put you off tonight.'

His chest tightened and a rush of gratitude swept through him. For the first time since becoming a civilian, he felt he might've found his place. His people. The old quote about no man being an island was true. He'd always been self-sufficient, but there was a massive difference between that and loneliness. The latter could pull a person into dark, hopeless places. He should know because he'd been there and had no desire to return.

'I plan on sticking around.'

'Good.' Nathan slapped his shoulder. 'Now, get these drinks in before we die of thirst.'

Gage straightened his stance, turned to face Tamara's group and flashed what he hoped was a fair approximation of John Travolta's intense look. Her conspirators treated him to a mix of suggestive smiles and flat-out curious stares.

92

'Evening, ladies.' Two could play the teasing game. And it might just put them off their quiz game.

* * *

'Right, ladies, this is our chance,' Evelyn said chidingly. 'We're tied with *them*.' A severe nod went in the direction of Proper Choughed.

Tamara caught Melissa's eye and winked. If they didn't pull their socks up, they'd get a rap on the knuckles or be forced to write out a hundred lines of *I must pay attention on quiz night*. She'd only answered a couple of desultory questions so far and knew she wasn't pulling her weight tonight. Most of the blame for her absentmindedness lay at Gage's door. That famous self-control of his had been rattled when he'd first seen her, but he'd refocused to help his new team and so far the men hadn't missed a single question.

But she wasn't the only distracted member of the Back of Beyond Brains tonight. Melissa had given an almost unheard-of wrong answer to a question on American football. Amy flat-out admitted her brain was fried after losing a difficult case at work. Laura had dragged herself in after being up all night with a teething toddler, her white ghost costume only adding to her exhausted look. Even Evelyn wasn't on her A-game and spectacularly messed up a literature question, which opened the door for Nathan to ease his team ahead. Josie and Becky were the only two on form, but it wasn't enough to carry the rest of them.

'The last round is General Knowledge,' Pixie announced.

That might or might not help their fading chance of pulling off a victory. Old Jimmy Trevail shuffled around the room to put the question sheets face down on each table and when he was done, the bell rang as the signal to turn them over. Tamara couldn't decide if it was a good omen when they swiftly answered the ten questions. They swapped papers with the Jam

93

First Geniuses and by the time Pixie started running through the answers, she was afraid to look at Evelyn. They'd got the name of The Beatles' last UK number-one hit wrong by putting 'The Ballad of John and Yoko' from 1969, instead of one called 'Now and Then', which Pixie declared topped the charts in 2023.

Evelyn's hand shot up. 'That song was made with the use of artificial intelligence — surely that doesn't count.'

'I'm sorry, but it does. All the official charts list it as The Beatles' most recent hit. That means Proper Choughed regain the coveted trophy and win the traditional round of drinks.'

'Don't be a sore loser, Mrs Taylor,' Micky Broad yelled and tapped Gage's shoulder. 'Our new member has you on the run. You might want to do a bit more studying before you challenge us again next month.'

'I believe I'm off home, ladies.' Evelyn slipped her camel coat back on and found her handbag. 'I'll see you all on Tuesday at my house.' She exhaled a weary sigh. 'Ophelia will almost certainly be there, so I hope she'll be cordial to you.'

It'd been a relief when the other woman didn't turn up tonight, and no one asked where she was.

There was a general move to leave, so soon only Tamara and Becky were left.

'I'd better get back to work,' Tamara said reluctantly. 'See you at book club.'

She needed the loo first, so started weaving her way through and headed down the dim hallway to the toilets. A couple were standing by the wall and Tamara was about to walk around them when she realised that the man was Christos. The young woman he was talking to was Emily, Becky's daughter, who looking distinctly uncomfortable.

Christos glanced back over his shoulder and his bleary eyes made it obvious he'd been drinking. Pixie never touched alcohol while she was working, but her fiancé clearly had no such reservations.

'Everything all right, Emily?' Tamara gave the girl's arm a reassuring squeeze.

94

'She's fine. Just having a friendly chat, weren't we?' Christos's overly hearty response only elicited a shrug from Emily.

'There you are, Tamara. I wondered where you'd got to.' Gage smiled at her, then threw a worried look at Christos. He'd clearly heard enough of the conversation to be concerned.

She'd never been so pleased to see him. 'You haven't met Emily yet, have you? She's Paul and Becky's oldest.'

'Oh, hiya, it's good to meet you.' Gage smiled at Emily, and introduced himself, then turned his attention to Christos again. 'About time you got back to work, isn't it?'

'I was going anyway.' Christos made himself scarce.

'Are you sure you're okay, Emily?' Tamara asked again, needing to be sure.

'Yeah. Thanks. I only wanted the loo, but he stopped me and chatted a bit . . .' Emily's voice trailed away.

'After you're done in the loo, why don't you join your mum?' Tamara suggested.

Emily nodded and hurried away.

'I might try and have a quiet word with Becky,' Tamara told Gage. 'Not right now, though, to spoil the evening.'

'Thanks for stepping in,' Gage said in a low voice.

'You did your bit too. I've got to get back to work now, but I'll see you later.' She hurried off.

95

CHAPTER TWELVE

Gage tore off his tie and tossed it on the bed. This was a casual Sunday lunch with his family, not a job interview. So why did it feel more like the latter?

'Paul is here.' Tamara popped her head in around the door.

The walk to Becky's house would've given him time to clear his mind, but that wasn't an option on crutches. Even if he surpassed the doc's predictions, it would be nothing short of a miracle if he could manage without them by the shop's opening day next weekend.

'You look as though you're going to your execution. Chin up, and smile. Don't forget these.' Tamara thrust a bunch of red roses wrapped in gold tissue paper at him.

Paul gave a wry smile. 'The wife likes a flower. She's always complaining I never buy any.'

Gage appreciated the support. The poor man kept tugging at his white shirt collar. Paul was squeezed into a dark-grey suit that probably hadn't seen the light of day since the last wedding or funeral he'd been forced to attend. The garish red tie dotted with hearts could've been a Father's Day gift and worn to please his children. Maybe it was just as well

96

things had worked out as they had with his ex-wife, because what did he know about being a good dad anyway? Sod all.

'We'd better get a move on, lad. Becky will have my guts for garters if we're late and her Yorkshire puds sink.'

'We can't have that.'

Out in the van, Gage wasn't sure whether to raise the subject of his parentage, but in the end fell back on the classic English conversation stalwart and commented on the nice weather.

'Make the most of it. We're supposed to have rain by Tuesday. Typical. Our Daniel's got footie in the evening and the parking over Polcren is in a field. Last time the van got stuck.' He nodded as they drove past the bookshop. 'Coming on all right, is it?'

'Yeah. Tamara's been a great help.'

'So I heard.'

The butterflies started fluttering again in Gage's stomach as they turned onto Wesley Lane and pulled into the driveway of number nineteen.

Paul clambered out and jogged around to open Gage's door. 'Leave the flowers on the dash and hand me the crutches.'

A petite blonde whirlwind raced out of the house. 'Yay, I got here first. Uncle Gage, I'm Lily.' She flashed a smile brightened by a mouthful of metal braces.

'My youngest. She's thirteen going on thirty aren't you, my handsome?'

'Mum's in a proper tizzy because the gravy's gone lumpy. Ollie's sulking in his room because she said he's got to eat his dinner with us instead of going to McDonald's with his friends.' She turned back to the house, screwed up her face and stuck out her tongue. 'Emily's hiding behind the curtains to spy on us. She pretends to be cool, but she's as made up as the rest of us.' Lily hooted with laughter.

He'd have to pretend to be surprised when he met Emily again. 'Well, I can't wait to meet you all. It's not every day a man acquires an instant family.' Gage held the flowers out to her. 'These are for your mum. Would you mind taking them?'

97

'No probs.' She grabbed them and sprinted back to the house.

He caught sight of Paul's relieved expression, as if the other man hadn't been sure whether this would work out. Gage hadn't been certain either. But now? He had the idea it might be okay, or with luck maybe a darn sight more than okay.

* * *

Being alone in the bookshop was a new experience for Tamara. She wasn't helping with Sunday lunches at the pub these days and had ignored Gage's plea for her to take the day off and join him and Becky's family. After Friday's Halloween party, things had shifted yet again with Gage. The frisson of attraction sizzled hotter than ever, making living in the same house even more of a challenge — but their friendship had deepened too.

They'd had a great time swapping stories and jokes while they worked. A man without a sense of humour wasn't worth having, in her opinion, and his was witty, dry and more than a little dark — very similar to her own. The only fly in the ointment was Toby. All she could hope was that when he'd calmed down and asked around about Gage, he'd hear only good things.

Tamara wandered outside to take a look at the window. They needed to get cracking with decorating it for Christmas, so customers were tempted to buy their presents here rather than ordering online or going to the larger, fancier bookshop in Truro. Mariah Carey's ubiquitous Christmas hit 'All I Want for Christmas is You' came to mind. Replace 'you' with 'books' and they'd have the perfect theme. Perhaps they could do some sort of fireplace scene with Father Christmas reading? The sound of approaching footsteps made her turn.

'Oh, hi, Melissa. Are you out for a walk while Nathan cooks? You've got it made.' It was a standing joke that

98

Melissa's husband banned his American wife from the kitchen on Sundays. After years of bachelorhood, he knew all the tricks of making a proper Sunday roast. Tamara would never say this in front of Rocky, or Pixie, but having sampled Nathan's golden-brown crispy potatoes and superb mile-high Yorkshire puddings, she thought they even put the pub's excellent ones to shame.

'Yeah, I have.' She sounded wistful.

'What's up? Something's wrong, isn't it?'

'Why would you say that?'

'Oh, come on. Your eyes are red like you've been crying and your make-up is smudged.' She glanced down. 'Plus, you're wearing odd shoes. Very odd shoes.'

'Am I?' Melissa looked shocked to see a black ballet flat on her left foot and the right one sporting a bright-red sneaker. 'I guess I ran out in a hurry.'

'Why?'

Her friend's face crumpled and tears oozed out of her swollen eyes.

'Let's go inside,' Tamara said. 'Before someone else spots us and you race to the top of Penworthal's gossip list. You definitely don't want that. Trust me. Been there, done that.'

'Yeah, me too. It wasn't pretty.' Melissa grimaced.

Neither spoke for a moment, remembering the time when her friend's financial problems, caused by her late husband's recklessness with money, had become village news.

'Come on.'

'What about Gage? I can't—'

'He's not here.' Her swift explanation erased a couple of Melissa's worry lines. 'I'll stick the kettle on. I'm ready to take a break anyway.'

'Oh, wow isn't this gorgeous?' Melissa had followed her in and now gazed around with wide eyes. 'I can't believe how much you've achieved in such a short time, especially with Gage's bad knee.'

'We work well together.'

99

They'd developed a seamless system where she did the heavy lifting and stacked books on the higher shelves, while he sat on a rolling chair and wheeled himself around to do the lower ones.

'It's more than that, though, isn't it? Your eyes sparkle talking about him.'

'It's early days.' Sharing this newfound joy with even one of her best friends could be tempting fate. 'This isn't why we came in, is it?' She gently eased Melissa away from the temptation of the books on the shelves and pushed open the swing door to the kitchen.

'I'd no idea all this was here.'

The large rectangular room with its industrial-sized stainless-steel appliances had shocked her too when she'd first seen it. 'The shop's been a lot of things in its time, but the last was a café that closed shortly before you moved here.'

'One day you'll talk Gage around and we'll see your famous cakes on sale. No one would make their own Christmas cakes or mince pies if they could buy yours instead.'

'Maybe. Sit down while I stick the kettle on and tell me what's got you all upset.'

After making their drinks, she raided the emergency stash for a packet of chocolate digestives.

'It's nothing really.'

'Don't talk rubbish.' Tamara scoffed. 'Out with it.'

'My youngest brother, Bryan, called me late yesterday and he was over the moon with excitement. He and his wife, Sue Ann, are expecting their first baby next June. I'm happy for them of course and managed to say so, enough to fool them, I think, and hopefully Nathan too, but they've only been married five minutes.' Melissa's voice broke. 'Last month I was five days late and hoped against hope that we might be in luck.'

Tamara covered her friend's hand and gave it a squeeze. 'I'm sorry. That's tough.'

Pointing out that a smart man like Nathan would soon realise something was wrong, if he hadn't already, wouldn't

100

help. Their book group was close, but some topics were too private even to lay in front of good friends. It'd been the case with Laura, whose numerous miscarriages had led her to desperate measures and almost destroyed her marriage in the process. Despite the promises they made to be more open with each other, they all kept secrets.

'I won't be offended if you tell me to mind my own business, but I assume you've both been to the doctor?'

'Oh, yeah. Loads of them.' Her cheeks pinkened. 'We've had every godawful test you can imagine and there's nothing officially wrong with either of us.' She reduced her biscuit to crumbs with her fingers. 'I try to be philosophical and accept it probably won't happen now, but then I see little Josephine and . . .' Melissa crumpled and her distress filled the room.

'Have you thought about adoption or fostering? What about IVF?'

'Yeah, of course I've thought about all those things, but I shut Nathan down when he dared raise the subject. To my mind, it's admitting we've given up. Stupid, I suppose, but there it is.'

She could make a dozen different arguments to the contrary, but Melissa's realisation needed to come at the right time for her and in the right way.

'Do you know what I dread most?' Melissa's shoulders drooped. 'Maybe I shouldn't say this to you of all people, because it's horribly mean, but I worry how I'll react if Chloe gets pregnant.'

Tamara almost choked on her coffee. 'I'm not ready to be a grandmother so I hope that's not anytime soon. They aren't in a position yet to . . .' Was this how her parents had felt all those years ago? And at least Chloe and Toby's partnership was loving and equal, unlike her and Fred's one-sided romance that had never stood a chance. 'I don't see Nathan as great-uncle material yet either. He's too—'

'Hot?'

'Not the word I'd use unless I want you ripping my eyes out.' Nathan's title as Penworthal's hottest and most

101

confirmed bachelor had flown out of the window when he had been whisked, very willingly, down the aisle by Melissa. 'But seriously, you're too nice to be anything but lovely if that happens one day. It might hurt a bit, but you wouldn't take it out on them or the baby.'

'I hope you're right.' Melissa's smile inched back. 'I feel much better for talking to you.'

Now they both had tears in their eyes. Her developing relationship with Gage was lifting her spirits, but she'd never make the mistake of abandoning her friends.

'Let's lighten the mood for a minute,' said Melissa. 'I hear Gage and Evelyn are pretty friendly these days, so have you heard anything about what's going on at *Shangri-La*?'

'You tell me. He turned into a clam when I tried to probe.'

'Nathan's the same about Quinten. They've met for a pint a couple of times — well away from here — but he won't spill the beans either. He gets all pompous and starchy — a bit like I imagine his father was.'

'That describes old Mr Kellow perfectly.'

Melissa coloured. 'I know I'm being unfair because if Nathan wasn't honourable and trustworthy, I would never have fallen in love with him.'

'That's true — but we'd still like to know, wouldn't we?' Tamara gave a sly smile.

'Are you through with your coffee? I know I am.' Neither had taken more than a couple of sips. 'I should've warned you it was Vernon's half-price special last week.' Tamara dumped the dregs in the sink and rinsed the mugs out, leaving them on the dish rack to dry. 'Do you want another look around?'

For the next few minutes, she watched Melissa behave like a little kid in a sweet shop, oohing and aahing at the enticing way they'd arranged the different sections.

The stunning floor-to-ceiling maple-wood bookcases around the walls housed the used books. It'd been an insight into Gage's mind, when they'd been sorting these out, to see the changes to his reading and buying tastes over the years.

102

The smaller shelves that ringed the centre of the space featured new books, curated with advice from the independent booksellers' group he belonged to. To her mind it was the perfect combination of old and new, both in the stock available and the chosen décor.

An old manual till sat on the counter. She'd bought it at a car-boot sale, purely because it appealed to her, but it had sat in the attic until finding its new home here. The fancy modern one next to it would actually be used for sales.

Whipping out her phone, Melissa took pictures of all the books she planned to buy when Gage opened on Saturday. Miraculously, her normal wide, infectious smile had returned to full strength, and there was a distinct spring in her step. Tamara couldn't help thinking that people who insisted books weren't important were deluded. They were missing out on one of the simplest mood-lifters, with the bonus they were calorie-free and with no artificial stimulants.

'There's only one thing missing. You need comfy chairs scattered around to tempt customers to sit down and get so into the lovely books they won't be able to leave them here.'

'We're on it. If all goes well, that'll be put right on Wednesday.' Tamara explained about the estate sale they were targeting near Tintagel. Gage was in full agreement that new chairs wouldn't fit the cosy atmosphere he was determined to create. 'Think squishy. Comfy. Mismatched. Vintage. We need small tables too, for people to set their books down.'

'And teacups when you get the café going.'

Tamara ignored the last remark and suggested Melissa might want to head off unless she wanted Nathan on the warpath.

'Thanks again for everything. I feel it in my bones, by this time next year, you and Gage will be all loved up, and we'll have winkled Evelyn's annoying sister out so she and Quinten can have their happy-ever-after too.'

'You read too many romances, Melissa Kellow.' Tamara shooed her friend out and closed the shop door with a wistful sigh.

103

CHAPTER THIRTEEN

'Are you going to tell me what's eating at you or do we keep pretending nothing's wrong? According to you things went well at Becky's on Sunday, but you've been like a bear with a sore head ever since.'

Gage squirmed under the force of Tamara's fierce glare. 'You might want to slow down. The sign says sharp bends for the next half mile.'

'Really? And there was me thinking the zig-zaggy symbol on that pretty red sign is warning me to beware of drunk pedestrians wandering in the road.'

He couldn't blame her for the heavy dose of sarcasm. After all, she'd opened her home to him and slaved away beside him in the shop until she was dropping with tiredness. Now she was forced to cope with the large, unwieldy van he'd hired for the day because he was out of commission where driving was concerned. And in the pouring rain, no less. And how did he repay her? By shutting her out.

'So?'

'Lunch was great. The kids are awesome and I can't wait to get to know them better. Paul's a friendly, easy-going chap and not thrown by any of this.'

'I knew he wouldn't be. We'll be there in five minutes, so you're running out of time to confess all to Aunty Tamara.'

He was aware the driver's door controlled the power locks and didn't doubt she would hold him hostage if necessary.

'As I was leaving, Becky asked something that threw me.' He cleared his throat, but that didn't help. The words remained stuck there.

'Do I get three guesses?'

'She asked if I'm still in touch with our father.'

'Are you?'

'I thought he was dead, didn't I? He and my mum split up when I was about eleven and we never saw him again. That's when I started going off the rails. When Mum threatened to hand me over to social services and I said I'd go live with my dad if she didn't want me, she laughed and wished me good luck with that because he was six feet under. Killed in a car crash.'

'Oh, Gage. How could she lie to you?'

How wrong he'd been to assume that he'd come to terms with his fractured relationship with his mother because now, thanks to Tamara's unstinting sympathy, tears filled his eyes. No matter how hard he blinked, they continued taunting him.

'We're stopping,' Tamara said and pulled off the road into a farm gateway. 'The chairs can wait.'

'I was a handful. She couldn't cope.'

'That's no excuse. Don't you dare blame yourself.' Her face flamed. 'I've not been a perfect mum, but I've never trashed Fred to Toby.'

'Even though many people would say you had every right to?'

'They'd be wrong,' she said softly. 'My son doesn't need that burden.' Tamara straightened her shoulders. 'These are broad. They can take it. Toby's better off hearing Fred was a good man who wasn't ready to be a father.' A faraway look appeared in her eyes. 'Maybe that's the truth.'

'But you stepped up. What does that say about your character compared to Fred's?'

105

She shrugged off the question.

'Does Toby have any contact with his dad these days?'

'No.' Tamara said firmly. 'Apart from paying child support, Fred's had nothing to do with us since he left. When Toby was little, he used to ask about his dad all the time but then he stopped.' A sigh slipped out. 'A few years ago, I asked him if he wanted to track Fred down because I would've helped if he did. Toby didn't want to know, so I've never mentioned it again.' She shook her head. 'We're getting off track here.' The undercurrent of strength and steel he'd spotted in Tamara the first day they'd met returned. 'So where is your dad?'

'Living in Edinburgh, with yet another family on the go.' He managed a faint smile. 'Becky hasn't had a lot of contact with him over the years, mainly Christmas and birthday cards and the occasional phone call. He had another couple of kids with a different woman after my mum, and now he's on his fourth lot, so we've more half-brothers and half-sisters scattered about the country. It might explain why I've never settled down. Must be the genes.'

'That's rubbish. Look at Becky. You couldn't find a more down-to-earth, grounded person.' She looked thoughtful. 'Perhaps the upset of her dad and everything pushed her the other way. Becky married straight out of school and the kids came one after the other, all before she was twenty-one.'

'Whereas I'm the original rolling stone.'

'Until you came to Penworthal.' Her voice wobbled. 'At least, I hope you're not going to throw it all in now you've got what you came for.'

'Reconnecting with Becky isn't the only reason I'm here and you know that.' Gage could hardly bear to look at Tamara, but couldn't look away either, so he briefly closed his eyes. 'At least, I hope you do?' He held his breath.

'I do.'

* * *

106

Tamara relaxed as relief inched over Gage's conflicted expression. Pushing too hard and too fast wouldn't help either of them. Determined to change the subject and get back on schedule she said, 'If we don't hurry up, we'll run out of time to check out the different lots first to decide which to bid for.'

'I've never been to an auction before. Probably best I superglue my hands to my body and let you take charge. I'm afraid I'll end up spending thousands on an antique Chinese pot.'

'Don't worry. If the auctioneer is on the ball, they're expert at telling the difference between a genuine bid and someone scratching their nose.'

She started the engine, put the van in gear and checked to make sure no one was coming before pulling back out. This was her first time driving a vehicle this cumbersome, although she'd kept that nugget of information to herself because Gage was edgy enough today.

'There's the sign. Boscarrek Manor.' Gage frowned. 'Looks posh. Are you sure we'll—'

'It's fine. Trust me.'

Tamara turned the van and drove through the intricate wrought-iron gates. Although impressive at first sight, the metal was badly rusted and the gilding on the ancestral crests had long since disappeared. From her research she'd discovered the family behind today's auction had owned the estate for almost four hundred years, but the new heir had sold it to a developer who planned to turn it into 'executive apartments'. In other words, fancy places for people attracted to living a simpler life in the country, in theory, but with none of the drawbacks.

'I scoured the online catalogue and we'll be good. This sort of thing is my happy place.' She giggled. 'Don't worry, I won't go over the allotted budget.'

'Unless you see a pig you can't resist.'

She smacked his arm. 'I should never have told you that.'

One of their many conversations had drifted to hobbies and he'd been stunned to hear about her porcelain pigs. The

107

only comparable thing he could come up with was hardly a secret — it was his inability to walk past a bookshop without buying something. Gage had blushed like mad when she'd asked how much he'd spent over the years on a storage locker to house his growing collection of books while he'd travelled around the globe. One reason for the bookshop was his realisation that he wouldn't live long enough to read them all, so sharing the pleasure with other booklovers made sense.

'I don't mind admitting I'll have to do the sitting-on-my-hands thing when a certain Wemyss pig comes up. It's very rare, from the 1930s. There are very few of the Irish-shamrock designs around. It'll cost an absolute fortune.'

After navigating around a ridiculous number of pot-holes, she was relieved that all the tyres had survived and the windscreen had no noticeable scratches from the onslaught of drooping branches and overgrown bushes. The glossy online pictures of the Elizabethan house must've been Photoshopped because the grimy building in front of them was covered in scaffolding, a good number of the leaded windows were shattered and weeds sprouted up around the house's foundations.

'Not quite what I expected.' Gage commented with raised eyebrows.

Tamara followed the car in front to the temporary parking area in a field and pulled into a spot at the end of a row. 'I should've dropped you off so you don't have the uneven ground to deal with.' At least the rain had finally stopped.

'I'll be fine.' Gage grimaced as he eased out of the van, but she held her tongue. The stubborn man insisted he didn't need crutches today because Evelyn had lent him a stout walking stick. He didn't protest, though, when she linked her arm through his and matched his slower pace.

The spacious marble hall was full of people milling around, but she steered in the direction of the viewing room and picked up a catalogue on the way. The furniture was towards the back, so they headed there first to examine the chairs they'd marked out as possible purchases. Some she

108

marked with a tick in her catalogue, and others were crossed through because they wouldn't suit for a variety of reasons.

'Right, let's get a good seat before the rush starts.'

'At the front?'

She laughed. 'Absolutely not. You want a clear view to scan the room and size up the competition — especially when we start bidding.'

Gage's cockeyed smile made her tingle all over.

They headed for the far side of what must have been a spectacular ballroom in its day, its ornately panelled ceiling adorned with fading but beautifully painted scenes from Greek mythology. Its inlaid wood floor only needed sanding and polishing to restore its glory.

Tamara plonked down at one end of the back row. This was when her height was a plus because it was easy to look over the heads of the people in front of them. An hour later she was beaming with satisfaction after securing the chairs they wanted.

An adorable Victorian wingback upholstered in faded dark-green velvet. A matching pair of tan leather 1930s club chairs, whose every scratch and worn spot showed how well loved they'd been. The prize for the best deal went to the two-seater Edwardian love seat she'd picked up for a song — no one else had wanted it because it'd been tastelessly re-covered in bright pink brocade. In the short term, they'd use it with enough scatter cushions to dim its garish colour and later she could reupholster it. They also bought half a dozen mahogany dining chairs that weren't wonderfully exciting, but serviceable for extra seating, and several small tables. Gage had done as promised — sat on his hands and not uttered a word.

'Right, that's us done. Are you ready to pick up our winnings?'

'Where do we go for the stuff?

'There's a door around the back for loading.'

'Fine. I'll go pay if you bring the van around. I'm sure I can find someone to help us load since I'm useless.'

'Nothing's overly heavy. I can manage.'

109

'Of course you can. Superwoman.' There was no hint of sarcasm, only good-humoured admiration. Very different from when they'd first met. 'I'll see you outside. I'll return that if you like.' He snatched the bidding card away from her.

'Cheers.' Tamara's spirits soared. They were good.

* * *

Gage swiftly paid for their purchases then sneaked back into the auction, just as the auctioneer announced they were moving on to the decorative pieces and gestured to his assistant, a thin young woman in black, who held up a large porcelain pig.

He waved the card in the air as the auctioneer started the bidding at a hundred pounds. If he was successful, he could claim it'd been bought as a lucky mascot for the shop. In truth, this had nothing to do with the shop, but everything to do with them. Gage wasn't a man for grand romantic gestures and she'd already told him flowers and the like weren't her thing. This would hopefully be a different story.

An older woman with a hooked nose, fierce eyes and a tightly pursed mouth stared fiercely at Gage and raised her own card as the auctioneer called for another fifty pounds.

'One thousand pounds,' Gage shouted, wanting to cut to the chase.

A gasp ran around the room.

With an angry headshake at the auctioneer, and a vicious glare at Gage, the woman conceded defeat. She rose from her seat and swanned out of the room, followed by a small ferret-faced man who scuttled behind her like the White Rabbit in *Alice in Wonderland*.

Gage made his way as fast as he could to collect his prize pig. By the time he reached Tamara, she was closing the van doors.

'Typical man, turning up when all the work is done.' She glanced back over her shoulder and all the colour drained from her face. 'Tell me you didn't buy that?'

110

'Nah, they let me bring it out for a minute so you could stroke it.'

'Very funny.'

'I thought the shop needed a lucky mascot.'

'A bloody expensive one. How much did you pay for it? Or don't I even want to know?'

He blurted out the truth before he could think better of it.

'You have lost your mind.'

Gage shrugged. 'I'd say it's the opposite.'

'But that's money you could really use for other things. Like paying the sky-high electric bill in a few months?' Her ribbing didn't dent his wicked grin.

'Don't you love it, though? What're we going to call her?'

'Why're you so sure it's a her?'

'Look at that face. It's obvious.'

'If you say so.'

'It needs to be something literary.' Gage frowned, deep in thought.

'I don't always choose one straightaway. Sometimes, I wait and get to know them first. It's a bit like having a baby, or at least it was in my case. Fred had zero interest, so I picked the name George. But when they placed Toby in my arms, I knew he wasn't a George. After about ten days, it fell into place and he was Toby from then on. Does that sound mad?'

Gage shrugged. 'I wouldn't know.'

'I've never thought to ask if you're married or whatever?' She gave a nervous laugh. 'I suppose I should've done before we kissed.'

'I was married once, but it didn't last long. I don't mention it because it's not important to me any longer. Before now it's not really mattered.' His heart thudded, waiting for her response.

'Did you have any kids with your ex-wife? I assume that would've mattered enough for you to tell me.'

Gage didn't blame her for either the pointedness or the questions, but he couldn't help being pissed off. It was a

111

touchy subject for him, but she couldn't know that. 'Time we got going, isn't it?'

'I don't get an answer?'

'I don't have kids, okay?' Gage swung away from her, almost losing his balance in the process. If he dropped the pig, that really would be the end.

CHAPTER FOURTEEN

Gage watched Tamara across the crowded shop. This should be one of the happiest days of his life, but a pall of guilt hung over him.

He'd been blown away this morning when she'd come downstairs wearing a dark-navy over-the-knee dress closely following every one of her luscious curves, her hair swept back in a fashionably messy bun and enough make-up to enhance her natural beauty without being what he called shouty. No one seeing her rest her hand on his arm earlier and smiling broadly at all the people piling in — an interesting mixture of serious booklovers and the curious — would guess they were at odds. Apart from working together to get the shop ready and discussing the business details surrounding today's launch, they hadn't spoken to each other for three days. Quite an achievement for two people sharing a house. First thing this morning, he brought out the Wemyss pig and set it at one end of the counter, hoping to use it as a peace offering. But she only broke her silence to say it wasn't safe there and would be knocked over. Dutifully he returned it to the storeroom out of sight.

She'd asked a perfectly understandable question at the auction about his relationship status and whether or not he

113

had children. His overreaction had been appalling. That silent drive home from Tintagel had seemed interminable, and they'd barely grunted to each other as they'd unloaded the van — correction — *she'd* unloaded the van. Even deciding where to place the new furniture around the shop had been accomplished by a series of grunts and nods. A few of the chairs were arranged in companionable groups, and the rest were dotted where people could sit and read in peace. The fact that most of the upholstery had seen better days and much of the wood was scratched and scuffed added to the general impression of comfort and homeliness.

'You've done a fine job, Mr Bennet, and I hope it'll be a huge success.' Evelyn stationed herself in front of him. 'I don't know what you've said or done to upset Tamara, but remember she has a lot of friends here.'

Now he knew how her old pupils must've felt when she'd torn them off a strip. Gage didn't try to defend himself and watched her leave with a heavy heart.

Out of nowhere, someone gave him a hearty slap on the back. 'Wotcha, Prof, you've done good.' Taff Morgan stood there grinning like a loon. 'Perhaps you'll prove me wrong after all. Who are the bunch of geeky-looking chaps in the corner?'

Gage laughed. 'They're the military-history nuts. I put the word out online and dropped a few teasing hints about certain books that were on sale, so here they are.'

'Another few weeks and you'll be swamped with their friends and relatives looking for Christmas presents.'

'That's the plan.'

'Whoa! Who's that gorgeous creature?' Taff's intense green eyes gleamed.

'That's Tamara. She's . . .' The words to describe what she was to him wouldn't come.

'Oh, mate, I get it and don't blame you. I'll steer clear. Don't want to step on your toes.' Taff threw up his hands. 'Although crocked as you are, you're hardly going to catch me, are you?'

114

He couldn't take that sort of ribbing from anyone else, but the first genuine smile he'd managed in days broke free. 'Bastard.'

'If she's not up for grabs, I'll leave you to your adoring fans and see if there's anything else to appeal to me, apart from a good book of course.' Taff grinned and sauntered off. Almost immediately he homed in on an attractive redhead.

If Gage were kinder, he'd find a way to warn his friend off. He could explain that Josie was a fiery nurse who'd eat Taff for dinner, and the stocky man with salt-and-pepper hair standing next to her was Harry, Josie's police detective husband. But he didn't.

With what he hoped was a welcoming smile, he ploughed back into greeting people.

* * *

'So, what's up with you and our wounded hunk?' Laura tapped Tamara's arm. 'He's thrown a few sad looks your way when he thinks no one is watching, and you've got that false-front thing going on. The one that says Tamara Pascoe isn't intimidated by anything, and will grit her teeth so hard they fall out rather than admit to any weakness.'

For a brief moment, Tamara contemplated what it might feel like to pour out all her problems and ask for advice.

'And, yeah, we both know I was a total prat about the baby thing.' Laura lowered her voice. 'Learn from my mistakes. I'm damn lucky to still have Barry. He'd have been well in his rights to scarper and leave me to it. If I'd told you and the girls in the first place, my marriage wouldn't nearly have fallen apart.'

'I'm tired. That's all. We've worked non-stop the last ten days.' Tamara forced a smile.

'Fine. Be an ostrich. But if someone comes along and kicks your feathered ass, don't blame me.' Laura tossed her blonde hair and stomped off.

115

She didn't have the energy to blink away the tears filling her eyes.

'Isn't this awesome?' Melissa looked vibrant and elegant today in a silky purple shirtdress and black patent heels. 'Oops, don't tell me. Mark Darcy has turned into Daniel Cleaver. The rotter.'

Her confusion must've shown because Melissa's tinkling laugh rang out.

'I'm immersed in the world of *Bridget Jones's Diary* at the moment, ready for book club. Poor Nathan is tearing his hair out this month.'

A pang of envy stabbed her heart. At one point she'd nurtured a stupid hope that Gage might take after Nathan, who always read the book-club selections and happily discussed them with his wife. When the couple had been dating, he'd even planned wonderful trips to many of the locations in the Cornish books that had been the theme for the year. Another dream out the window.

'I haven't had time to read it yet.'

'Why don't you come to mine after you close here? Nathan's going for a drink with Quinten, so we can open a bottle or two and eat junk food.' Melissa squeezed her hand. 'It might cheer you up.'

The tears welled up again. She didn't deserve such good friends. One had gone off in a huff already. Tamara couldn't afford to lose another. 'Thanks. Did you talk to Nathan?'

'He'd already guessed that Bryan's news upset me. There's not much my dear husband misses. He was sad too. That kinda helped.' Melissa straightened her shoulders. 'There's always next month.'

'Of course there is.'

She wasn't convinced by Melissa's casual response, but would have to be satisfied for now. There was a queue of people waiting to pay, and Gage looked tired and drawn from standing for far too long. Being in one position for an extended time was hard on his knee anyway, these days, but while he was still in recovery mode?

116

'I need to go help serve.'

'You do that. While you're there, make sure he gets a good eyeful of you in that dress. I bet you haven't paid any attention to all the admiring glances you're getting today?'

'Me?' Compared to the jeans and T-shirts she practically lived in, she might not look too bad, but Melissa was undoubtedly laying the compliments on with a trowel to boost her confidence.

'Oh, Tamara. You're worse than I was.' Melissa gave her a shove. 'First, make him regret pissing you off and then make him beg. Go on.'

Pulling back her shoulders, she headed towards Gage. It childishly boosted her ego when he spotted her and turned pale. *Regret, then beg.* She repeated the words like a mantra.

* * *

He wasn't sorry to see the crowd had tapered off and was down to the last few stragglers. His aching knee was making its presence known now. About an hour ago, Tamara had marched over to him like an avenging Valkyrie. She'd shoved him towards the high stool they'd bought for behind the counter, pithily telling him that it hadn't had any use today. Then she'd stated in no uncertain terms that she'd stand there and take the money while he wrapped people's purchases.

'You should be able to manage now while I start tidying the shelves. I don't know about you, but I'm knackered. We can come in tomorrow to restock for Monday.'

'Can we talk?' he asked.

'What do you think we're doing now? Playing chess? Ice skating?'

Gage cleared his dry throat. 'I've been a stubborn idiot.'

Tamara folded her arms across her body as if to ward him off. Unfortunately, that tightened the dress over her generous breasts and lifted them to his direct line of vision. Gage's only saving grace was the fact he was sitting behind the till, so he could shift around on the stool to minimise his discomfort. As their eyes met, her triumph was unmistakable.

117

'I won't argue with that.'

'Didn't think you would. You caught me off guard.' She opened her mouth to speak, but he pre-empted her. 'But that's no excuse for how rude I was to you.'

'You're right it's not.'

'Do you think we can stop being—'

'Childish?' Tamara gave a wry smile. 'I think so.' She stuck out her hand. 'Friends again?'

As they exchanged a firm handshake, he was hyper-aware of her warm skin and subtle perfume. 'Yeah.' He longed to ask what the chance was of moving to a little warmer than 'friends', but didn't have the nerve.

'We'll see, Gage, okay? Let's take it slow.'

A flush of heat prickled his neck. She'd read him like the proverbial book from day one.

'I'm sorry, but I can't stay any longer tonight. Melissa's on her own because Nathan's playing amateur psychologist to Quinten again, so I'm going over for a girly chat.'

'About useless men?'

Her chin tilted. 'I'm sure we'll have a meaningful discussion about a wide range of subjects.' A giggle slipped out. 'And drown our sorrows in chardonnay. Hopefully I won't be too hungover in the morning because I know Pixie wants to get the Christmas decorations up after we've finished serving the Sunday roasts.'

'Already? It's only the eighth of November.'

'I know but it gets customers in the festive mood, which means more sales, so it's good for business. You need to think about decorating here too. I had a few ideas today, so we can talk about them tomorrow.'

'Yeah, sounds good.'

Gage was sorry to see a customer approaching the counter, forcing an end to the conversation. A tiny seed of hope lodged in his gut that if he didn't mess up again, Tamara might give him a second chance.

118

CHAPTER FIFTEEN

According to Gage's personal weather forecasting system — his aching knee — it would start raining soon. He made sure Evelyn's precious book was safely wrapped in plastic before he stepped outside and locked the shop for the night. The short walk up to her house would be good exercise for his knee. He crossed the road and noticed someone had been busy. The shop window display had plunged headlong into Christmas. No doubt that was the plucky Chloe's doing. She cheerfully browbeat Vernon on a regular basis and used his tiny shop as a place to experiment with the modern business practices she was studying at uni.

Fairy lights twinkled around a veritable festive wonderland. The chubby red Father Christmas in the middle was surrounded by slightly manic-eyed elves. What Gage assumed to be a snowman naturally turned out to be a snowwoman, and she was surrounded by dancing candy canes. Heaping piles of fake snow showed off boxes of mince pies, chocolates and the fancy tins of biscuits no self-respecting British family celebrated the season without. Encouraging people to buy locally this early, before they started hauling things home from the supermarkets, was a smart move.

All this gave Gage a sharp nudge. Tamara was right. He should get cracking himself on that score. According to his independent bookseller group, this was the crucial time to maximise profits in the run-up to the new-year slump. In January, no one had money to splurge on non-necessities, although he would personally argue books were crucial to life, and the weather was usually against casual shoppers.

He reached the little white bungalow and was about to ring the doorbell when he noticed the door was ajar. Raised voices drifted out.

'You're a liar!' Evelyn yelled. 'I know Sam wasn't perfect but he would never—'

'It was easier for you to put the blame on me than face the fact your precious husband . . .' Ophelia's sobs muffled the rest of her words.

Before Gage had a chance to turn around and creep away, Ophelia burst through the door. Automatically he shot out his hands to stop her barrelling into him. Over her shoulder he spotted Evelyn.

'Oh, *mon Dieu*, I'm sorry.' The mixture of French and English showed her confusion, and her wild eyes struggled to focus.

'It's fine. Is there anything I can do to help?'

Ophelia shook her head at Evelyn. 'I hoped we might finally . . . but she won't listen . . . it's hopeless. I have to leave.'

'I believe that will be for the best.' There was ice in Evelyn's voice and her blue eyes were equally cold.

'I don't know what's kept you at odds for forty years, but I *do* know your time to sort it is running out. If you aren't careful, you soon won't have the chance to listen to each other's side of the story and you'll never know who was right.'

Evelyn scoffed. 'I know compared to you we must seem ancient, but neither of us has one foot in the grave yet.'

'I do,' Ophelia whispered. Silent tears tracked down her face.

'I should go.' Gage shifted awkwardly from one foot to the other.

'No, stay. Please.'

'I only came to return your book, Evelyn.' He turned to his newly acquired friend. 'It was wonderful and I'll definitely read more of her work.'

'I'm glad you enjoyed it.' She gave him a cool nod. 'I don't have a problem with you remaining if that's what Ophelia wants. Why don't you both go into the living room while I make tea?' She nodded to her sister. 'I assume you'd prefer coffee? If you trust me with your fancy machine, that is.'

He noticed Ophelia's jaw tighten and was prepared for another caustic comment, but none came. She wandered off in the direction of the living room, shoulders slumped and every slow step a massive effort.

Gage followed behind and sat in the chair closest to the window. He spotted a couple who'd been in the shop this week out walking their miniature white poodle. They waved and smiled, so he did the same. Running a business was far different from what he'd expected. Harder in some ways because everything relied on him, but that same aspect made it incredibly satisfying. After a career spent following orders and an agenda made by others, Gage revelled in the freedom to carve his own path. It might prove an abject failure in time, but at least he'd only have himself to blame.

Ophelia nestled in the corner of the sofa furthest away from him and kept her eyes down.

'Right, here we are.' Evelyn bustled in with a loaded tray and set it down on the low wooden table before passing them each a cup and saucer. No mugs here. She considered them a sign of lowered standards. 'Now, Ophelia, I want to know exactly what you meant by that dreadful thing.'

'Dreadful? Really? That's the nicest thing you've said since I arrived.'

'I opened my home to you and put my life on hold. What more do you want?' Evelyn bristled. 'I wouldn't leave you

121

homeless, but it's no good pretending we're close and loving sisters, is it?'

'I suppose not.' Ophelia's head drooped. 'Gage saw it straight away, but you didn't.'

'Saw what?' Evelyn's attention switched to him. 'Do I get an answer?'

'Sure.' Gage planted his hands on his knees and leaned forward. 'I don't know the details because Ophelia didn't share them, but anyone with eyes can tell she's seriously ill.'

'Ill?' Evelyn set down her cup and stared at her sister. 'She's terribly thin, but I never . . .' She shook her head. 'What is it?' she croaked.

'My lungs. Too many cigarettes. I didn't listen to the warnings. But that's me all over, isn't it?' The attempt to sound blasé might've worked if her eyes weren't brimming with tears.

'How long?' Evelyn whispered.

'Have I been sick or have left?' Ophelia's brittleness returned. 'About a year ago, I could no longer ignore my persistent cough and tiredness, and the doctor confirmed what I already guessed. They don't care to be too precise when it comes to handing out death sentences, but if I make it to next summer . . .' Her voice faded.

Rain beat against the window now, darkening the room until they were all in shadowy profile. It pinpointed a strong likeness between the two women he hadn't recognised before now.

Evelyn rose and sat by her sister, reaching for her hand. 'I'm sorry.' The faint smile she sent his way tugged at Gage. 'Thank you. If you weren't so—'

'Nosy?'

'I'd use the word astute. But I'm grateful.'

'How about I leave you to talk now?'

'You might as well hear the rest. Hadn't he, Ophelia?' Evelyn murmured. 'Your side and mine.' Shoulders straight again, she patted her sister's hand and sucked in a breath. 'I was twenty-three and newly married. Dizzy with love, and excited about my first job at the school. Ophelia still lived at

122

home with our parents, but she visited Sam and me a lot. It made me happy they got on so well.' Her expression hardened. 'One day I came home from work and saw her kissing Sam in the kitchen. Next thing, he pushed her away and shouted for her to leave him alone. He said it was sick, that he thought of her as a sister.' A sob caught in her raspy throat. 'She spun a story about Sam trying to force himself on her.' She shook her head. 'I do admit that later I discovered a different side to Sam, but at that time he was crazy about me, so—'

'You chose to believe him.' Regret laced Ophelia's words. 'He'd been making suggestions to me for weeks, every time he got me alone. It's why I never came to visit unless I knew you'd be there, but that day you were late. He cornered me in the kitchen and started trying to kiss me. When I tried to push him off, Sam smirked and said he'd spin the story so you'd believe *I* came on to *him*. You were like a mum to me, Evelyn. Who explained what was happening when I got my period? Whose shoulder did I cry on when Joe Wilson dumped me for that awful Blewett girl? For sixteen years we were the closest of sisters, and you wouldn't even hear what I had to say. You told Mum and Dad that if they didn't throw me out, you and Sam would leave the village and move away. You even threatened if you had children, they'd never see me. I saved them the anguish of deciding between us and I left.'

Evelyn exhaled loudly with a shudder. 'I've been so stupid.' When she glanced back up, her eyes shimmered with tears. 'Can you ever forgive me, or is it too late?'

Now he really did need to leave. Gage stood. 'You'll be okay now.'

Evelyn's hand found Ophelia's again. 'We've a lot to talk about.'

'We certainly do. For a start I want to hear more about Quinten and why you've been so terrible to the poor man.'

He slipped out, leaving them bickering companionably like normal sisters.

* * *

123

Acting was so not Tamara's forte. Evelyn ambushed them all as soon as they arrived for book club and announced she had something to tell them. It was sure to be about Ophelia, so she would have to act surprised. She'd been absolutely shocked when Gage had told her everything that had happened when he'd visited Evelyn. The sisters sat side by side on the sofa, and an eerily pale Ophelia listened silently as Evelyn calmly recited the whole story of their estrangement and her sister's health troubles. A collective gasp ran around the group before the sympathetic questions and offers of support started. They weren't women to hold grudges, so nobody held Ophelia's previous haughty attitude against her now.

'So, that's it.' A flush tinged Evelyn's gaunt cheeks. 'I'm sorry for being so close-mouthed before, but nowhere near as sorry as I am for letting Ophelia down.' She squeezed her sister's hand. 'We do seem to be finding out an awful lot of each other's secrets recently. It's far healthier, isn't it?'

Becky sneaked Tamara a wry smile, as if to say it might be healthy but that didn't make it easy. Despite it being common knowledge that she and Gage were half-siblings, Becky was still close-mouthed when it came to talking about their tentative relationship. Neither seemed sure what to expect or hope for from the other.

'Right, now let's get down to the book,' Evelyn said firmly and picked up her copy. 'What did we all think of *Bridget Jones's Diary*? Tamara, why don't you start us off?'

This reminded her of being at school when teachers always picked on her when Tamara either didn't know the answer or was reluctant to give one. Being completely truthful meant exposing herself in a way that made her uneasy, even with her best friends. Melissa's encouraging smile helped and she took a deep breath.

'I was only twelve when the book came out so Mum wouldn't let me read it, but when the film was released five years later I went to see it with friends. I left the cinema wanting to smack Bridget because I was seventeen and pregnant,

124

married to a man who didn't give a shit about me or our baby, and there she was, a self-absorbed thirty-something with a glamorous job, and two hot men literally fighting over her. All I could think was what the hell did she have to whine about?'

There was silence and a few uneasy glances flickered between her friends.

'I would say you make a very valid point,' Evelyn said staunchly. 'As someone from a very different generation, Bridget and her friends often struck me as incredibly annoying but also terribly sad. There's a comment Bridget makes along the lines of older people not reading self-help books, but simply getting on with life. Does anyone else wonder if the more you fret and try to analyse whether or not you're "happy", whatever that is, the less content you are?'

A trace of satisfaction settled inside Tamara as the arguments ping-ponged around the room.

'But surely you can sympathise with Bridget's body-image obsession?' Amy aimed the question straight at Tamara. 'You're always complaining about your latest failed diet, even though you're incredibly fit, healthy and strong. Didn't you connect with the part when Bridget finally managed to lose weight, but her friend Tom declared she looked better before? She felt she'd wasted all those years of counting calories and deprivation for nothing.'

'Well, yes. Maybe.' And leaving the room backwards so no man would see Bridget's wobbly bum? Been there, done that. There was no need for a mirror to know an ugly flush mottled her face.

'Just as she is. That's the toast they make to Bridget. That's the theme of the book and it comes out even more prominently in the film.' Amy's colour heightened. 'I was thirty before I had the courage to come out and stop hiding my sexuality. Penworthal was very old-fashioned and traditional when I was growing up, which is the main reason I went to uni in London and stayed away for years. I wasn't sure how

125

we'd be received when Tessa and I came back to live, but it's been fine — most of the time anyway.'

This was certainly turning into a night for revelations. Amy had never spoken with such deep honesty before.

'So what are our thoughts on the book in comparison to the film?' Evelyn nudged them back to the discussion. 'The parallels with *Pride and Prejudice* are far more obvious in the book. The film cut out the part about Mark Darcy tracking down Bridget's mother's boyfriend and recovering the money he'd stolen from their friends. That storyline was clearly taken from the book, when Mr Darcy pursues the despicable George Wickham, ensures he marries Lydia to save her reputation and settles Wickham's debts.'

'I know I'm shallow,' Melissa's laughter was completely unashamed, 'but is anyone else not surprised that Bridget was under Daniel Cleaver's spell? There's something about a bad boy that attracts women, despite themselves.'

'Does anyone mind me joining in?' There was no trace of a French accent in Ophelia's quiet voice.

'Of course not.' Becky beamed. 'You've experienced so much, dear, living abroad and that. Paul's been my man since I were a girl, see, so all this is foreign to me.'

'You're too kind. All of you.' Ophelia's gaze darted around. 'I only came here because I didn't know where else to go, and there was a faint chance of putting things right with my sister before it was too late. The last thing I expected, or quite honestly even wanted, a few weeks ago, was to be brought into your fold. I was incredibly rude at first and I'm terribly sorry.'

'We're sorry you're having a hard time, my love, but we live by the Cornish motto — One and All — and you're one of us now,' Becky said kindly.

Ophelia's thin throat worked as if holding back tears. 'Thank you.' She straightened and blinked rapidly. 'Back to Melissa's comment.' Tamara heard echoes of Evelyn in her firmer tone of voice. 'In my experience, those of us who've been

126

tempted by so-called bad boys live to regret it. They made the film version of Daniel Cleaver much less awful than the book character, but he was still untrustworthy and rotten at the core. I spent far too many years involved with a French version of Daniel. He was a handsome charmer called Lucien, who totally had me wrapped around his little finger, always dangling promises that he never kept. I didn't have the courage to break things off with him for good until I got sick. So I've ended up alone.'

Evelyn grasped her sister's hand. 'You're not alone. You've got me.'

Tears pricked Tamara's eyes. A vivid picture of her own sister floated into her head. She couldn't remember the last time Tracy had contacted her, as opposed to the other way around. When she did reply to an email or text, the answers were brief and impersonal. The ten-thousand-mile distance between them seemed to have erased their old closeness. She missed it. Badly.

'Right, girls. Refreshment time.' Evelyn clapped her hands. 'I didn't think anyone would appreciate Bridget's notorious blue soup or lumpy marmalade pudding, or the Boxing Day turkey curry buffet. Ophelia has baked the most amazing Cointreau-and-orange-marmalade biscuits, and I've made curried devilled eggs and ham-and-pickle roll-ups. All washed down with a delicious vodka cocktail, courtesy of my sister's deft hand. Of course, we also have tea, coffee and soft drinks for anyone not indulging.'

A general swarm started towards the kitchen and as soon as they all had their food and a cocktail, everyone regained their seats and settled down for the far more serious business of the night.

'So we're having a village Christmas tree.' Tamara happily made the announcement. 'Vernon had a word with the parish council and they don't have a problem with it.' She gave a wry smile. 'Mainly because it won't cost them anything. The vicar thinks it's a great idea too.'

127

'Well done,' Evelyn said. 'I suggest we have a tree-lighting ceremony. Penworthal might be small, but that doesn't have to stop us doing things properly.'

'Other places have carol singing and craft stalls and food and drink to pull visitors in.' Laura bubbled over with enthusiasm.

'Let's not run before we can walk, dear,' Evelyn said firmly. 'Another year maybe. I think if we sing a few carols and have some of your wonderful mince pies, Tamara, that will make a nice evening of it. Perhaps you could put our suggestions to Mr Bull and offer to take charge of the event, with all of us helping of course?'

What could she do but say yes?

When Ophelia brandished a silver cocktail shaker in front of her face, Tamara knocked back her drink and held out the empty glass for a refill.

CHAPTER SIXTEEN

After he'd straightened the display of new books, stationed inside the door so they would be the first things customers saw, Gage checked the time. A quarter of an hour left until opening time at nine. Tamara wouldn't be here for at least another hour, needing to finish her early-morning stint at the pub. With less than six weeks to go until Christmas, they'd hopefully get really busy soon and he was already worried about how he'd manage without her when she started working her day shift at the pub again. At least that problem was a thousand times better than most he'd dealt with over the last twenty years, in the sense that no one would die if he managed it wrong.

But, for now, his tea-making supplies were running low, so he'd better pop across to Vernon's and treat himself to a dose of the man's morose grumblings. Whistling happily, he locked up and strolled across the road.

Nowadays he almost bent in half entering Vernon's emporium to avoid a repeat of the ignominious knee incident. While he debated whether buying orange custard creams as opposed to the regular ones was a step too far, two women around the next aisle were discussing the new houses.

129

'Bloody great monstrosities, they are. Don't fit in the village at all. Some folk got more money than sense. Next thing, they'll be barging in here telling us what to do and complaining when poor Mr Bull doesn't stock avocados or whatever other fancy nonsense they eat.'

He smothered a smile. The great Penworthal Avocado War. Villagers against outsiders. Instead of duelling pistols, they could throw avocados at ten paces.

'Are you the owner?' A stern-faced woman, whose tweed suit strained over a well-upholstered chest, glared at him.

'Me? Uh, no, ma'am.'

'I was hoping to be served, as opposed to insulted.' Her booming voice carried around the shop. 'I'm Monica Wyndham-Smythe and I moved into one of the "monstrosities" at Trelawney Court last week.'

He stuck out his hand. 'Gage Bennet. I own the Mighty Pen bookshop across the road.' The woman's brisk handshake resembled Tamara's and left him wincing. 'If you'd like to pop over when you've done your shopping, I'd love to show you around. We do a twenty per cent discount on purchases for new customers.' He was prompted to make the offer after hearing about the similar scheme Chloe had initiated here in the shop. 'I'm a newcomer too and I've found everyone very friendly. Some of the locals might take a while to come around, but plenty of others will go out of their way to welcome you.' He'd raised his voice so the eavesdroppers hopefully heard every word.

Gage spotted Vernon and beckoned him over. 'This is Mr Bull and he's the gentleman you need.'

'You've been most kind, Mr Bennet.' She managed a tight smile. 'I'm sure I speak for all the Trelawney Court residents when I say we each want to become an integral part of this community.' Her mouth twitched at one corner. 'And for your information, Mr Bull, I'm highly allergic to avocados.'

'That's good, my love, because we ain't got any.' Vernon gave a nervous laugh and rubbed his hands together. 'You come with me and I'll show you what's what.'

130

Gage struggled to keep his amusement in check. The shopkeeper would do anything to make a sale, even going against his naturally grumpy nature to ingratiate himself with the incomers. Tamara would get a kick out of hearing about this later. He recklessly grabbed a packet of Garibaldi biscuits off the stack. Some people cruelly called them squashed fly biscuits but he'd loved them as a boy, possibly because they weren't overly sweet, and he hadn't eaten one in years. He dropped the money on the counter and made his escape.

* * *

Gage perched on the stool for a breather. Thankfully five o'clock was looming. Closing time.

'Hello, my love.' Becky bustled in. Emily trailed behind her and, judging by his niece's mutinous expression, she wasn't here willingly. 'This one's got something to say to you.' She jabbed her daughter's elbow when the girl didn't speak.

'Thanks,' Emily mumbled.

'What for?'

'Stepping in—'

'Tamara had a word with me,' Becky interrupted. 'Quiet like, after book club, and told me about Christos being a bit over-friendly with our Emily on Halloween night in the pub.'

Before Gage could open his mouth to say it was Tamara who deserved most of the credit, his sister ploughed on.

'That Christos struts around like he owns the place. I wouldn't trust him as far as I could throw him. Pixie won't see it though.' Becky sounded exasperated. 'She'll find out the hard way, you mark my words.'

'We'll see, I suppose.' An idea struck. 'Do you have a Saturday job, Emily?'

'Nothing round here, is there?'

'I can't pay much, but I could do with a hand here.'

His niece didn't look too thrilled. Being stuck with her uncle and a load of old books might not be cool in her eyes.

131

'If you aren't interested, that's fine.'

'I s'pose I could if you like.'

'Give you a bit more pocket money, won't it?' Becky nudged her daughter again. 'Say thank you.'

He suppressed a smile when Emily looked exasperated. An almost forgotten memory struck so hard he bit his lip. Before his relationship with his mother had deteriorated, she'd often talked to him the same way. Mildly despairing, but loving all the same. It gnawed that they hadn't had a chance to at least try to put things right before cancer had stolen her from him. He hadn't even made it back from Afghanistan for her funeral.

'Got brains, she has. She's at Truro College taking A levels in computer science, art and design and English literature, and her teachers say she's more than bright enough for university. First in our family, she'd be.' A veil of tears clouded Becky's eyes and she sniffed. 'Apart from you maybe?'

'I did get my degree while I was in the marines. Much later, though,' he explained. 'I don't suppose you have a couple of hours free now, Emily?' he asked.

His niece tossed him a wary look.

'Good, because I'm not these days.'

'Yeah. I guess your crappy knee sucks.'

'You could say that.'

'Just did, didn't I?'

'Emily, don't be rude to your uncle.' Becky tutted.

'It's okay. Perhaps we've both inherited the same weird sense of humour.' Like it or not, half of his make-up came from Wally Harris.

'Mebbe,' Becky said. 'Dad always had a joke at the ready. Mum used to get annoyed when he wouldn't take anything serious.'

His sister rifled in her handbag and pulled out a small scrap of paper. 'You never asked for this, but I've been carrying it around in case you did or if I got the guts to give it to you. It's Dad's address and phone number.'

132

If Emily hadn't been scrutinising them both like they were zoo exhibits, he would've told Becky to toss it in the bin. The last person he wanted to contact was the man who'd screwed up by fathering him in the first place, then had done a bunk and moved on without a backward glance. Gage grunted his thanks and snatched the note away.

'I need a few bits for our tea so I'm off to the shop.' Becky angled her daughter a sharp look. Pausing at the door, she stopped and turned. 'I'm ever so glad you came back, Gage.'

The heartfelt outburst touched him. 'Me too. Off you go so I can put this young lady to work.' He turned to Emily. 'Let's go outside first to see if you can come up with ideas for a Christmas-themed shop-window display.'

'Me?'

'Yep. Tamara and I have some thoughts, but I'd like your opinion.'

Her clear surprise indicated no one had asked her such a thing before. That reminded Gage of his first boss after he'd completed basic training. He hadn't treated him as simply another clueless grunt, but had asked pertinent questions and had listened to his answers. Never calling them stupid, he'd always given them proper consideration before either agreeing or pointing out what might be a better solution.

'Come on then. No offence to Mr Bull's display, but I'm thinking of something a little less—'

'Tacky and tasteless?' She chortled. 'Appeals to the oldies, though, doesn't it? Chloe's smart.'

'She certainly is.'

Finding out they had a new part-time assistant would be another surprise for Tamara later.

* * *

It wasn't in Tamara's nature to be jealous, especially of her friends, but tonight was a challenge. She stopped wiping down the bar for a moment and watched Melissa and Nathan

133

enviously, cosied up by the fireplace over a bottle of wine. Evelyn and Ophelia huddled around a table by the window, laughing over one of Quinten's stories. Thanks to Ophelia's persistence, the couple had been reunited and he was once more a fixture at the bungalow. Evelyn was looking particularly pretty tonight in a turquoise wool dress. Her burnished silver hair was caught back loosely at the sides with a pair of antique silver clips fashioned into twisted Celtic knots.

Now their children were older, Becky sometimes left the older kids to look after the younger ones and eat pizza, so they must've done this tonight as she and Paul were enjoying a meal together. Josie and Harry were chattering and laughing while they played darts, badly. Even Laura and Barry had popped in for a quick drink because her mother was babysitting little Josephine.

Was it foolish to imagine she and Gage could be the same one day? She stared greedily at Gage, propped on a stool at the other end of the bar, listening to Jimmy Trevail's woes. After the bookshop had opened a week ago, he'd moved back into the flat over the shop so there were no more friendly chats over breakfast or late-night cups of tea. No kisses either.

She and Gage were very much at ease with each other these days, and the shiver of excitement that ran through her every time she set eyes on him hadn't lessened one bit, but neither seemed ready to take the next step. Or at least they hadn't said so aloud. If she made the first move and it frightened Gage off, where would that leave them?

Right now, though, all she wanted was to go home, unwind in a hot bubble bath and crawl into bed. Even that would be far later than it should be, because Christos had bailed again. His excuses were sounding thinner and thinner to her, but when she'd hinted along those lines to Pixie it hadn't gone down well. No one wanted to believe their dream was falling apart.

Gage met her gaze and ended his conversation with Jimmy to start heading her way. Before she'd had a chance to

134

beg Pixie for a ten-minute break, another customer pounced on her.

'Any chance of getting served tonight, gorgeous? Or you can flash your tits. Either will do.' The ruddy-faced man leered at her breasts.

His crude comment was no worse than a million others she'd tolerated over the years, and a sharp putdown was usually all it took. For some reason she saw red. It must've shown on her face because out of the corner of her eye, she spotted Harry keeping a wary eye on them. Despite being off duty, his policeman's internal radar was still switched on.

'You don't speak to my staff that way.' Pixie muscled her way in. 'Get out of my pub and don't come back. You're barred.'

'I'm pretty sure you don't want to do that, little lady. I'll spread it around Trelawney Court — and they're people with plenty of moolah — that this place is a dump.' He looked around the pub with a sneer. 'You can't afford to lose our business.' He ogled Tamara again. 'Maybe you haven't been in the job long, love, but keeping the punters happy is what it's all about.'

'Thanks for the advice.' Her sweet tone should've been a warning, but the idiot was too full of himself to realise. 'I hope this keeps you happy.' Tamara leaned forward to give him another eyeful of cleavage. The distraction worked perfectly, and he never noticed her picking up a full pint off the bar. 'Beer makes a great shampoo, and your pathetic comb-over certainly needs help.' She ceremoniously dumped the whole thing over his head.

'What the fuck! You stupid cow.' He pushed strands of wet hair out of his face and glowered at Pixie. 'If you don't fire her, I'll sue you.'

Although she trusted her friend to step up and defend her, Tamara knew she'd overstepped the line.

'Don't worry, I quit.' A tangled knot of guilt and relief took up residence in her stomach. 'Sorry to leave you in the lurch, Pixie, but you don't want me here any longer today, trust me. We'll talk tomorrow.'

135

'I'll take you home.' Gage's dark, flinty eyes bored into the other man and she guessed his self-control hung by a thread.

All she could do was nod, desperate to get out of there before she broke down. Tamara stuck her chin in the air and took Gage's arm.

Long before they made it to the door, loud clapping filled the pub, accompanied by the noisy stomp of feet on the wooden floors. She didn't dare turn around when raucous cheers of 'you go, girl' from her friends and regulars rang out. Only when the fresh air hit, along with the full impact of what she'd done, did her knees buckle and threaten to pull her to the ground. If Gage hadn't kept a firm grip on her waist, she would've faceplanted on the pavement.

'I was damn proud of you back there. You know I would've—'

'Thumped him. I got that impression. I should've handled it better. I've been doing this job for a decade and never physically assaulted a customer before tonight.'

'He deserved it.' Gage's eyes crinkled. 'If it'd been left to me, he'd have more to worry about now than wet hair.'

Tamara buried her head in his chest and sobbed.

Gage's arms wrapped around her, so she felt safe and cared for.

'Let's get you home.'

It hovered on the tip of her tongue to ask him to stay with her, but she couldn't force the words out.

'I want to be with you too, but not because you're angry and frustrated about what just happened.' His face creased into a wry smile.

Knowing he'd read her mind gave Tamara the courage she needed. She was aware of throwing caution to the wind, but was too fired up to stop now. 'It might not be "sensible" but I detest that word. Absolutely detest it. In fact, I'd ban it from the dictionary.'

Her vehemence made him smile.

136

'I've had to be sensible since I was seventeen and it gets to me sometimes.'

'I get it. Totally. In many ways I've done the exact same thing.' Gage pressed a soft kiss on her mouth. His fingers stroked through her scrappy ponytail that'd long since lost its oomph.

'But?'

'I still need to know you're sure and won't regret this in the morning.'

'Would you like it in writing?' she teased.

'Oh, Tamara, what am I going to do with you?' Gage chuckled.

'I could suggest some things if you're out of ideas.'

'I've plenty of those. Trust me.'

'I do.' Her quiet response sent a glorious smile spreading across his face, and his eyes turned as dark as the night sky. A flutter of nervousness ran through her, but she pushed it away and tucked her arm through his. 'Sensible' could take a back seat tonight.

137

CHAPTER SEVENTEEN

As soon as he nudged Tamara's front door closed behind them, Gage's hands slid to her waist and he started kissing her. He stopped briefly to tug her emerald green T-shirt over her head and tossed it to the floor. Next to go was the plain white bra. She automatically crossed her hands over her exposed breasts. Gently and swiftly he moved them aside.

'You're beautiful. Don't hide from me. Ever. Let's get rid of these too.' Gage helped Tamara wriggle out of her black leggings. 'I'm pretty sure my knee won't cope with much more standing up. Would you mind if we shifted this to a level surface somewhere?'

'Absolutely.'

He appreciated that she refused to patronise him by waffling on about only teenagers finding it a turn-on to make love up against a wall or in the back seats of cars.

'There won't be any carrying you romantically up the stairs either.'

'Bloody good thing too. Any man stupid enough to try that needs his head tested. And he'd probably require back surgery afterwards.' Tamara took his hand. 'Come on, and I'll show you my—'

'China pig collection?'

'Oh, much better than that.'

* * *

Gage was desperate to straighten his stiff knee, but was afraid of waking Tamara so lay there immobile. He caressed the strand of her soft hair tickling his chest, but resisted the urge to wake her up. It challenged his self-control to behave like a man of thirty-seven who'd been around the block more than a few times, instead of a randy teenage boy. The stupid fears he'd clung on to about going to bed with a woman for the first time since his injury had proved to be exactly that — stupid. Yeah, he wasn't as agile as he used to be, but when he warned her his chandelier-swinging days were over, Tamara joked back that her Asda lampshade wasn't strong enough to survive being used as a sex aid anyway.

He hadn't been the only one with reservations and hers, which revolved around her body and previous less-than-stellar experiences in the bedroom, had proved groundless too. He hoped it wasn't boastful to think that his intuition about what she might like, or might not, had something to do with it.

'Feeling pretty pleased with yourself, Mr Bennet?' Her wide blue eyes gleamed up at him. 'Quite the creative one, aren't you?'

'I like to think I have my moments.' He shifted slightly and stretched out his leg. 'I hate to say this but—'

'You could do with walking around before your knee freezes up.' A gentle smile creased her face. 'It's okay. But nothing is stopping us doing this again whenever we want.' A flush of heat raced up her neck. 'If you want to.'

'Want to?' Gage's eyes drifted down his body and her gaze followed.

The blush was instant and fierce now.

'There's your answer.' His fingers danced over her warm skin, skin that smelled of him.

139

Tamara cleared her throat. 'You must be famished, so would you like breakfast . . . or . . .' Her fingers did the walking and a groan slipped out of him when she reached her target.

'Definitely or.'

* * *

Tamara dragged the last bite of toast around to soak up the smear of sauce from the baked beans and popped it in her mouth. Breakfast had turned into brunch, and not exactly a gourmet Sunday one either, but Gage insisted it worked for him. 'For pudding I've got a couple of choc ices in the freezer.'

The less-than-enthusiastic offer made him laugh. 'Don't worry. You know I'm not one for sweets.'

'Christmas is one long round of temptations for me.' She couldn't help sighing. 'Sweet things are the hardest to give up when I'm on yet another diet. And don't try to convince me it's foolish to keep fighting the scales. Not today.'

He placed a hand dramatically over his mouth, then swiftly removed it again. 'I can't believe I forgot to tell you this but I suppose we've been . . . busy.' Gage smirked. 'Since yesterday we've got more help in the shop.'

'What do you mean?' She was surprised when he told her about Emily. 'That's awesome.'

'We even put all the Christmas decorations up inside the shop. She told me what to do and I followed orders.' Gage said with a chuckle. 'It worked well. Looks good too.'

'I can't wait to see it. Now do I get to hear about your ex-wife?'

'And spoil a perfect morning?'

Tamara wrangled with her conscience. 'As a compromise, go with the bare details.' A selfish part of her didn't want to hear too much about her last rival.

Gage's countenance lost some of its cheer. 'It sounds juvenile, but I'd gone through some rough times and coming back to no one waiting for me was the final straw.'

140

'There's nothing juvenile about that.' She covered his hand with hers. 'We all need to matter.'

'Yeah, I suppose.' Haltingly he ran through the story of meeting Victoria at a party and being amazed when she appeared to fall wildly in love with him too. A whirlwind romance led to a swift, glamorous wedding. 'Real life didn't work so well for us. We had little in common and soon drifted apart.'

'You were defensive when I asked about kids the other day. Can you tell me why?'

He stared down at the table. 'At the time I thought I wanted them. Turns out she didn't. Simple as that.'

Something told her it wasn't simple at all. Or the whole truth. 'I see. Fair enough.' Relief poured off him as though he'd expected more of an inquisition. 'What can I do about Toby? Chloe seems to think it'll work itself out.'

'I don't know her anywhere near as well as you do, but she doesn't strike me as the sort of person who lets things drift.'

'You're right.' Now it bothered her too.

'I don't suppose he's off work today?'

'I've no idea.'

'We could both do with some fresh air, so how about a brisk walk?' A mischievous smile played around his mouth. 'You've told me about Melissa's old house before and how lovely it is, but I've never seen it.'

'Really? We need to put that right.' Tamara played along. 'The people who live there might not be home though.'

'The exercise will still be good for my knee.'

She sniggered. 'You mean it hasn't had enough?'

Gage put on a stern expression. 'You are a debauched woman, Tamara Pascoe.'

'And who did the debauching? Does anyone even use that word these days?'

'It suited my purpose. Come on.' He levered up off the chair. 'We've got a walk to take.'

'I'll get some shoes on.'

141

'Not a bad idea. It's chilly, so you might want . . .' He smacked his head. 'Stupid me. I'm talking to the woman who thinks coats are for wimps.'

'I've got serious waterproof rain-gear.' Tamara pretended to be affronted. 'And I've got regular coats too.' Using the word in the plural wasn't strictly accurate. One coat. A long black wool number she'd picked up for a fiver at a car-boot sale and kept for funerals. 'It might be cool enough for a thin jumper over my T-shirt.'

'Woah, don't go mad. We don't want you having hot flushes on the way.'

'I'm not *that* old.'

* * *

'You've got a lovely home.' That sounded more like estate-agent talk than normal family conversation, but Gage was unnerved by Toby's silent glares. At least dealing with the Taliban, he'd been armed and somewhat prepared.

'We adore it, don't we, Toby?'

Chloe's forced cheerfulness was equally disconcerting. When she'd opened the door, a brief burst of shock had been swiftly replaced by an overly effusive welcome as she'd ushered them in and gushed about how wonderful it was that they'd dropped by. Tamara's earlier determination had evaporated at that point, leaving him to stutter out a pathetic explanation about being out for a walk and stopping to admire the house.

'I'll make tea.' Chloe sprang off the sofa.

'I can give you a hand.' Tamara jumped up too.

Gage steeled himself not to let the panic coursing through his body show. Beads of sweat popped out on his brow and if he dared lift his hands from his legs, it'd be impossible to disguise how badly they were shaking.

Left on their own he waited for Tamara's son to speak, but nothing altered the young man's mute glower. If he hadn't taken the initiative, they'd still be sitting like two carved stone statues when their other halves returned.

142

'Toby, if there's anything you want to know about me, go ahead and ask. I promise I'll answer as best I can.' A couple of steadying breaths regulated his racing heartbeat and he ploughed on. 'I care for your mother very much. She's an amazing woman—'

'I know that! You don't have to tell me how wonderful she is.' His pale skin flushed with anger. 'I know I'm being childish and selfish, okay? Chloe's been on at me about it for weeks. Last night she had another go and I shouted at her. Told her to shut up because she didn't understand.' He grimaced with pain. 'That's not me.'

'We all behave out of character sometimes and you had good reason. Chloe will understand.' He risked a fleeting smile. 'Although I'm pretty sure she'll make you pay. Your mother is everything to you. I get that. And I admire that you're trying to look out for her.' Perhaps his sincerity resonated because Toby appeared to see Gage properly for the first time. 'You don't know me from Adam but if we could start putting that right, you'll hopefully see I only want the best for her too. I would never want to push you out of her life.' If anyone knew how it felt to be sidelined by family, he did. Some of his background was public knowledge by now, but he'd assume the young man wasn't up to date with village gossip and dive in. By the time he finished sharing with Toby a brief recap of his childhood, his connection with Becky, and the highs and lows of his career in the Royal Marines, there was a subtle change in the atmosphere.

'Where do we go from here?' Toby sounded puzzled. 'Sorry for being a dick. I'm just overprotective of my mum.'

'Quite right too.'

The agreement brought out the other man's engaging smile and his resemblance to Tamara was unmistakable.

'We could have a drink together sometime and talk some more. And if you haven't been in the shop yet, I could show you around?'

That last question was a misstep. Toby turned pink. They both knew he hadn't ventured inside.

143

'I was too pig-headed to come to the opening the other day.'

Gage cracked a smile. 'Pigs' heads are one thing we're never short of around your mum.'

They were in fits of laughter when Tamara and Chloe walked back in.

'Have you stopped being an idiot, Toby?' Chloe didn't mince her words.

Gage wouldn't care to be in his shoes later.

'Yeah, and I'm sorry I—'

'Didn't listen to your far smarter partner?'

'Exactly.'

'I'm just glad we're talking again.' Tamara's voice wobbled. 'We've all made mistakes.'

How true was that? Gage had certainly made his fair share. But the chance to put things right didn't always drop into someone's lap this way. Knowing this could've wrecked his relationship with Tamara made him turn hot and cold.

'Teatime, I think.' Chloe's resolute tone made it clear the soul-baring part of the visit was over. Fine by him.

144

CHAPTER EIGHTEEN

Doing his best to creep out without waking Tamara went well until Gage stubbed his toe on the leg of the bed, swore, lost his balance, dropped the armful of clothes he'd been holding and fell back on top of her.

She wriggled out from under him with a laugh. 'Don't ever apply for the part of the handsome prince waking Sleeping Beauty with a kiss. You won't get the job.' Tamara's sleepy eyes rested on him.

'I was trying to be thoughtful,' he said wryly, giving her an apologetic kiss on the forehead and getting himself back up.

He'd done a lot of thinking while she'd slept, but wasn't convinced this was the moment to share his new ideas.

'Spit it out. Tell me what's going through that devious mind of yours.'

Tamara glanced at her bedside clock.

Shaped like an unnaturally pink pig, its alarm was — at least to his mind — a disturbing sequence of loud oinks.

'You've only got an hour before opening time, and I assume you'll want to shower at yours and put on clean clothes before facing the customers.'

145

'You're right. If I don't get a move on, Emily will beat me to the shop.'

'I'll get dressed and join you downstairs.'

Soon they were sitting at the kitchen table with the teapot in front of them.

'You'll say I'm out of my mind, but hear me out before you roll around laughing, okay?' He took a deep breath. 'I'm sure you could go out and get another job in a pub easily enough, but I don't think it's what you really want. Your dream is to open a café. I've got a shop with a full kitchen that only needs an upgrade. Bookshops with cafés get a lot more business. I know you don't have spare cash to plough into a business, but I'm guessing the bank would give you a loan against your house.'

'But what if it fails and I lose my home? I can't risk that.'

He understood the whole safety net thing and didn't take it personally.

Gage wrapped his hands around hers, drawing her close. 'We can do this. Together. You won't be the strong, capable woman I know you are if you let this opportunity slip by. This will give us more time together and fulfil one of your dreams. Take the plunge.' His heart thudded in his chest, waiting for her response.

Tamara's eyes glittered. 'Okay! You're right. If I don't seize the chance now, I'll always regret it. I can do this. We can do this.'

* * *

'I can't believe you're leaving me in the lurch this way,' Pixie said sadly. She continued polishing glasses and stacking them behind the bar. 'I know last night you said you'd had enough, but I didn't take you seriously.'

'You should've done.'

'Why now? What did that man do or say different from all the others with too much drink in them? Don't get me wrong — he absolutely shouldn't have said what he did, but we're used to that.'

146

Her friend genuinely sounded puzzled. Was she shooting herself in the foot? Did it make sense to give up a couple of month's wages when she'd almost certainly lose her job in January anyway? Gage's words flooded back and stiffened her spine.

She told Pixie the whole story.

'Wow, you're not doing things by half, are you?'

'You could say I'm following your example. Remember the advice you gave me weeks ago?'

Pixie's brow furrowed. 'Are you sure I'm the best person to pay attention to? I'm starting to question my judgement.'

'Why's that?'

'Come on. You don't miss a thing that goes on here. I've seen you watching Christos like a hawk.'

If she tried to spin a line about observing Christos to make sure he didn't need help with anything, it'd be a miserable failure. Her friend was far too shrewd.

'He's good with customers, but—'

'We both know he's got flirting with women off to a fine art. That's about it. He's useless with the rest of the job.' Tears glazed her eyes. 'Am I right?'

Inwardly squirming, Tamara nodded.

'Despite all of that, I still love him. I've got a lot to lose all around. I paid for our aeroplane tickets and put down a deposit on a house, because Christos's savings are tied up in investments that he can't touch without paying a penalty.'

If you believe that, you believe in fairies and the Loch Ness monster.

'Can you imagine what a field day the village gossips will have if this all blows up in my face? I've got to believe that Christos and I can make this work. Surely you can see that?'

'I can, but—'

'But?' Two blotches of heat flared in Pixie's cheeks. 'I thought you were my best friend, but I clearly got that wrong. I think you'd better go.' She shook her head sadly. 'And don't come back either.'

Anger filled Pixie's voice now and Tamara knew there was no point trying to defend herself.

147

Rocky came out from the kitchen and his sharp blue eyes checked them both out. 'Is everything okay?'

'Ask Pixie.' Tamara said with a gulping sob. 'I'm leaving.'

* * *

One of the downsides to being tall was the need to continually scan the environment around him for low-hanging objects. The shop was now a danger zone that included ropes of fake greenery with clumps of bright-red holly berries and swags of gold tinsel.

His niece's college had a staff development day, so she'd come to work. This morning Emily had sat cross-legged on the floor, sorting through boxes of old books discarded from libraries that he'd picked up for next to nothing on eBay.

She'd seen a TikTok video of a 'tree' made out of books, so they'd created a Christmassy twist on that for the centre of the shop and now she was decking it out in fairy lights. It seemed safest to leave her alone.

Doing the window display was on the agenda for when they closed tonight. Earlier he'd helped Emily to cover up the window with her ingenious Christmassy sign, which told customers to watch for a big reveal tomorrow morning.

'I blew it.' Tamara burst through the door and flung herself at him. The tears trickling down her face and huge, sad eyes told him something was badly wrong, so he checked to see what customers were left. Only two older men engrossed in rifling through the military-history section.

'Ems, would you mind keeping an eye on the counter for a few minutes?'

Her flash of pleasure amused him.

He'd discovered a lot about his niece already: she hated her full name; Greta Thunberg was her idol; her love of hard-core American rap (mostly to piss off her parents) equalled that for traditional Cornish folk music; she was an avid computer coder, but also a voracious reader — and always printed

148

books, never the digital versions. Like so many people these days, she was into fantasy novels, but also had a secret liking for Sherlock Holmes and Jane Austen.

Gage took Tamara's arm and steered her towards the kitchen. 'Tea? Coffee?'

'I don't need any drinks. I need . . . Oh, I don't know.' She sank into the nearest chair and clasped her head in her hands. 'I should've been more honest. She might not have wanted to hear it, but at least I'd feel now that I did all I could.'

He lifted her chin so she was forced to look at him. 'Tell me the whole story.'

Tamara brushed back a strand of hair. 'Perhaps I'll have that tea after all.'

Gage listened to the whole dismal tale while he made their hot drinks. 'Do you think she'll give Christos the elbow?'

'I'm not sure. She's still very much in love with him but I think she feels made a fool of. The idea of being gossiped about all over the village horrifies her.'

'We both know Penworthal has a short attention span when it comes to scandal.'

'Thank goodness.'

Emily poked her head around the swing door. 'One of the oldies wants to buy a couple of books.'

'I'll come,' he said. 'Another day, I'll show you how to use the till.'

'Yeah, that'd be great. I told them they should open one of our wish-list accounts.'

'Our what?'

'All the online shops have them and it's catching on with regular ones too now. Customers make up a wish list from the inventory and give the link to whoever is interested so they can buy direct from us. We could offer gift wrapping as well. I could add it to our website later if you like?' A tiny frown settled between her eyes.

'I think it's a great idea and I'll happily take you up on the offer.' He grinned. 'It'll mean a bonus in your pay too.' Gage

149

touched Tamara's arm. 'You two can plot the finer details of our window decorations while I go pretend to be the boss and sell some books.'

Their laughter followed him out.

His phone dinged with a new text from Taff. He'd have time enough to take a look at that later. Right now, he had business to drum up.

CHAPTER NINETEEN

Tamara watched Gage's face light up when they stopped at the Kellows' gate. The beautiful Victorian home was looking its best tonight. Welcoming lights flooded out from the windows and the jewel-like stained glass above the front door glowed like a handful of wine gums.

'It's quite a house, isn't it?' he said admiringly.

'Wait until you see the inside,' Tamara said. 'It's seriously gorgeous. Melissa is so excited about hosting this Thanksgiving dinner. Her first husband, Robin, was never really into it, but now I think Melissa is making up for lost time. She told us it's always on the fourth Thursday in November and is a really big deal apparently.'

'I remember being invited to a Thanksgiving dinner in Kabul at an American base. There was tons of great food to pig out on before we watched one of their football games on a massive screen. It was a bit like Christmas, but without the presents. No decorations either really, apart from a few paper turkeys and pumpkins.'

'I think we're in for a good evening and I'm definitely ready to have a fun time,' she said. 'It's been such an awesome week so far.' Excitement bubbled out of her.

151

The adjustment to working together, while setting boundaries between that and their newly intimate personal life, was going smoothly. The café plans were well underway, and Georgie Rowe and his crew were scheduled to do the kitchen refurbishment, including putting in a new door from the kitchen to the space designated for the café. There were a few legal hoops to jump through, including acquiring food-service and hygiene certificates, and she still needed to work on the menu and branding. Realistically it'd be the new year at the earliest before they could open.

'What're you two doing lurking out here? I hope you aren't snogging in our garden?' Melissa's cheery voice rang out, heavily laced with the southern accent she'd never lose. 'Everyone but Josie and Harry are here already, and we've started on the appetisers. Josie wasn't due to finish work until six, so we knew they'd be late.'

Inside, Tamara couldn't help smiling. Melissa clearly didn't get Gage's memo about not doing much in the way of Thanksgiving decorations. Garlands of fabric leaves in stunning vibrant autumn shades were woven around the intricate Victorian bannisters, and bright orange fairy lights twinkled everywhere. She gave up trying to count the number of pumpkins dotted around the place, real and ornamental, and a couple of life-sized cardboard cutouts in Pilgrim costumes guarded the entrance to the living room.

'Wow, this is beautiful.'

'Thanks.' Melissa beamed. 'I went a little overboard, but Nathan didn't mind.'

'That man's so nuts over you, he wouldn't mind if you decorated him too. You could drape a strand of lights over him and stick a pumpkin on his head.'

'Are my ears burning?' Nathan came to join them and kissed his wife's cheek.

'The only thing burning will be the sweet-potato casserole if you don't hurry up and whip it out like I asked you three minutes ago.' Melissa hugged Nathan's waist and returned the kiss.

152

'Already done, my love, and it's sitting on the counter as instructed.'

'You're the best. I'll see y'all later. The kitchen is calling me back.' Melissa flashed a wide grin.

'Anything I can do to help?' Tamara asked.

'No, thanks. You're good.' Melissa smiled and hurried off.

Tamara scanned the room for somewhere to sit.

'I'll hang with the guys and leave you to your girly gossip,' Gage said.

'That's a very sexist remark, Mr Bennet.'

'Blame everyone else for splitting off into two groups before we got here.'

He pointed to where Tamara's group of girlfriends were clustered around Evelyn by the seating in front of the fire, while the men were huddled around the television at the other end of the room watching a football match.

'Here you go.' Nathan, as if by magic, produced a beer for Gage and a glass of white wine for Tamara. 'Have I got the drinks right?'

'You certainly have. We're creatures of habit,' Tamara said with a laugh.

'And you two are playing catch-up with appetisers. Stop by the table and help yourself to what I'm supposed to tell you comprises a layered taco dip, a warm spinach-and-cheese dip, and chilled prawns with a slightly spicy American cocktail sauce.'

Tamara and Gage headed towards the table as instructed. After they loaded a couple of small plates, they sneaked a kiss before parting ways.

'Right, girls, what've I missed?' Tamara plumped down next to Laura on a sweet two-seater sofa covered in rich burgundy floral fabric, one of Melissa's new additions. Their cross words at the bookshop opening were long since forgotten. She dipped one of the succulent giant prawns in sauce and popped it in her mouth.

'Evelyn's got some news.' Amy and Tessa spoke in unison, grinning like mad.

153

'Hey, don't tell yet — I want to hear too.' Josie rushed over to join them, glass in hand, and squeezed into the group.

'Goodness, you're making something out of nothing.' Evelyn's colour rose and her fingers worked at a tortilla chip, breaking it into a myriad of crumbled-up pieces. 'For some unknown reason, Quinten wants to marry me, that's all.'

Loud cheers and claps broke out, so loud that the men stopped what they were doing to turn and stare. It didn't take a genius to guess the only one who knew what was happening was a very red-faced Quinten. He hovered at the edge of the group as if wishing he could disappear like the genie in *Aladdin*, back into his lamp in a puff of smoke.

'That's all?' Josie squealed. 'You sly old goose. When did this happen? We want details.'

Despite her pretended indifference, Evelyn pinked like a young girl. Quite shyly, at least by her standards, she told them how Quinten had surprised her by proposing at their ballroom-dancing club in the middle of their favourite dance, a Viennese waltz.

'So when's the big day?' Laura asked eagerly.

'I'm not sure yet. Neither of us wants a lot of fuss, so it'll be very quiet.' Some of the brightness left her face. 'And it depends on Ophelia. She wasn't well enough to come tonight and the last doctor's appointment I took her to wasn't terribly encouraging.'

'Oh, Evelyn, we're so sorry.' Laura spoke for them all.

'Thank you. But Quinten's moving in with us next week, so that will be lovely. I'll find his presence a huge help and support.' A trace of her usual arch smile returned. 'The two of them get on really well. I suppose they don't have the history Ophelia and I do. We've done our best to put it all behind us, and I know she never came on to Sam that time, but these things linger.'

Forgiving was one thing. Forgetting, quite another.

Nathan moved over to the mantelpiece and picked up a small brass hammer. He used it to hit an ornately engraved

154

Chinese gong. 'I'm instructed by the chief cook to announce that our feast is ready. If you could all head for the kitchen, you can help yourselves to the buffet. There's a seating chart pinned up on the wall so you can find your allotted place. The dining room table isn't big enough for everyone, so a few of us will be relegated to the kitchen.' He grinned. 'I'm informed that's usually where they put the children, so my assumption is the most immature of us will end up there.' He picked his way through the crowd and Tamara noticed him stop briefly to congratulate Evelyn.

There was a light-hearted rush for the food and Tamara's jaw dropped when she saw the huge spread.

Melissa clapped her hands to get their attention. 'I think you'll recognise almost everything. There's the standard roast turkey, a glazed ham, cranberry sauce, bread rolls and mashed potatoes. But the bowl of green beans isn't like y'all have because they're cooked southern style, low and slow with chunks of bacon. The long dish that looks like it's nothing but burnt marshmallows is my mom's famous sweet-potato casserole.' She pointed to another platter. 'That's cornbread dressing. Cut into squares. It's another southern thing, which we have instead of stuffing. And the fruit salad is another of my mom's recipes. It's not a dessert, so you eat it with the meal.' Her face lit up. 'It's wonderful to have y'all here tonight, and later we'll follow one more Rutherford family tradition and go around the table, or tables in this case, so everyone can say what they're thankful for.'

Tamara's heart skipped a beat and a blush rose in her cheeks when she caught Gage watching her.

* * *

Gage forced himself to slow down. Tamara had pointed out the other day that he tended to shovel in his food at a rate of knots. She'd done so very tactfully and gently. He supposed he'd acquired the habit out of self-preservation when it paid

155

to wolf your meals down and hurry out of the mess hall in case of a rocket attack. Learning how to relax and take life easy was one of the many challenges he faced that no civilian could hope to understand.

'Your shop-window display is really cool by the way,' Josie said, interrupting his wayward thoughts.

'Sorry, I was wool-gathering.'

He was annoyed with himself for ignoring her. Tonight, all the couples had been split up because their hosts thought they saw enough of each other at home. He and Josie were squeezed together at one end of the main table while Harry was in the middle, flanked by Evelyn and Laura. Tamara was with Melissa in the kitchen.

'I didn't mean to be rude.'

'Don't worry about it.'

Suddenly Gage had a longing to be more honest. 'I'm not great at navigating social situations like this. My only excuse is that I joined the forces at sixteen, so this is my first real experience of civilian life as an adult.' He managed a wry smile. 'It's been an eye-opener.'

'It must have. You may never be the life and soul of the party, but that's okay. Not everyone has to be loud and opinionated like me,' she said with a laugh. 'Harry's teaching me to be a little less brash, but it's an uphill battle some days.'

Gage couldn't help smiling.

'You've had to deal with the physical and emotional after-effects of your traumatic knee injury too. It adds to it.'

'Yeah.' His gaze swept around the room, full of people laughing and enjoying themselves. 'It's hard to accept I've the right to be happy sometimes when I've seen so much suffering all over the world.'

'I get that.' She glanced around. 'I have the same problem switching off after a tough shift at work. Harry's much better at compartmentalising.'

'Men are supposed to be, but it doesn't always work that way.' Gage took a gulp of beer. 'Being part of the military force

156

in a particular place, we were often the root cause of people's distress. That's a conflict you don't have to deal with because you're simply there to help your patients. End of story.' He hadn't meant to sound bitter. 'Sorry. I'm being a downer and spoiling a great night.'

'Maybe this isn't the place to say this, but I wonder if you might find it helpful to—'

'Speak to someone?'

'Or isn't that for tough, invincible marines?'

'We both know I'm not that.' He grimaced. 'This proves it.' Gage tapped his left knee. 'I had counselling afterwards and it helped. I'm trying to learn to put distance between myself and all that happened, and move on.'

Josie's compassionate smile said she knew it wasn't that easy.

'Anyway, forget that. You were complimenting me on the shop display.'

'It's awesome. I was there for the unveiling.'

He'd been surprised when quite a crowd had gathered outside the shop on Tuesday morning to see Emily, wearing a bright-red-and-green elf costume, dramatically pull back the paper covering from the window until the whole scene was visible. When that was done, she sprinted around to pass out colourful flyers advertising their Christmas specials.

'I had very little to do with it. I arranged a few things under instruction and fixed the lights, but that's all. Oh, and played "It's Beginning to Look a Lot Like Christmas" on my phone when Tamara gave me the cue. Tamara came up with the theme of "All I Want for Christmas is Books".'

Between her and Emily, they'd created the scene of books tumbling out of stockings hanging at a fireplace, while Father Christmas sat in a rocking chair, engrossed in reading the books that'd been left out for him instead of mince pies.

'I think it's brill. Becky says she hasn't seen Emily so enthusiastic about anything in ages. She's really grateful to you.'

157

'I'm the grateful one. Having the opportunity to help my niece, and get to know her better in the process, is incredible.'

'And as for the transformation you've worked on Tamara.' Josie lowered her voice. 'She needed dragging out of her rut. We'd all failed miserably, though not for lack of trying. Then along you came.' She patted his hand. 'You're a good, decent man. Stop being so hard on yourself.'

Gage's eyes prickled and he blinked hard. The last thing he needed was to break down in front of all their friends.

'Can I whisk my man away for a minute because there's something I need to show him?' Tamara appeared by his shoulder.

He pushed back his chair and mumbled a quick apology to Josie for abandoning her.

They meandered through the kitchen and stepped outside the back door, making sure to shut it behind them.

'I was helping Melissa collect the dirty dishes when I saw Josie haranguing you and thought you might need rescuing. She can be a bit forceful at times.'

'She meant well.'

'The most damning words in the English language.' She chuckled. 'Melissa tells us the southern equivalent is "bless her heart" said in a syrupy, sympathetic tone.'

'Actually Josie was really understanding. She's very observant. I suppose the best nurses always are.' He hesitated briefly. 'We talked about stuff I'd like to share with you too. Not now though.'

The soft night air, the myriad of stars twinkling in an ink-black sky, and the hum of conversation that drifted out through the open kitchen window. All of those faded away. Telling her the full story would be a relief.

'Anyone would think you were horny teenagers instead of a respectable middle-aged couple.' Melissa's laugh rang out and they turned to see her watching them from the kitchen door. 'Get inside. Now. Dessert is on the table, so you've more eating to do. Then there's our thankful thing.'

158

'We're coming in a minute.' After that promise Gage lowered his voice to a whisper. 'It'll be late when we get away from here. Too late to talk?'

'Not for me. Let's go stuff ourselves with pumpkin pie, or whatever Americans eat at Thanksgiving. I'd happily eat a whole bowl of that sweet-potato casserole for pudding.' She giggled. 'Don't look so horrified. You and not liking sweets! From my experience most men love their sweets. You're an exception.' A giggle slipped out. 'In oh so many ways you're a very unique man. Maybe that's why I fell for you.'

'You're unique too. Smart, witty and beautiful. You'll do me very well.'

'Oh, will I indeed, Mr Bennet? We'll see about that.' Tamara grabbed his hand and dragged him along with her. 'And if I'm not on your thankful list, there'll be trouble.'

'You top it.'

That silenced her. A rare-enough occurrence to make them both laugh and he couldn't help giving her a quick kiss.

* * *

Tamara's heart fluttered as she glanced across at Gage. He'd chosen to sit in his old favourite chair when they'd walked into her living room, leaving her to drop down on the sofa. They'd been the first to leave the Thanksgiving dinner and had had to put up with a lot of teasing smiles and suggestive remarks about why they'd been so keen to go.

'It's hard for me to talk about some things, but I need to try. If nothing else it should help you understand me better.' Gage puffed out a breath. 'Earlier at dinner I had to apologise to Josie for not doing the polite thing and chatting to her.' He leaned forward and rested his hands on his large, muscular thighs. 'Until recently I've spent all my adult life in the military, where so many of the so-called rules are different.'

'I get that and I'm sure Josie understood.'

159

'She did. Too well.' He gave a rough laugh. 'I didn't plan on admitting so many of my demons, but she wriggled them out before I knew what was happening.'

'That sounds like Josie.' Tamara needed to tread carefully. 'Tell me more.'

Her heart broke a little more for him with each wrenching word he dragged out. The lamp behind his shoulder cast shadows on his face, showing the pain evident in every line of his stern profile.

'From the time you were a teenager, you've done a job not many of us could manage and did it to the best of your ability. Josie was right when she said you're a good man and not to be so hard on yourself. You'll get there and I'll do everything I can to help.'

Gage got up and came to sit by her. He draped his arm around her shoulder. 'You're good for me, you know that?'

'I hope so. You certainly are for me.' She nestled into him. 'I'm going to offload on you now for a minute. Melissa's worrying me. When we were in the kitchen, her face kept falling into a dark kind of sadness when she thought nobody was looking. And Nathan was throwing her worried looks. I think it's the baby thing.'

Gage's expression altered.

'Don't panic. Just because I'm around the same age as Melissa, that doesn't mean I want to have another baby.' She softened her voice. 'I might've been tempted if we'd met ten years ago, but I wouldn't fancy going back to dirty nappies and sleepless nights now.' Tamara faltered. 'You said that when you were married, you wanted kids but your ex-wife didn't. I sense there was more to it. Am I right?' The breath caught in her throat when he didn't rush to answer.

* * *

'Yeah, but there are other things I need to get off my chest first.' Gage grimaced. This was never going to be easy, so the

160

sooner he got it over with, the better. 'I told you I met Victoria at a party, but I never said how much she dazzled me.' He could see the stark admission had taken Tamara aback. 'Most of all I need you to know why. The only excuse I've got is that I'd recently returned from my third tour of Afghanistan and was wiped out, mentally and physically. I'd seen so much . . . ugliness. I can't explain it . . .'

'I can. She was the opposite of everything your life was about and you clung to that like a drowning man to a lifebelt. How long were you married?'

'Five years on paper. She came from a wealthy family whose lineage goes back to William the Conqueror, and it was an act of defiance on her part to marry a common soldier. Yeah, I was an officer by that point, but that didn't make me any more acceptable.

'The novelty soon wore off for both of us. She was never going to fit into my life and I'd no interest in fitting into hers. We limped along for a while and kept up the pretence of being a couple.' Gage swiped at his eyes. 'The final curtain came when I returned from a month-long NATO exercise to find a taxi waiting outside the front door and a pile of suitcases in the hall. As her parting gesture, she told me that while I was away she'd found out she was pregnant. I was still reeling from that when she casually tossed out that she didn't want my baby, or any-one's. As it happened, she'd miscarried — at least that's what she claimed — but I've never been certain.' He stared at the floor.

'No wonder my thoughtless comment about not wanting another child struck so hard.' She rested her head against his shoulder.

'That's different.'

'Yes, it is. And you need to absolutely know that.'

Her fierce response made him smile. For the first time in days, he thought about Taff's enigmatic message. He'd worried over it at first before concluding that his old friend must've got the wrong end of the stick. No way was his ex-wife interested in tracking him down to rekindle any sort of relationship.

161

'But . . .' Her voice trailed away.

'But what? You can say anything to me. Surely you know that now?'

Her breath trembled. 'I don't want to hold you back from becoming a dad if that's what you want, but I really can't see myself with a baby at this point in my life. Perhaps it's best we break things off now before we get in any deeper, so you could find someone to have a family with.'

'Oh, Tamara.' Gage gazed into her troubled eyes. 'You want me to go out and find some random woman to father a child with? Seriously?'

'Well, when you put it like that — no.'

'What we have together is more than I've ever dared to hope for and you're all I need.' This wasn't the right moment to say anything more about his deepening feelings for her. He gathered her closer so he felt her heartbeat against his own. 'Are we okay now?'

'I'd say we're more than okay.'

162

CHAPTER TWENTY

Why was the aroma of books so intoxicating? Tamara held Richard Osman's latest bestseller up to her nose and sniffed.

'You're as weird as Uncle Gage.'

Emily's caustic comment made her smile. It must be hard-wired in children that overnight, on their thirteenth birthday, they acquired the knack of sardonic disdain for all adults.

'I caught him fondling one of those grubby old books about some battle everyone else has forgotten about. Talk about creepy.'

The girl had determined that working in a bookshop demanded that she dress all in black, and wander around quoting poetry at random moments. Echoes of Virginia Woolf.

'Have you restocked the biography section?' asked Tamara.

Much to Gage's bewilderment, books about pop-culture celebrities were hugely popular as Christmas presents so there was another order from the wholesalers to shelve.

After the first week of officially working with Gage full time rather than juggling it with her old commitments at the pub, Tamara's spirits were sky-high.

163

Despite a few misgivings, she'd agreed to his suggestion that they use her ceramic pig collection as the focal point of the proposed café. Georgie was lined up to build display shelves in the same rich maple wood as the bookcases to show them off. Tamara still wondered if some customers might be put off by some of the negative connotations surrounding pigs, so that was the main reason why the café's name was still up for debate. It sent Emily off in a huff when her suggestion of 'Babe's Bakery' was turned down. The girl had thought it the perfect nod to the famous pig from Dick King-Smith's 1983 novel *The Sheep-Pig*, but Tamara envisioned them trending on social media for all the wrong reasons.

The only fly in the ointment came every time she glanced across the road at the pub. Last night she'd been a coward and insisted Gage went to the pub quiz on his own while she'd bailed out with a fictitious headache.

'Yeah, and I've updated our Instagram and TikTok feeds.' Emily shuffled her feet and didn't quite meet Tamara's eyes. 'Any chance I can leave a bit early today?'

Despite the fact Emily was officially an adult, Gage took his responsibilities towards his niece seriously. If he were here, he'd be quizzing Emily about where she was going and with whom. But he wasn't, and wouldn't be back until after closing time.

The ever-patient man had taken the van and driven to Redruth to pick up a set of two dozen pale-pink plastic chairs, steel-framed with tubular legs, which she'd bought online. They were cheap knockoffs of the famous Eames chairs from the 1960s and would fit perfectly with the slightly kitsch style she had in mind for the café.

'I don't see why not.'

'Cheers. I'm getting the bus to Truro and meeting a friend.'

'That's fine. Why don't you run along now? We won't get many more customers. I can manage.'

'You're the best. Cheers. See you next Saturday.' Emily's smile filled the room, the cool teenage front momentarily forgotten.

164

The girl's dark ponytail swung in time to her excited, bouncy stride as she hurried out of the shop.

Tamara smiled to herself as she tweaked the Christmas book display before standing back to survey it. She jerked around as the shop bell jangled, and tried not to gawp. The stunning redhead who strutted in looked familiar, but she couldn't think why. Dressed as if she'd stepped off a catwalk, the woman's cream wool dress fitted like a second skin, emphasising her jutting hip bones and Bambi-like legs.

'Is GG around?'

The upper-class drawl put her teeth on edge.

'GG?'

'Gage. Or maybe you call him Mr Bennet?' Her languid stance contrasted with cold blue eyes that darted around, sizing everything up, including Tamara.

'He's not here at the moment. Can I help?'

'It's personal. Private.'

The air of dismissiveness irked her and she considered putting the stranger right about her own relationship with Gage.

'If you'd care to leave a message with your name and contact details, I'll pass them on when he gets back later.'

'My name?' That seemed to amuse her. 'GG knows that, and where to contact me. You can say Victoria popped in to return his call.' In a cloud of expensive perfume, she swanned out of the shop.

The penny dropped. Victoria was Tori G. The face of a dozen iconic brands, and so well-known that Tamara could kick herself for not recognising her immediately. Her reaction wasn't a million miles from William Thacker's to the famous Anna Scott when she'd dropped into his Notting Hill bookshop. Even the idea of Gage *knowing* Tori G was bizarre. Like an odd jigsaw piece from a totally different puzzle, nothing about it fitted. It'd be interesting to hear him explain this away later.

* * *

165

Humming to himself, Gage parked the van and almost sprang out. He couldn't wait to show Tamara the chairs, along with a surprise that should make her smile even brighter. The owner had forgotten to include the matching tables in the advert, but had offered them at a knockdown price when he'd arrived.

'Sorry it took me a while but the A30 was backed up around Truro.' Gage breezed into the shop. 'People have started Christmas shopping already, I suppose.'

Tamara stopped in the middle of straightening books, but stayed where she was instead of rushing to him. It was childish for him to feel a niggle of disappointment. As Melissa said the other night, they weren't teenagers with their first crush, but regular middle-aged people. He went to her instead. No matter.

'Has it been busy while I was gone?' Gage wrapped his arms around her and breathed in her soft, warm scent. The wonderful sensation of coming home overwhelmed him. For too many years that hadn't been a feature in his life, which was why he treasured it so much now.

At the last second, Tamara turned so his kiss missed her mouth and landed awkwardly on her jaw.

'Is something wrong?' He stepped back. 'Where's Ems?'

'She asked to leave early to go meet a friend. I couldn't see any harm letting her go.'

Why did she sound so defensive? 'That's fine. Are you okay? You seem a bit—'

'I'm tired, that's all.' She pushed a loose strand of hair away from her face. 'Before I forget, you had a visitor. I'm supposed to tell you that Victoria — or Tori G, as she's better known — popped in to return your call.'

He spluttered and turned bright red. 'Bloody hell. She came here? I told her not to.'

'How do you even know . . .' The blood drained from Tamara's face. 'Don't tell me she—'

'Yeah, she's the Victoria I mentioned. My ex-wife. I know it's unbelievable.' He crammed his hands in his pockets. 'She

166

went through a stage of imagining herself as a regular person instead of a top model. I should've told you the other night.'

'Yes, you should've done.' There was an unmistakable edge to her voice.

He couldn't blame her for being annoyed because right now he could kick himself for not being totally honest.

'So why's she here now?'

'I don't know. Not really, I . . . look, let's get the van unloaded, then we'll close the shop early and go upstairs for a chat.'

'Fine.' Tamara's tone and her sardonic smile told him it was anything but fine.

They worked silently until all the chairs were in.

'Hang on.' He leaned into the van and whipped off the old blanket the man had given him to protect the tables on the drive home. 'Call these an early Christmas present if you like. They match the—'

'OMG, they're perfect!' Tamara dragged the first one forward and together they lifted it out onto the pavement. 'You're such a thoughtful man.' She flung her arms around his neck, but swiftly let go. 'How could you not tell me you were married to that . . . glamorous creature? I suppose now you're the one slumming it with me.'

Gage had experienced the same gnawing at his self-confidence when he and Victoria had been together.

He shook his head dismissively, then reached for one end of the table and nodded for her to pick up the other.

They stacked the new furniture at one end of the kitchen before balancing the till and putting the money in the safe. After their chat the other night, he'd done a whole lot more thinking. He'd almost decided to throw caution to the wind and tell Tamara how he really felt about her. Trust his ex-wife to screw things up for him again.

* * *

167

'Now I totally get why you said your ex-wife dazzled you,' Tamara blurted out.

By the time they'd walked up the stairs and sat down, she'd almost convinced herself to deal with the bizarre discovery rationally and reasonably. In truth, she was eaten up with jealousy.

She couldn't fake it any longer. 'No man has ever said I dazzle them, and I'm pretty certain they never will, so I'm trying my best to be nice here.'

Sadness flooded his face. It hollowed his cheeks and pulled down his mouth. 'I can't win now. If I claim you dazzle me too, in a different sort of way, you'll think I'm lying to make you feel better. But if I shrug it off, you'll feel smaller and less worthy.' Gage placed her hands against his thudding heartbeat. 'I should've known she would blight the best thing that ever happened to me. Pass my phone over, please.'

It hovered on the tip of her tongue to ask why he couldn't leave it alone while they had a serious conversation, but something stopped her. After all, he was the one who'd suggested early on that they set them aside at meals and on dates, so there must be a good reason for his request. Tamara grabbed it off the table and handed it over. The table was one of her recent bargains. A genuine Edwardian occasional table she'd picked up for a fiver in an auction because 'brown furniture' wasn't fashionable these days.

In between everything else they'd been busy with recently, she'd helped him to choose the furniture for his newly redecorated flat, including his only non-negotiable — a sofa at least two metres long. The dark-navy L-shaped sectional she'd tracked down from an online discount warehouse fitted the bill perfectly and had come at a bargain price. Georgie and his crew had ripped out the dated kitchen and bathroom, and installed all new fittings. They'd painted the walls a cool grey and white, and fitted matching blinds for the windows.

168

'My old mate, Taff, who you met at the bookshop opening, sent this and I should've shown you right away.' He scratched his head.

Heads up, mate. Victoria's on the warpath and says she needs to see you. She conned your address out of me. Sorry.

'I rang and left her a message, telling her not to come and see me. In case you have any doubts, I am one hundred per cent not interested in anything she has to say.'

'Tell me some more about your marriage because try as I might, I can't see the two of you together.' She sensed him deciding how much honesty she could take. 'Don't hold back. I'm not a fragile plant. I suppose the sex was amazing. I'm sure Tori can bend into positions my poor body couldn't copy in a million years unless I wanted to end up in A and E.'

'Oh, Tamara.' His voice cracked. 'I am so angry with her right now. But I'm actually angrier with myself for not telling you straight away. It was stupid.' Gage caressed her face with his hands and gazed into her eyes. His mouth was inches away from hers and if they kissed, one thing would lead to another.

But a vivid picture of his ex-wife, supercilious and arrogant from her sleek red hair to her ankle-breaking designer heels, filled her head.

'*Was* the sex great?' The question burst out and she sat back, crossing her arms and putting some space between them.

Gage paused before saying softly, 'Yeah, at first it was. But after a while, it palled because at the end of the day, physical satisfaction on its own leaves you empty.' He visibly swallowed. 'There was no affection, Tamara, no real caring.'

Tamara shuffled over to close the distance between them. 'I suggest you ring Victoria again and make it crystal clear you don't want her coming here.'

Her fierce response brought the first smile she'd seen on Gage's face all evening.

169

Despite that, a sliver of her old insecurity returned. 'If that's what you want . . . If I'm poking my nose in and you want to—'

'Stop it. Please. We've both got pasts. There's no getting away from that, even though it'd be a bloody sight easier.'

The crooked tug of his smile loosened something inside her.

'Victoria is part of mine. That's all. A small part in the scheme of things.'

'I need to stop being immature, don't I? And dig out a pair of my old Bridget Jones big panties, the sort I used to wear before you came along.'

A wicked grin burst out of him. 'So all the sexy silk and lace was bought in my honour?'

'I didn't know I was competing with a supermodel, either, did I?'

'You have never — ever — been in competition with Victoria. She was a mistake when I was vulnerable. You're a choice I've made from a good place, mentally and literally.'

'Any minute now you'll start singing "You're the One that I Want" and beg me to get my Sandy outfit on.' That was a cowardly attempt to make light of his unequivocal statement.

'I can't hold a tune, so that's not happening. The Sandy outfit — well, you know I won't ever turn down that offer. But . . .' Gage's cheeks flushed.

There was the sense he wasn't saying something, so she decided to pre-empt him. 'The level of commitment we've got now works great for me, if that's what you're worried about. My teenage dreams of white weddings and happy-ever-afters flew out the window long ago. I've clung onto my independence all these years and never let any man get as close as you.'

'I know. And that means a lot. What we've got is great.' The loud breath he exhaled emanated relief.

It'd shocked her a minute ago to realise she wanted more. Lying had been the only way.

170

CHAPTER TWENTY-ONE

If she'd ever wondered how many men it took to put up a Christmas tree, Tamara now knew the answer. Vernon Bull was directing operations, of course, with Wilf, Paul and Quinten good-naturedly following orders that mainly consisted of moving the tree a minuscule amount one way, and then the other.

Early this morning, they'd dug up the tree and planted it in a large red ceramic pot generously given by Monica Wyndham-Smythe. Although Tamara hadn't met the woman who lived in the new development yet, Gage had bumped into her in Vernon's shop and said she'd seemed keen to become involved in village life. The tree had been loaded on a wheeled trolley and pushed down to the village. They'd already cleared a spot in front of the church, and now Wilf's fir stood tall and ready for its lights.

She should be home, baking the mince pies for the official light-up later on, instead of lingering here. It had seemed a long way off when she'd agreed to Evelyn's suggestion, but the first of December had rolled around faster than she'd bargained for. Numbers were tricky because she didn't know how many people would turn up. She'd heard some villagers complain that

171

it was a waste of time and typical of the new folk moving in, wanting to change things. In their view, Penworthal had never had a Christmas tree, so why did it need one now?

A ladder appeared and Paul nimbly climbed up, holding a thick strand of lights under one arm. He started wrapping it around the tree and Tamara suppressed a grin when he patently ignored Vernon's harried instructions. Although plumbing had become his main line of business, he was also a qualified electrician so they'd put him in charge of that side of things today.

'Looks good, doesn't it?' The vicar came to stand next to her. Tamara didn't know Tim Killigrew well, but the young tousled-haired man struck her as refreshingly down-to-earth. He'd been heard to joke that he'd become a vicar to make up for some of his ancestors' misdeeds. In the sixteenth century, Lady Mary Killigrew had been possibly Cornwall's most notorious pirate. Tim was responsible for three other churches apart from Penworthal and lived near the largest of those, about ten miles away.

'It certainly does. You'll be here tonight?'

'Wouldn't miss it for the world.' He pointed to a smartly dressed ash-blonde hovering near the tree. 'Karen Buckingham, Wilf's wife, is going to lead the carol singing.' Tim chuckled. 'Be glad she offered or you might've been stuck with my out-of-tune efforts.'

'I'm no singer either, although I can't resist a Christmas carol. I ought to get a move on or we won't have any mince pies.'

She wasn't totally unprepared because she'd been making and freezing blocks of pastry for the last few weeks and they were all defrosted now, ready to use. It was a pity the book-shop's large oven hadn't been overhauled yet or she could've used it.

'Good luck.'

She debated popping in to see Gage, but resisted the temptation and went straight home.

172

A couple of hours later, Tamara made a cup of tea, popped two warm mince pies on a plate and flopped down in a chair. She picked up one to take a large bite. The pastry was golden-brown, light and flaky, her homemade mincemeat perfectly spiced. She had baked two hundred, which sounded excessive, but it wasn't boasting to say that from experience, Tamara knew few people could stop at eating just one. Any leftovers would surely find good homes among her friends.

Once her unconventional lunch was finished, she put one mince pie in a bag to take to Gage. He might not appreciate it, but would eat it for her sake. To pacify, she added a sandwich on his favourite crusty wholemeal bread, filled with juicy thick-cut ham, sharp cheddar cheese and a layer of crisp lettuce.

Tamara hummed to herself as she strolled down the road, checking out what new Christmas decorations had popped up. When the short-lived winter sun started to fade, everyone's lights would come on and start twinkling like the starry sky.

The only snag was that Victoria still hadn't responded to Gage's multiple attempts to call her, and they didn't know why. Despite that, Tamara hadn't looked forward to the festive season this much since Toby had been full of wide-eyed childish excitement about the holidays.

* * *

'I'm off to help Paul set up the refreshment stall.' Gage shouted upstairs to Tamara. She was in the flat, clearing away the scratch meal of scrambled eggs, bacon and toast they'd pulled together after the shop closed for the day.

'Okay. I'll be along soon with the first batch of mince pies. The girls will be there with the drinks in a few minutes too.'

He tugged a thick, dark-green jumper on top of his checked shirt and pulled a black beanie over his head. To his

173

mind, it'd turned chilly, although a certain tough lady would laugh at the idea of wearing any warm clothes.

Outside he stopped for a moment and mused at the wintry scene in front of him. During long, dark winters, it was no wonder people found ways to brighten the days until spring, all the way back to the first caveman's fire. The soft glow of the streetlights. A flickering Christmas tree shining through a house window. Vernon's festive shop display. And last, but certainly not least, the well-lit pub. Pixie had gone all out with a spectacular laser light show projected onto The Rusty Anchor's front walls.

It bothered him that Pixie and Tamara still weren't speaking. A couple of times, he'd dared to raise the subject but had got his head bitten off for his troubles. Christos was still around because Gage saw him behind the bar on quiz night. Not that the man looked very happy about it.

Gage rubbed his cold hands together and strode off towards the church. He was early, as usual, and there was no sign of Paul yet, so he headed towards the tree. A rough curse broke out of him.

'What've the buggers done?' Paul's gruff voice rang out behind him and he turned to see his friend, red-faced with anger.

The tree lay on the ground with several of its limbs lopped off. Shards of the red plant pot were spread over the grass along with glass from the shattered lights.

'I know some weren't happy with us having the tree, but they didn't have to spoil it for everyone else. The little kiddies are going to be some disappointed.'

'Then we'll have to make sure they aren't,' Gage said firmly.

'Well said.' Tamara hurried over to join them.

His brain went into battle mode. 'First thing is to get it upright and see how bad the damage is. We need to spread the word and see if anyone's got any spare lights. I doubt anyone will have a pot big enough, so we'll dig a hole and stick it in the ground for now.'

174

Between the three of them, they righted the tree and leaned it against the churchyard wall. By now more people had started to arrive, including Wilf and Karen, who stared at their decimated tree in disbelief.

'Who would do this?' Karen was close to tears.

'Someone who resents us moving here and trying to do our bit,' Wilf said sadly.

'Well, they don't represent the majority.' Tamara's no-non-sense statement was typical. Any sort of unfairness and prejudice got her back up. 'It doesn't look too bad. Once we get some lights back on, it'll be fine.'

He wasn't so sure, but, if the tree wasn't a perfect speci-men, did that matter? With an inward smile, he compared it to himself. It also reminded him of a children's book he'd put out on the shelves today. *The Last Christmas Tree* was about a misshapen tree missing several branches that no one chose to buy, until the right family came along who it suited perfectly.

Next thing, a couple of men whom he'd seen in the pub but didn't know by name turned up with a garden shovel and pair of loppers. One started digging a hole while the other trimmed the tree to even it up. By the time the tree was nestled in the ground, willing neighbours had brought over more than enough lights to replace the broken ones, so Paul went back into action and set the lights up all over again.

'I've got just the thing to finish it off and prove the light of Christmas will keep shining no matter what.' The vicar passed a large, bright gold star up to Paul, who fixed it to the new, slightly flatter top.

The crowd had swelled while all this was taking place, and Gage blinked back an unexpected rush of emotion at the sight of the community coming together. Tamara's hand clasped his tightly and he noticed a shimmer in her big blue eyes.

As the designated turner-on of the lights, Vernon stepped forward, but, instead of launching into a long speech as every-one had anticipated, he beckoned Wilf over to join him. Some muttering went on between the two men, then Wilf took hold of the big red switch Paul had engineered for the occasion.

'I don't deserve this honour, but Mr Bull is most insistent. My wife and I love Penworthal already and hope it will be our home for many years. After I turn on the lights, we're going to sing "Silent Night" and then some more carols. I'm told our book-club ladies have a stall set up with warm mince pies and a mulled cranberry punch. There's no cost, but donations for the Spirit of Christmas meal will be gratefully received. And now let's count down from ten and get Christmas in Penworthal started!'

Gage held his breath that the hastily erected lights would work, but at the press of a button the tree blazed with a mixture of all shapes, colours and sizes of lights.

'Oh, ye of little faith,' Tamara murmured. 'And with the vicar standing next to you too.' She snuggled into him and Gage kissed the top of her head.

Karen's crystal-clear soprano voice rang out and soon others started to join in. He left the singing to them and gave himself up to recognising the feeling of contentment that had settled around his heart.

176

CHAPTER TWENTY-TWO

Gage snatched the foaming pint from Nathan and took a large gulp. 'Boy, you've no idea how I needed that.'

'Your undue haste is something of a clue.' Nathan dropped into his seat and grinned around the table at their friends. 'That's what Book Club Refugees night is for.'

Even before Gage had arrived in the village, it had become a habit for the abandoned spouses and partners to meet in the pub while their other halves attended the monthly meetings, and he'd become part of it now. The only one missing tonight was Tessa, who was stuck at home with a stinking cold.

Tamara had prickled like a threatened porcupine and snapped when he'd asked if she'd mind him coming for a quiet pint or two. Her tart response had been that he didn't need her permission for anything.

It didn't help that they were both on edge about Victoria, who still hadn't responded to his calls or texts, despite being so insistent on hearing from him when she'd come to the shop on Saturday. It was still only Tuesday and she might be busy with work, so he was trying to cut her some slack.

'Busy day?' Quinten asked and went back to munching contentedly on his cheese-and-onion crisps. Evelyn had a

177

violent dislike of them because they made his breath stink, so as a compromise he only indulged on rare occasions. He was on his second bag already.

'Yeah, but that's good. Four blokes drove all the way from Bristol to check out the military transport section. They left loaded with far more than they intended buying.'

'So, has everyone done their Christmas shopping?' Nathan chuckled. 'No escaping it, you know. We're into December.'

'No escaping it anyways with this place decked out like Santa's grotto.' Harry gave a good-natured chuckle. Pixie didn't do minimalist, so every inch of the pub sparkled with tinsel, lights and shiny glass balls. 'Not that our Greek friend looks full of the festive spirit.'

Up at the bar, a grim-faced Christos was scurrying madly from one end to the other.

'Having to work for a living doesn't suit him,' Harry continued. 'I reckon he's in the doghouse with Pixie for some reason and on a short leash.'

Gage kept his mouth shut.

'Nathan will hate me for this.' Quinten's boast came with a cheeky smile. 'I've bought a signed first edition of one of Daphne du Maurier's lesser-known books — *Mary Anne* — for Evelyn. It's one of the few she doesn't have in her collection.'

'That must've cost a pretty penny.' Nathan sighed. 'Ah, well, I might get invited to come and look at it if I'm lucky.'

Gage's heart sank. Maybe it was just him? He seemed to have landed in the middle of a bunch of men who actually bought gifts for their significant others before Christmas Eve. During his brief marriage, Victoria would buy something she wanted, wrap it up and give him the bill. His only job was to stick it under the tree and hand it over on Christmas Day so she could pretend to be surprised.

'You aren't saying much.' Harry nudged him. 'Tamara's easy, surely. All you've got to do is buy another of those ugly pigs she's crazy about.'

That'd be easy. But predictable. Did she expect a surprise?

'I'd better be off.' Barry lumbered to his feet. 'Laura's mum likes an early night.'

'I'll head out too.' Quinten crammed the last handful of crisps into his mouth and screwed up the bag. 'The girls will be home soon, so I need to brush my teeth a couple of times first.' He shrugged on his long tweed coat, settled the familiar black fedora on his head and adjusted his dark-red silk scarf. 'See you, gents.'

'Ready for another?' Gage gestured at Nathan's empty glass. 'My round.'

'Cheers. I'm in no hurry.'

That struck him as odd. Nathan always made a point of being home when Melissa returned so they could dissect the book-club discussion together.

'Have you eaten? I didn't have time myself.'

'Uh, no. I told Melissa I'd make myself something before I came here, but I never got around to it.'

'Will a pasty suit you?'

'That's fine.' Nathan sounded indifferent.

Gage could do with his friend's opinion on a couple of things, but considered he might not be the only one who needed to talk.

* * *

The morning had been nerve-racking because Tamara had had an appointment at the bank to sign the loan documents, using her house as security. On the way back, she'd stopped by Georgie Rowe's to pass over a hefty deposit to secure his go-ahead with the kitchen refurbishment. Then she'd started her preparations for tonight with a speedy clean of her neglected house, making her aware how little time she'd spent there recently.

It was a sort of unwritten rule that if you hosted the December meeting, your house should look suitably festive, so she'd spent another hour or so putting up her decorations.

179

The artificial tree she'd dragged out of the attic had lost a lot of its needles, but she'd still covered it in all of the ornaments she'd collected over the years, including several lumpy clay Christmas puddings made by Toby in school. Festooned with the ornaments, draped in an excessive amount of tinsel and decked out in plain white lights, the tree cheered up the room. Vernon had been pushing the bright-red poinsettias he'd had on sale this week at the shop, so she'd bought several yesterday and dotted those around too.

Now she was indulging in her favourite part of the whole day — the baking. There were the traditional mince pies and sausage rolls everyone would expect, but the star of the show in her eyes was one of her own recipes — a festive take on Battenberg cake. She sandwiched individual fingers of sponge cake together with a homemade cranberry jam and covered the whole thing with red and green striped marzipan. It was the same recipe she had planned on using yesterday for the first day of the pub's December Dessert specials. Presumably that idea had gone by the wayside now.

As the last job before everyone arrived, she set a large pan of mulled wine on to warm through and fragrance the whole house.

It was something of a squash, but Tamara somehow squeezed all nine of them into her living room. Their usual seven-strong group had expanded to include Ophelia, and tonight they had another visitor. Evelyn had invited Monica Wyndham-Smythe, from the new Trelawney Court development, because she was interested in starting a similar club among her new neighbours and was keen to see how theirs worked.

'Are we ready, girls?' Evelyn clapped her hands and bestowed a wry smile on Monica. 'You'll find you have to take control, or it can disintegrate into nothing more than an excuse to drink and gossip.'

'And wouldn't that be terrible?' Josie said with a grin. 'Sorry, Evelyn. I'll behave.'

'That would be a first, Josephine. You never did at school, so why start now?' The tart response set off a round of giggles.

180

'Books out.' She peered over her glasses. '*A Christmas Carol*. We'll have opinions on the book first and as our resident nurse is in fine voice tonight, I suggest we start with her.'

Tamara and Laura shared a smirk. They often placed imaginary bets on who would get picked first.

'You all know I'm practical, a bit cynical at times and not one for sentiment.' Josie's cheeks glowed. 'But I don't mind admitting I shed a tear reading the book. The part with those pitiful children — Ignorance and Want — was heartbreaking and tore me up. We're reading it as historical fiction, but, when it was published, that was contemporary life to Dickens with all its warts and horrors.'

'Absolutely, and part of its brilliance is the way you could change the setting to modern times and it works equally well.' Amy chimed in. 'Scrooge would be a modern-day business tycoon, consumed by greed and riding roughshod over the so-called little people.'

'I love the hopefulness of it the most,' Becky said. 'It's about redemption, isn't it? If someone as dreadful as Scrooge can change his ways, then there's hope for everyone.' Her shoulders straightened. 'If we all made the same promise as old Scrooge when he said he'd honour Christmas in his heart and try to keep it all the year, the world would be a kinder, gentler place.'

'I hadn't read the book until yesterday.' Tamara made the admission reluctantly. 'Good thing it was short.'

Evelyn's eyebrows shot up.

Gage had been so sweet and had suggested a speed-reading session to race through it over their lunch. He was determined to copy Nathan's habit of reading along with every one of the book club's selections next year.

'I've never seen any of the films either, except for *The Muppet Christmas Carol*. It was Toby's favourite and we still watch it every Christmas.'

'Of course you do. Miss Piggy is probably your favourite actress.' Laura's good-natured teasing made everyone laugh.

She noticed Monica's bewildered expression and hurried to explain about her pig obsession.

181

'Ah, I see.' The colour rose in the woman's plump cheeks. 'I'm diffident to voice an opinion—'

'Don't be, please,' Melissa said encouragingly. 'Everyone has one and they're all different. That's what makes the group so much fun.'

Tamara was relieved to hear her friend sound more animated. She'd been unusually quiet recently and almost seemed lost in a world of her own. In the bookshop a couple of days ago, Gage and Nathan had been in deep discussion about the Cornish books section he hoped to start soon, so she'd asked Melissa how she was. Melissa had fixed on a bright smile, and insisted she was fine. Later, Tamara might try to have a word with Josie to get her opinion. The two used to be neighbours and were still very close.

'If you're sure.' Monica folded her hands in her ample lap. 'I'm something of a film fan, especially the old classics, even back to the first silent films.'

Tamara always found it fascinating to see what emerged through their group discussions. The books they read were only a part of it and simply opened the door.

'Believe it or not, the oldest film based on this wonderful book was made in 1901 and was called *Scrooge, or, Marley's Ghost*. It's obviously a silent film and only lasted a little over six minutes, and sadly about a minute of that has been lost over the years.' Monica perched on the edge of the chair. 'Remember, Charles Dickens didn't die until 1870, so people watching the film when it was released could've been old enough to remember the book being published. They might even have heard Dickens read from the work publicly. Isn't that incredible? Oh, goodness, I could rattle on for ever about all this. My poor husband tries to rein me in, but when I get started . . .' She took a breath. 'Most film buffs consider the 1951 version starring Alastair Sim to be unrivalled. He brought Ebenezer Scrooge to life quite incredibly and it's the best adaptation as far as staying true to the story. It still makes people shiver, cry and laugh after all these years.' Monica sat back, pink with embarrassment.

'I can't believe I've come across another film aficionado.' Ophelia's eyes shone. 'I became interested when I lived in France where it's such an art form. I'm particularly fond of forties and fifties classics with the old stars like Brigitte Bardot, Alain Delon and Catherine Deneuve.'

Was it wishful thinking to believe Evelyn's sister looked brighter tonight?

'I love those too.' Monica nodded enthusiastically. 'Perhaps you'd care to come over for coffee one morning? We can happily bore each other talking about films, rather than all these dear people.'

'I'd enjoy that very much, thank you.'

Tears pricked Tamara's eyes to see the club working its magic again. She left them all talking and slipped out to put the mince pies and sausage rolls in the oven.

'Anything I can do to help?' Josie popped her head around the kitchen door.

'You can put the kettle on.'

'When are you and Pixie going to stop behaving like five-year-olds who've fallen out over a favourite doll?'

'I'm not discussing that.' Apart from Gage, no one knew the full story of why she'd thrown in her job and hadn't ventured inside the pub since. 'I'd rather talk about what you think we can do to help Melissa.'

'Fine. Be that way.'

She busied herself fetching a selection of sparkling waters and fizzy drinks from the fridge and setting them on the countertop. 'Melissa claims she's not bothered about the baby thing, but I don't believe it.'

'Sometimes people find not facing up to the truth the only way of coping. I see it with patients all the time. The secret is trying to work out if they want to be pushed into it, or not.'

'So, what's your opinion in her case?'

'Yeah, do share.' Melissa marched in with eyes blazing and her American accent significantly stronger than usual. 'Am I tonight's group pity-project?'

183

'It's not pity and you know it.' Josie sounded quite fierce. 'We care about each other and if one of us is hurting, we all hurt. If we can help, that's what we try to do. You know we share our joys too. The whole package.'

'As I told Ms Nosey here—' a dismissive nod came Tamara's way — '*I've* absolutely accepted that it's extremely unlikely Nathan and I will ever be parents. *He* doesn't seem able to do that.' Melissa shook her head. 'Ironic, isn't it? I was the one full of having a baby in the first place, whereas he was happy either way. That's why I never mentioned the possibility of IVF, adoption or even surrogacy to him. Now he doesn't understand why I won't consider either. I simply want to enjoy the wonderful life we already have. If a baby comes along, that's great, but if not it'll be fine. I expect Chloe and Toby will have kids one day, so we can look forward to spoiling them instead.' Her smile was unnaturally bright. 'By the time I come back from visiting my family, I hope he'll be more . . . accepting. Then we can move on together.'

'When are you going?'

'In a couple of weeks. For Christmas.'

'Without Nathan?' Tamara couldn't hide her dismay and Josie looked equally bamboozled.

'We're married. Not joined at the hip.' Melissa bristled. 'He's fine with me going alone.' She glanced at the food on the table. 'I've lost my appetite, so I'll leave y'all to dissect me over the mince pies.' With that, she flounced out of the house.

'I'd say we well and truly put our gigantic feet in it.' Josie picked up the ladle and sloshed mulled wine into two red heatproof cardboard cups, then passed one to Tamara. 'Drink that. There's no way we can share this in front of Monica, so it'll have to go around the phone tree later.'

They'd set up a cascading list for passing on critical group messages — more often than not, gossip they didn't want the others to miss out on. The lines would burn up later.

184

CHAPTER TWENTY-THREE

'I'll be up as soon as I've locked the shop for the night.' Gage kissed Tamara's cheek.

'Okay. I'll put the kettle on.'

He stepped outside first to enjoy one of his favourite parts of the day. It'd become something of a habit to take a few moments to soak up the village's increasingly festive vibe. Today, the house three doors up from the shop had fixed a couple of gaudy plastic reindeer, a sleigh and Father Christmas to their roof. Presumably because, at least in their view, the giant inflatable candy canes and Christmas stocking on the front lawn didn't make enough of a show.

He glanced towards the brightly lit village tree and smiled. No one had dared to mess with it again, probably because they knew the wrath of most of the locals would come down on them.

The sound of Noddy Holder's raspy voice drifted out from the pub's open door. If Gage never heard Slade's 'Merry Xmas Everybody' again he'd be a happy man.

He wished he could come up with something to get Tamara and Pixie back on speaking terms. Nathan hadn't been any help the other night because he was too caught up

185

in his own misery. Instead of bringing him and Melissa closer, their inability to get pregnant was straining the marriage. His friend had teetered on the edge of breaking down when he'd mentioned his wife's travel plans. Tamara had naturally shared what had happened at book club, so he knew it wasn't all in Nathan's overactive imagination.

'Goodness me, GG, you do look miserable. Not that it's any wonder in this place. Whatever made you bury yourself here?'

'Victoria?' His ex-wife materialised in front of him and he noticed the taxi she must've arrived in pulling away. 'What on earth are you doing here? I thought I made it clear that you weren't to come.'

'I needed to talk to you.'

'That's what phones are for.'

'In person. I need a favour.'

A trickle of uncertainty edged into her voice and his heart sank. Whatever it was, Gage was pretty sure he didn't want to hear it.

'Don't I at least get invited in for a few minutes? I've come all the way from Exeter in this awful weather. I've been on my feet all day, shivering and dressed in next to nothing while being forced into every conceivable pose by an incredibly arrogant photographer who thinks he's the next Nick Knight.'

'Nick who?'

Victoria rolled her eyes. 'You're such a philistine. He's the iconic fashion photographer every model would give his or her soul to work with. Of course he's done me many times.' She shuddered. 'Are you going to keep me standing here all night?'

'I suppose you'd better come up to the flat.'

* * *

At the top of the stairs, Gage flung the door open and shouted to Tamara, 'We've got a guest.'

She drifted out from the kitchen in the middle of drying her hands on a towel. 'Oh, who—'

186

'So you're his little girlfriend. I should have guessed.' Victoria looked smug. 'I hope I'm not interrupting your evening, but I absolutely have to talk to GG.'

'I'd prefer it if you stopped calling me by that idiotic name.' Gage gritted his teeth. In the beginning she'd used it as an affectionate nickname, but when their marriage had started unravelling and she'd realised the name irked him, Victoria had wielded it as a petty act of revenge.

Tamara plastered on a bright smile. 'Would you like a cup of tea, Victoria? We were just about to have one. I've got some freshly baked mince pies as well. With Cornish clotted cream of course. Now it's December we have free licence to eat them every day, not that Gage indulges so I have his share too.'

'Oh, gosh, not for me, but thank you.' His ex shuddered. 'I rarely touch carbs because they show up dreadfully on camera.' A tiny frown marred her smooth brow.

Botox, had to be.

'The younger models can get away with it, but when you reach your thirties, things change.'

'Thirties?' Gage spluttered. 'You're—'

'That must be so hard. You have amazing discipline and self-control,' Tamara interrupted.

Now he felt guilty as relief skittered across Victoria's face.

A lot of people, and women in particular, were sensitive about their age. Who could blame them if it threatened their livelihoods? Men in the public eye tended to get a lot more latitude when it came to showing grey hair and a few extra kilos. Women were frequently sidelined in favour of younger replacements. He should've thought before he spoke.

'I don't know why I was surprised when Taff told me you'd opened this place. At least you're getting paid for sticking your nose in a book now, so that's something.'

Victoria's pointed remark almost made him blow up at her again, but Tamara caught his eye and gave a tiny shake of her head. She was right. He had no need to be petty and vindictive.

187

Gage surprised himself by talking about Becky and his newly rediscovered family.

'My eldest niece, Emily, is working in the shop on Saturdays. She's a great character and not at all shy. Ems absolutely loves books too, although she despairs of what she calls my dull taste in reading. She just turned eighteen and gets mad when her parents still treat her like a child, at least from her point of view.'

'She's lucky her parents care so much,' Victoria said. 'Mine were always very distant and packed me off to boarding school as soon as they could.'

'Your grandmother was different, though. A really lovely lady.' His gaze clouded over. 'I always found it amazing that she liked me and was supportive of us.' The corners of his mouth dragged down. 'I wish I'd kept in touch with her. How is she?'

'Grandmama is actually the reason why I'm here.' Victoria dabbed her eyes with a white lace handkerchief and he noticed her hand shaking.

Gage felt his colour drain away. 'She's not—'

'Dead? No. I'd hardly make a big deal of seeing you in that case, would I?'

'I suppose not. So why then?'

'It's a bit awkward, but I need a huge favour.'

Here we go.

'I expect she took our divorce hard?'

Victoria squirmed in the chair. 'I'm sure she would've done if I'd told her. Mummy and Daddy persuaded me to keep it from her because they were furious with me. They insisted if I'd been what they called "a good wife", you wouldn't have left me.'

'That's totally unfair.' Gage couldn't let her take all the blame. 'Our lifestyles were poles apart and we didn't love each other enough to compromise. Anyway, your parents always made it plain I wasn't good enough for you, so I assumed they were pleased to get rid of me!'

'Yah, well that's typical. As if it wasn't bad enough that their only daughter became a model, she insists on marrying a common soldier and it's an abject failure.' Victoria gave

188

a resigned shrug. 'I'm afraid Grandmama isn't well and for some reason she keeps asking for you.'

'Me? Where does she think I've been the last two years?'

A flush crept up his ex's long, thin neck. 'On assignment in Australia. A secret mission where I wasn't able to join you.'

'Australia?' Gage spluttered.

'I didn't know what to say, GG.' Her eyes turned misty with unshed tears.

Victoria's love for her grandmother was genuine. Maybe the only real thing about her.

Tamara wasn't famous, wealthy or classically beautiful, but at least her life was grounded and authentic. He caught her eye this time and as they locked gazes, her thoughts seemed to mirror his own.

'So.' He cleared his throat. 'What do you need me to do, Victoria? No offence, but I'm not marrying you again.'

'I'm not suggesting we go that far!' Her shock might've been laughable under different circumstances. 'All I need is for you to come to Kingston upon Thames and visit her with me.' Her voice wobbled. 'Just once.' She shot a worried look Tamara's way. 'You wouldn't mind, would you?'

'Of course not. Although, Gage doesn't need my permission for anything because that's not how we are together.' She reached for his hand and gave it a squeeze.

'When do you need me?' He sounded resigned.

'I don't suppose you could come tomorrow?' Victoria shot them another anxious look. 'It's about a five-hour drive, so I'm afraid you'll pretty much have to stay the night. My taxi is coming back for me in about ten minutes to take me to Exeter. I'll get the quarter-past-ten train tomorrow morning and there are only two changes, so I'll be at Kingston by about a quarter to two. We could meet at the station.' Her brow furrowed slightly. 'I hope that's all right?'

'Yeah, that's fine.'

Tamara did her best to stifle a yawn. 'I think I'll make a move. It's been a long day. I could do with a lie-in, and I can

189

get that better at my place if you're going to be up at the crack of dawn tomorrow. If you'll be staying the night in Kingston that means you won't be back to open the shop on Monday morning, so do you want me to do it?'

'Bloody hell, I hadn't given it a thought.' Gage smacked his head. 'Are you sure that's okay?'

'Daft question. Of course it is.' She slipped her coat on and found her bag. 'Bye, Tori — I'm sorry, but that name comes more naturally — you don't mind?'

'Why should I? It's who I am these days.' There was little joy in the statement.

'I'll come down and lock the door behind you,' he said, his eyes locking with Tamara's.

The twinkle in her eyes relayed that she knew he had in mind much more than a simple good night.

They were both in fits of giggles by the time they reached the bottom of the stairs. He pressed her up against the wall with his mouth crushing hers. There was a wonderful illicitness about sensing each other's frustration through their clothes.

'This will be quite a story to spread around book club.' Gage felt Tamara's hot blush against his skin. 'Hey, it's fine. I'm good with you telling them. It doesn't need to be a secret.' He dropped a soft kiss on her mouth.

'I was proud of you tonight when you didn't let Victoria needle you.'

He lifted his broad shoulders in a shrug. 'I'm working at being more laid back. Those of us connected to the forces, or emergency services or the medical profession, deal with making life-or-death decisions all the time. It's one reason that so many struggle with regular life. We don't understand when someone makes a fuss over things like their cubicle being smaller than their workplace neighbour.'

'I need to put things right with Pixie, don't I? We have to find a way to deal with the situation without ripping apart a decade of incredible friendship.'

190

'I wasn't getting at you. That wasn't over something trivial. All you tried to do was help an old friend see that she was being made a fool of by an unscrupulous man. I know you held some stuff back, but I'm pretty sure she would've been even angrier if you'd told her everything.'

'Maybe, but us not talking to each other needs to end.' She eked out a smile. 'Apart from anything else, the choice of entertainment venues in Penworthal is limited and if I let my quiz team down again this month, Proper Choughed might start thinking the trophy is permanently theirs.'

'Maybe I shouldn't encourage you to hold out an olive branch after all,' he mused. 'They might ostracise me if they find out.'

'All the more reason for me to put on those Bridget Jones panties again. While you're away I'll go to the pub and sort this out once and for all.'

'I love when you turn all fierce and take charge.' Gage's voice turned husky. 'You'd better go before I behave in a very ungentlemanly manner, in public, where anyone might see us.'

'It's dark. Who's going to see?'

'You're wicked.' Gage wriggled his hand under her red T-shirt and stroked warm, bare skin, making her shudder.

'So are you, and you're making me want to do all sorts of naughty things to you right now.' With a reluctant sigh, she pushed him gently away.

'I'll hold you to that when you get back.'

'You could hold me to anything, anywhere and I wouldn't object,' Tamara said teasingly and his laughing response followed her down the street.

191

CHAPTER TWENTY-FOUR

Tamara yawned and rolled over. Five a.m. The clock must be wrong. She propped herself up on one elbow and grabbed her phone. It confirmed the time. Was it her imagination or did the Petunia Pig clock face look extra smug this morning? During the long, mainly sleepless night, she'd made her plans.

Pixie always arrived at the pub first on Sundays, around eight o'clock, to spend a quiet hour catching up with paperwork before Rocky turned up to start on the roast lunches.

She swung her legs out of bed and shoved on her pink furry slippers. They had pig bobbleheads for the toes and were Toby's Christmas present from a couple of years ago.

After she showered and got dressed, it was time to hit the kitchen and bake a peace offering for Pixie. The one possible drawback with her plan was if Christos had changed his routine of clocking in just as the pub opened at noon. She would cross that bridge if she came to it.

By half seven she'd put the finishing touches to the cake and had time to sit down with a mug of tea. Her unique take on a Christmas yule log had turned out perfectly. The light, airy lemon sponges were pieced together to resemble a log and rolled up with a cream filling laced with limoncello liqueur.

Along with the whipped cream exterior, it played to Pixie's love of light, fresh, citrusy cakes. She'd decorated the top with miniature Christmas baubles in jewel colours, and they were some of the best sugar-work she'd ever done.

A message popped up on her phone and the sight of Gage's name made her smile.

Good luck with Pixie. Your day might even be easier than mine.

The row of horrified-face emojis he signed off with made her laugh.

The church clock started striking and she counted the chimes. Eight. Time to go. Tamara slipped an old black cardigan over her T-shirt as a concession to the frost whitening the grass outside her window and picked up the white cardboard box from the kitchen counter.

Why did distances shrink when you least wanted them to? Before she realised it, Tamara was knocking on the back door of the pub.

'It's open, Rocky. Why're you . . .' Pixie turned pale. 'Oh, it's you. What do you want?'

'To give you this. Can we talk? Please?' Tamara thrust the gift at her old friend and anxiously rattled off a description of the contents.

'I suppose you might as well come in.'

She nervously followed and watched Pixie open the box. Her friend studied the contents with wide eyes and gave an appreciative sniff.

'You didn't need to do this.' Pixie's lower lip wobbled. 'You should pelt me with it for being a proper cow, although it would be a shame to waste this beauty.' A burst of high-pitched laughter betrayed her nervousness. 'Is it okay to eat lemon cake this early in the morning?'

'Why not? It's almost Christmas and everyone knows that's the season of free passes when it comes to calories.' She

193

was swamped with relief. They weren't over the hump, but at least the door hadn't been slammed in her face. Perhaps the United Nations should use cake as a peacemaking tool. 'How about a coffee? I'll make it while you cut the cake.'

'Coffee sounds awesome. I didn't have time before I came here.' Pixie turned away and headed for the cabinet where they kept the dishes.

They busied themselves as they'd done so many times over the years and shared the task of getting their unusual breakfast ready. Soon they were sipping hot, fragrant coffee and digging into the cake. Tamara blushed with pleasure at Pixie's almost orgasmic reaction. Making food for other people was all about unselfish giving and nourishing, which was exactly what their shattered friendship needed.

'This was one of the recipes I planned to include in the December Dessert specials. Did that—'

'Go by the wayside? Yeah.' Pixie sighed. 'Rocky didn't have time for anything extra, so he stuck to the usual stuff. You must have this on sale in the café when it opens,' she said vehemently.

'How is Rocky? Has he had any luck finding a new job?'

'He doesn't need to, thank goodness.' Pixie's relief was obvious. 'I spoke to the new landlady last week and they're keen to keep him on. And with a pay raise too, so he's over the moon. How are your plans going for the café?'

'Really good. I should be able to open in the new year.' Damping down her enthusiasm for the project she'd dreamed about for so long was impossible, and her friend *had* asked, so she got the full rundown. 'We're still struggling with the name, though.'

They were soon convulsed with laughter at the various pig-related ideas that had been batted around so far.

Pixie's mouth turned down. 'I've missed this so much. I don't mean I resent you getting this amazing chance. If I'd simply lost you to that, I wouldn't be so bloody miserable.' A tear leaked out and trickled down her cheek. 'But not seeing

194

you. Not talking to you.' She touched her chest. 'It hurts my heart. You were right to leave . . . and you were right about Christos.'

Tamara reached across and gave Pixie's small hands a quick squeeze.

'I sent him packing a few days ago. The estate agency where he worked doesn't want him back, so he got a last-minute flight out to Santorini yesterday. I don't envy him having to explain things to his family, but it's his own fault. He deserves whatever grief they give him.' The sound of her deep, gulping breaths filled the kitchen. 'I watched him like a hawk after you left and for maybe a week, he couldn't have been more attentive and hard-working. Then he reverted to his usual lazy, charming self.' Bitterness flooded out of her. 'One of the new Trelawney Court women caught his eye. A wealthy, bleached-blonde divorcée. But she sized him up in a hurry, so he didn't get far. He started going out after closing time and rolling back in the early hours of the morning. If I asked where he'd been, he blew me off and said he deserved some fun after slogging away here all the time.'

Tamara metaphorically super-glued her mouth shut.

'A young woman came in yesterday looking for him. I mean really young — barely over eighteen is my guess. You should've seen his face when I fetched him, and she started blabbing on to me about how they'd met in a sleazy nightclub in Newquay and were madly in love. I suppose it would've put a damper on their romantic trysts if he'd mentioned living with his fiancée.'

'I'm so sorry.'

'So now I'm single again, broke and soon to be jobless.' The fake bright smile and pulled-back shoulders couldn't hide Pixie's distress. 'I'm sure Christos won't willingly give back the money I loaned him for the deposit on the house and our plane tickets, and I've no interest in shelling out more money to sue him. I don't need your hunky boyfriend and his mates hunting Christos down to knock some sense into

195

him either.' A flash of the old confident, take-no-prisoners Pixie re-emerged.

'Of course not!'

'I'm surprised you dragged yourself out of Gage's bed this early on his day off.'

'I spent last night at mine. You'll never guess in a million years where he's gone, and who he's meeting up with later. I've got some gossip you won't believe.' She wagged her finger in Pixie's face. 'Not to be shared, though. Not yet.' She didn't want to push her luck. The whole story poured out and her friend's reaction was priceless.

'Tori G? Bloody hell. I mean she's—'

'Gorgeous. Yep, I know. It's a bugger, isn't it? Luckily for me, he decided a while ago that high-maintenance, demanding women weren't his thing.' Tamara stabbed the last forkful of cake and popped it in her mouth. 'I don't usually praise my own baking, but that's amazing.'

'Told you so.'

'Anyway, what's *your* next move? Have you approached the pub to see if you can cancel your resignation?'

Pixie shook her head. 'That was my first reaction too, but you aren't the only one ready for a change. I also need to spread my wings and not just to get away from everyone's sympathy.' She planted her hands on the table. 'I'm going back to Wales. I've got a cousin who lives in Cardiff and she's asked me to stay with her for a while. I can pick up some odd bar work or whatever while I get my plans in order.' She glanced anxiously up through her long, dark lashes. 'I've always regretted leaving school at sixteen with only a couple of GCSEs. I know I'll have to start at the bottom again and a university degree might be unattainable, but I'll never know unless I try.' The worry lines deepened again. 'Do you think I'm crazy?'

'Absolutely not. Go for it.' She threw her arms around Pixie. 'We're more alike than we ever knew. Both of us needed kicking out of our comfortable ruts. I needed that shove to get my café and I'm sure you wouldn't have picked hitching

196

yourself to an unfaithful pillock.' Her hand flew to her mouth. 'Sorry. That was super tactless. The plans you made would've been awesome if—'

'Christos hadn't turned out to be an unfaithful pillock? It's okay. I can take it. At least I can now.'

'Morning.' Rocky breezed in and shrugged off the old khaki army greatcoat he lived in over the winter. 'It's great to see you again, Tamara. Please tell me you two have sorted out whatever turned you into a pair of idiots and you're coming back to work?'

'Yes, and no.' She beamed. 'We're besties again, which is awesome, but I'm all set to open a café in the bookshop and couldn't be happier. I'm thrilled your job is safe, though.'

'Me too.'

'Any chance you'll pop back in after we're done serving and have lunch with me like old times?' Pixie asked.

'Every chance.'

Tomorrow she'd thank Gage properly for making her see sense. Right now she had Christmas cakes to deliver or her girlfriends would start to wonder if she'd forgotten their gifts. A bright idea struck. Tamara pulled out her phone and sent out a group message inviting everyone over to her house later for tea and mince pies.

She strode off up the road humming 'We Wish You a Merry Christmas'.

* * *

'Push me over to the window, young man, so I can see you better.' Louise Hatton remained an imposing presence and although her body was pitifully frail these days, her pebble-like dark eyes were fixed on him with the same astuteness he remembered.

'Of course, Grandmama.' It was a relief to manoeuvre her wheelchair away from the blazing log fire. 'Would you like me to fetch you a shawl?'

197

'Don't you start fussing around me too,' she snapped. 'I sent Victoria away because I need the truth, and no one else will give it to me.' A faint smile crept over her face.

His heart sank. This wasn't part of the deal.

'I've always had a soft spot for you and I thought you'd be good for my wayward granddaughter.' Louise shook her head sadly. 'You might've been if you'd actually loved each other.'

He squeezed his eyes shut for a moment. 'When did you guess?'

'Guess?' She threw back her head and gave an unladylike snort. 'The last time you were here for my son and daughter-in-law's ruby wedding anniversary, you couldn't stand to be in the same room together. You barely spoke to each other unless other people were watching.' Louise shook her head knowingly. 'It didn't fool me.'

'I didn't know until yesterday that the family hadn't told you we'd got divorced soon after that. I should've stayed in touch, but I thought I'd make things awkward for Victoria.'

'I suppose Australia was a lie too?'

'I've never been there. That was another—'

'Falsehood they told to keep the old lady quiet and stop me asking where you were?'

'Apparently.'

'So where did you hurt your leg? I noticed you limping when you arrived.'

It would be easy to spin a tale about injuring himself in a car crash or a fall, but there'd been far too many lies. Gage told her everything. He didn't realise his cheeks were damp with tears until Louise leaned over to brush them away. The gentle touch from her gnarled fingers unlocked his emotions. After spending hours in the car, only to arrive here and be greeted by Victoria's parents with the same disdain they'd always shown, his resistance was at a low ebb.

She patted his shoulder. 'I didn't want to upset you, but we both know I don't have much time left and I very much wanted to see you again.'

198

'For what it's worth, I'm proud you were once my grand-mother-in-law. Is there even such a thing?'

'Just because you and my granddaughter didn't make a go of your marriage, doesn't mean you divorced me too. I want to hear all about your new young lady and your lovely shop.'

Gage cradled her hand as he spoke and by the time he finished, her head had dropped to her chest and she was snoring softly. Later, he would thank Victoria. Louise wasn't the only one to gain a measure of peace from today. He'd finally come to terms with the end of his marriage and looked forward to returning to Penworthal and Tamara tomorrow. Where he belonged.

* * *

Tamara smiled at the cakes lined up along her kitchen counter. It'd taken a few late-night icing sessions, but would absolutely be worth it when she saw her friends' faces. She had sturdy red boxes ready for them to be carried away, but knew from previous years that they would want to see everyone else's gifts too.

The doorbell rang, so she quickly turned the kettle back on and took a quick peek at the mince pies warming up in the oven before running out to answer the door.

'Come in!' She gave Amy a swift hug. Tamara had predicted correctly that the ever-punctual Amy would arrive first. The rest of the girls would come in dribs and drabs, with Josie inevitably bringing up the rear.

It wasn't long before her living room was full of lively chatter and laughter while Christmas music played softly in the background. Laura gave her a hand to bring everyone a cup of tea, and then her friend sat down while Tamara went back for the mince pies. For a moment she hovered in the doorway, briefly overcome with emotion as she thought about how lucky she was.

199

'Here we go, girls.' Tamara breezed in and set down a platter of warm mince pies. She'd already brought in plates, napkins and a pretty green glass dish full of rich clotted cream. 'Help yourselves.'

'No Melissa?' Evelyn said worriedly.

Tamara shook her head. 'I didn't get any response. She was pretty annoyed after the last meeting, so I'm guessing we aren't forgiven yet.' Her smile felt forced, but she was determined not to spoil this impromptu get-together. 'Anyway, right now you need to eat your mince-pie ration for the day. I don't want any slackers because Gage certainly won't eat the leftovers!'

Once it was clear everyone was finished, Tamara got their attention. 'I know you're all nosy, so you might as well pile into the kitchen and check out everyone else's cakes as well as your own.'

No one took offence and there was friendly jostling to see who could get there first. Each cake had a small white card standing in front of it with the name of the recipient.

'Oh, my, you've excelled yourself.' Laura clapped her hands in glee. 'That's little Josephine pulling decorations off the tree!'

'You've even got mine and Harry's faces.' Josie peered closely at the snow policeman and snow nurse holding hands in the centre of her cake. 'You're brilliant.'

She heard Gage telling her to accept the compliments instead of brushing them off, so she did her best and thanked them both.

'Quinten will absolutely love this.' Evelyn looked up with tears in her eyes. 'I can't believe you were able to do us in our ballroom-dancing clothes, waltzing around the Christmas tree.'

Becky chuckled. 'Mine is spot on. That'll be me Christmas Day evening. Swigging the sherry and falling asleep by the fire.'

'And this beachy Christmas scene puts me and Tess on the set of *I'm a Celebrity . . . Get Me Out of Here!*.' How cool is

200

that? You know it's our favourite programme!' Amy beamed at Tamara. 'I can't wait to take it home.'

'Is this one yours?' Ophelia pointed to a cake set off a little from the others. 'It has to be with the family of pigs sitting around the Christmas tree.' She gave a tinkling laugh. 'You even have their little snouts stuck in the book gifts they've opened.'

'Gage got a kick out of seeing it, even though he won't eat a bite.'

'This must be Melissa's,' Evelyn said quietly.

'Yeah.' Tamara's smile fell away. She'd spent ages crafting the miniature room with its couple snuggled together on a burgundy floral sofa that mimicked the Kellows' own. The fondant Melissa and Nathan had their heads together and were reading *A Christmas Carol*. She cleared her throat. 'I'll give it to her before she leaves, even if I have to abandon it on the doorstep.'

'Good girl,' Evelyn said with a firm nod. 'Now I for one am taking my cake home and cutting it straight away to have a taste.'

There was a flurry of boxing up cakes, thanks, hugs and promises to see each other soon. After they'd all left, Tamara decided that Evelyn's idea sounded good to her. She refilled the kettle and turned it on to boil, then cut a large wedge of cake from one of the thickly iced corners and bit into it. Perfect. This was Christmas.

201

CHAPTER TWENTY-FIVE

Tamara pulled her collar up around her ears and shoved her free hand in her coat pocket. Even she had to admit it would've been smart to wear gloves. Up until now they'd enjoyed Cornwall's normal mild and damp winter weather, with the occasional early-morning frost, but last night the temperature had plummeted. This morning, they'd woken to a scene that only needed a sprinkling of glitter to resemble a Christmas card. A light covering of snow changed the shape of everything and gave even the most pedestrian buildings a hint of the gingerbread cottage. You could almost smell Christmas in the air.

She'd left Gage in a grouchy mood. They'd been promoting Secret Santa Saturday all over social media, seizing the fact it was mid-December and people were starting to panic about their Christmas shopping. He was even interviewed on the local radio station for their daily segment on festive happenings. Their promise was to help people choose the perfect gifts for everyone on their lists. But this weather could send all their efforts down the drain if the roads weren't safe to drive on. It was a long-standing joke that Cornwall's idea of preparedness began and ended with a single snow plough that was shifted around the county as needed. It was a shame after such a good week.

202

Gage had been different after his visit to Victoria's grandmother. More relaxed and at ease with himself. His long conversation with Louise had clearly put more of his demons to rest, especially his lingering insecurity about never being good enough in the eyes of Victoria's family. The old lady had apparently told him with a wry smile that her son and daughter-in-law were snobs and would learn their lesson one day.

Gage had also been overjoyed to hear about her reconciliation with Pixie and hadn't minded at all when she'd helped out at the pub a few times. But Tamara's best gift to her friend was introducing Pixie to Wilf Buckingham. The man's experience in the hotel business made him ideal as a part-time barman and waiter to help the pub through the busy Christmas season. Rocky was doing all the puddings now and was happy with the extra pay boost. Tamara was officially off the hook.

The holly wreath pricked her bare fingers, so she picked up her pace, eager to get to the cemetery and her parents' graves. She and her sister had made it a Christmas tradition to do this every year, and her good mood slipped down a few notches thinking about Tracy and how much she missed her.

She pushed open the creaking gate and was hurrying along the snowy path when the sound of someone talking made her grind to a halt. The last thing she wanted to do was to disturb anyone's private moment. The path forked at the base of an ancient oak tree, but before Tamara could head over to the right the voice drifted close enough for her to recognise Melissa's strong American accent.

'Oh, Robin, I'm in such a mess. It's partly your fault because if you hadn't been so selfish and we'd had a baby together, this wouldn't be an issue. I almost convinced myself that if I pretended not to care any longer about getting pregnant, Nathan and I would go back to how we were, but it's not working. It's tearing us apart, and I can't bear it much longer.' An anguished sob ripped out of Melissa. 'I don't know what to do.'

On impulse, Tamara stepped out into her friend's line of sight. Melissa turned the same colour as the snow at their feet.

203

'Sorry, I didn't mean to overhear, but I couldn't help it.'

'You could've walked on by and left me in peace.' Melissa's voice shook, but Tamara couldn't be certain whether it was in anger or with the cold.

'I suppose I could, but you're my friend. I know Josie and I messed up at book club, but—'

'You meant well.' The corners of Melissa's mouth lifted. 'Bless your hearts.'

Was it wrong that they both burst out laughing? Tamara didn't think so. 'We really did.' She touched her friend's arm. 'Don't push us out when you need us the most. I'm learning my lesson too when it comes to that, so maybe we can do this together. As for Nathan, you've always been great at communicating with each other, so stop lying to him. Tell the poor man exactly how you feel, and listen when he does the same. Bawl your eyes out. Get angry. Rail at the injustice of it all. I completely understand you wanting to see your family, but don't leave Nathan here alone. Not at Christmas.'

'I keep trying to get the courage to ask him to come with me.' Her shoulders drooped. 'I'm afraid buying the ticket was a touch of defiance on my part.'

'You hoped he'd beg you not to go.' The realisation hit like a bolt of lightning. 'Nathan's not a man to play games. You know that. All he saw was you, miserable and desperate to get away from both here and him.'

'Pretty dumb, huh? Or as you say in these here parts, I'm a daft maid.' Melissa's mangled Cornish accent was the worst Tamara had ever heard. Worse even than the actors on telly who often tried and failed so miserably to emulate it. Melissa wiped her eyes and sniffed. 'I'd better go home and grovel to my poor husband.'

Tamara touched Robin's dark granite headstone. 'See, you did help her after all.'

'You don't think it's weird me chatting to him? I don't do it as often these days, but sometimes it still helps.'

204

'It's not weird at all. I'll be talking to my mum and dad in a minute. Tell them about Gage and our plans.'

'Do I hear wedding bells?'

'Absolutely not!'

The outburst made her friend smile. 'So you made one mistake when you were a teenager, but we've all done that. How long are you going to keep beating yourself up over it?'

'I'm just cautious.'

Melissa's expression softened. 'Caution isn't necessarily a bad thing unless it holds you back. You know that if I'd let my doubts win out, Nathan and I wouldn't be married now.'

'I'm not as brave as you.'

'Sure you are. Gage is great for you and you've done wonders for him. Everyone sees it. And now you're all set to open your dream café.'

'But would I have taken the plunge if Pixie hadn't forced my hand?'

'Stop being so hard on yourself. Sure, you got a little nudge, and Gage did his bit too, but in the end it came down to you.' Melissa squeezed her arm. 'You could've found a job somewhere else. Shied away from getting involved with Gage. But you didn't. Try to start seeing yourself as the bright, capable, strong-willed woman we all do, then nothing can hold you back.'

A film of tears blurred Tamara's eyes. For a moment she couldn't speak. Swallowing didn't help and neither did clearing her throat. 'I almost forgot,' she whispered. 'I've still got your Christmas cake.'

Melissa looked shamefaced. 'I'm sorry I ignored your invitation, but I couldn't face y'all.'

'I'll drop it off at yours tomorrow.'

'Thanks. I bet it's awesome. Now off you go and do your thing.' Melissa shooed her away. 'I need to go home and mend fences. I've really put him through it recently. I'd hug you, but the holly wreath looks lethal.'

205

'There's an answer to that.' Tamara set it down on the snowy grass and flung her arms around her friend. 'Always a way, right?'

'Always,' whispered Melissa.

* * *

Gage couldn't believe it. The constant stream of people coming to the shop for Secret Santa Saturday blew his mind. When the weather forecast had threatened to wreck everything, Emily had had the bright idea of putting up a big sign outside and spreading the word on social media that they would be offering free hot chocolate and mince pies to all their customers today. It'd already lured in a lot of villagers who hadn't ventured inside before. He'd been dubious from a legal standpoint, but Tamara had assured him that because they'd submitted their registration as a food business, it wouldn't be a problem. The premises would be inspected before the café opened properly, but that didn't stop them from serving now. He still hadn't seen how they could pull it off logistically in such a short time, but his negative attitude had made the two women burst out laughing, and he'd been told to watch and learn.

The first stop had been Vernon's shop, where they'd stripped it of all the ingredients to make hot chocolate, plus every jar of mincemeat and packet of ready-made pastry he'd had in stock.

Gage spotted Tamara hurrying out from the kitchen where Becky and Laura were tucked away hard at work. The silver jingle bells on her bright-red Christmas jumper bounced merrily away as she set down another platter of warm mince pies on the temporary café counter they'd created. In reality it was the old kitchen door balanced on a couple of Barry's woodwork trestles and covered with a green velvet curtain Evelyn had dug out of her attic.

The shop bell jangled and a group of four or five men bundled in together. They brought a blast of cold air with them and shed a flurry of snowflakes when they stopped to take off their heavy coats.

'Major Bennet?' A tall, burly man tugged off a wool hat to reveal a shiny bald head, and stuck out his hand. 'Captain Ronnie Marshal, Royal Marines Retired. This rabble still calls me Red Ron, although the red hair's long gone. Taff's description of you was pretty spot on, although with that shaggy hair you might be mistaken for a regular Jack Tar. Don't they have barbers in this part of the world?'

Gage smiled at the dig at the Royal Navy, who were traditionally mocked by the Royal Marines for being sloppy and unfit. Plenty of insults went the other way too, so no one took serious offence. 'You know Taff?'

The man guffawed. 'We know the old bugger all right. We all live in Bristol. Drink in the same pub. Play darts together — no one beats the Bootneck Brigade.' He stuck out his chest. 'Taff's outside parking the Jeep. He thought we needed a rabbit run to get Chrimbo gifts, so here we are.'

He dipped his head and swiped a hand over his eyes. The idea that Taff had dragged a bunch of men, who didn't know him from Adam, on a three-hour drive to Cornwall in crap weather was mind-blowing.

'It's great to see you all. Help yourself to hot chocolate and mince pies.' He gestured to where Tamara and Emily were busy serving. 'If you need help finding books or whatever, just ask and I'll be happy to help.'

'Come on, lads.'

'How's it going, mate?' Taff trotted in, rubbing his hands together. 'It's bloody icers out there. Not a bad turnout, eh?'

'More than I expected. Thanks for bringing the cavalry.' He nodded towards the group gathered around the free snacks.

'Anytime. Don't you miss it?'

He knew what his friend was getting at and thought carefully before answering. Like many other retirees, Taff had sought out fellow veterans when he left the Corps, whereas Gage had done completely the opposite. Apart from the

207

Welshman, he'd purposely chosen to have no contact with anyone from his old life.

'Certain bits, I suppose. Even yomping across Dartmoor with heavy packs in shit weather had its moments. There were a bunch of good times and I don't regret any of them.' He cracked a smile. 'Not many, anyway.' It was a struggle to explain the far better but very different place he found himself in now. 'At sixteen, we were gung-ho for whatever they threw at us,' Gage said with a shrug. 'The marines dragged me out of the mess I'd got myself in and it gave me purpose. I've found a different purpose now. It's quieter and much less stressful. There's nothing life or death about selling books, which is a huge plus from where I'm standing.' His gaze strayed towards Tamara and his mouth settled in a satisfied curve.

'Maybe I need to find me a good woman and settle down,' Taff muttered.

In the old days, his best mate had avoided actual relationships like the bubonic plague.

'It suits me, that's all I'll say.'

'I can tell.' Taff's colour turned ruddy. 'By the way, did your old woman come banging on the door? I screwed up and let it slip before—'

'It's okay.' He grabbed his friend's arm. 'In fact, I want to thank you.'

'What the bloody hell for? She wasn't after getting her claws into you again, was she?'

'No!' Gage told a brief version of what had happened with Victoria and ended by reiterating that Taff had done him a big favour. He noticed Tamara gesturing towards the people waiting at the till. 'I'm sorry, but I've got to get back to work.'

'No rest for the wicked. If the offer's open, I'll pop down another day and we can have a few pints for old times.'

'Anytime, Taff, you know that.'

'Off you go, Prof, and sell your precious books.' Taff chuckled. 'If you can bear to part with them.'

208

Out of nowhere he hugged his old friend, both unsure which of them was the most startled. Breaking it off to go and serve saved them both from further embarrassment.

At first, Gage had been stiff and awkward with customers, unsure how to act or speak, but gradually he'd learned to allow his love of books free rein. Gage made a point of delving into what customers were looking for in a way the online retailers could never emulate. They might be cheaper, but his shop's personal service couldn't be rivalled. The next challenge was how to build up his customer base once the initial novelty of having a local bookshop wore off, but he relished having something to get his teeth into.

'Come on, Prof. We've got books to sell.' Tamara appeared by his side.

With all the emphasis on Christmas today, it reminded him that the big day loomed in a little more than a fortnight and he still hadn't bought her a present. What could possibly top everything she'd already given him? Now that really *was* a challenge.

209

CHAPTER TWENTY-SIX

'Do you think anyone would miss us if we don't turn up for the quiz?' Gage flopped on one of the shop's easy chairs and his face fell into deep, tired creases.

Tamara could see one drawback to this new job was the need to be on his feet more than was ideal. Once the café opened and hopefully brought in more business, he should be able to afford to hire an assistant. She certainly couldn't be in two places at the same time.

'I suppose it was a good idea of Pixie's to shift the quiz and have it a week earlier than usual. No one would've wanted to do it on Boxing Day. I'm sure we aren't the only ones, though, who wouldn't have minded a bit if it was cancelled this month,' she said. 'I suspect it's all part of Pixie's determination to keep busy and stop her dwelling on Christos's shitty behaviour. She's far more shaken up than she's willing to admit. Betrayal takes a long time to get past. I know.' She shook her head. 'I let it rule me far too long.'

Gage's dark eyes locked with hers.

'Not any longer though.'

'Good.' He tugged her over onto his lap. 'Letting go of the hard stuff is . . . hard.'

210

His quirky smile melted her heart.

'What do you think I should do about this?' He pulled out his wallet and extracted a crumpled piece of paper.

Tamara recognised Becky's neat handwriting. This was the first time he'd shown any interest in discussing whether or not to reach out to his father. The old adage about leading a horse to water couldn't be truer.

'It needs to be your decision, not mine.'

'But if you were me, you'd contact him?'

'How can I know? I've never been in that position. My dad was the loveliest man, who worshipped my mum and treated Tracy and me like princesses.' She choked back a sob. 'Losing him when Toby was little, and then my mum not long after, was the worst thing ever.'

'I can't begin to imagine.' He looked stricken. 'Family dynamics are a minefield for me.'

'I totally get that. Even though it's been a long time now, every year when Christmas comes around, I feel their absence like it just happened. All the advertisers conjure up images of loving families gathered around the dinner table, smiling and laughing and opening presents together. But is that the reality for most people?' A few steadying breaths kept her going. 'That's the main reason Pixie started the Spirit of Christmas meal and I willingly got involved.' Her smile re-emerged. 'I know we haven't talked about how we'll spend Christmas, but I hope you're good with us joining in? There's generally about thirty of us from all around the village. We're a mixed bunch of couples who don't want to eat alone, families who can't afford to make a proper Christmas dinner and lots of singles of course. No one judges. No one asks why you're there. Everyone is welcome.'

'Sounds wonderful to me. It'll remind me of being back in the marines, but hopefully with better food.' Gage chuckled. 'It never used to bother me, being on duty over the holidays, but a lot of the younger blokes and the family men found it hard. We made the best of it, though.'

211

'Pixie likes to get a rough idea of numbers, so I'll sign us up.'

'What about Toby and Chloe?'

'He's already told me he's working Christmas Eve night, but he and Chloe will join us on Christmas Day at the pub. On Boxing Day morning, they're heading upcountry to see Chloe's parents.'

She suddenly remembered what they'd been talking about. 'We've got off track, haven't we? Your dad. The way I see it, the worst that could happen is that he's not interested in getting back in contact. You've lived without his presence all these years, so you'd survive. But if he was pleased and you had the chance to talk through things, wouldn't that help?'

'I suppose.'

'How about I go up to the flat and make us a sandwich while you phone him?' Tamara flashed an encouraging smile. 'Cheese and pickle?' It was a running joke that she hated even the sight and smell of the spicy brown chopped-up pickle mixture, and so he usually ended up making it himself. 'Just this once. But if you chicken out of ringing, you'll get peanut butter and honey instead.' Toby's favourite sandwich combination as a boy had become hers too, but it made Gage gag.

'Witch.'

She dodged his attempt to grab her and left him, all the while laughing like a drain.

* * *

Gage's attempt to focus on the question sheet in front of him was a miserable failure, but so far no one seemed to have noticed his lack of participation. His mind kept returning to his brief conversation on the phone with Wally Harris. He'd last seen his father about twenty-five years ago, when he'd told Gage's mum and his thirteen-year-old son that he'd be away on business for a few days. They'd never seen him again.

212

'Well, I'll be darned. Who would've thought it? Little Gage. How'd you track your old man down?'

The lack of any emotion other than mild surprise threw him. He answered his father's questions almost robotically.

'I thought I'd surprise your sister next week and pop down for Christmas. It's been a while since I've seen the grandkids. It'll be good to have a pint with you, meet your girlfriend and see this little place you've got.'

That's when Gage exploded and totally lost it. Wally's casual attitude hurt far more than being told to sod off and not bother him again. After telling his so-called father what he thought of him, Gage threw the phone across the shop in disgust, and it knocked several books off the top of Emily's creative decoration. Tamara must have heard the crashing sound and she rushed down to see if he was okay. Her quiet disappointment when she discovered the truth pained him. Not that she blamed him, or did she? Gage couldn't be certain.

Very quietly she put the books back in place and told him his sandwich was ready.

'Oi, Prof, wassup with you?' Paul gave his elbow a sharp jab.

He didn't miss Nathan's sympathetic glance. Melissa's husband was a different man tonight and all smiles. The couple were taking the train up to London tomorrow before catching the overnight flight to Nashville on Sunday to spend Christmas with the Rutherford family. They planned to return in time to celebrate the new year.

'None of us can answer the last question, but I'm pretty sure it'll be a piece of cake for you.' Paul grunted. 'We're neck and neck with the girls, so we need you to get your brain in gear and stop Mrs Know-it-all Taylor wiping the floor with us.'

'Sorry, mate.' Gage gulped down his beer and wiped the foam off his mouth with the back of his hand.

'Come on, Prof, we're running out of time.'

Pixie was standing by the bell, preparing to ring it as a signal to stop writing and swap question sheets with the group next to them.

213

He quickly scanned the question and couldn't help smiling. '*Per Mare, Per Terram*.' Gage whispered the answer to his friends and hurriedly wrote it down. The English version of the Royal Marines' motto, 'By Sea, By Land', was more well-known, but the Latin version?

The laughingly called Bell of Doom rang three times. Gage's spirits plummeted when he noticed Evelyn looking her usual serene self.

Nathan shifted into the vacant chair next to him. 'So, what *is* up with you, mate?'

It'd be easy to pass it off as nothing more than tiredness from working non-stop, but that'd be a lie and a slap in the face for a man who hadn't shied from sharing his own troubles. Morosely Gage repeated the tale.

'You've every right to be mad. I spent my whole life trying to please my father. Waiting for him to throw a crumb of approval my way.' Nathan rested his elbows on the table. 'It never happened and I've had to learn to live with that.'

'I realise no one's life is perfect and it's far healthier to make the best of what we've got and let the rest go. Doesn't make it easy.' Gage drained the last of his beer. 'The counsellor they made me see after my injury worked hard to steer me in that direction.' He tapped his knee. 'I was pretty down then.' If he was determined to spill his guts, it needed to be a hundred per cent. 'That's sugar-coating it. I teetered on the edge for a while and couldn't see the point in anything. I saw a strong body and strong mind as being the same, so one was useless without the other.' A rough laugh dragged out of him. 'I know — look at Stephen Hawking.'

'What does Tamara think?'

'She suggested I wait and see what happens when he comes for Christmas with Becky. If he doesn't reach out, then I've got to accept I've done what I can and move on.'

'Sensible woman.' Nathan picked up their empty glasses. 'Another?'

'Cheers. And thanks. It's good to see you and Melissa back on track.'

214

'Your girlfriend has a lot to do with that, so anything *I've* done to help *you* is small repayment.'

This sort of conversation would've embarrassed him no end in the old days, but the stoic Englishman mould didn't suit him as much now. Gage would never turn into a full-on New Age man, but loosening the straitjacket that kept his emotions in tight check could only be a good thing.

'Hurry up and get the drinks in before Pixie announces the results,' Gage said. 'I'd hate to think the Back of Beyond Brains are going to beat us — again.'

* * *

Tamara revelled in the sight of her friends laughing, chattering and generally enjoying each other's company. The discussion that'd been ongoing between quiz rounds was still in flow as they struggled to decide what theme to settle on for next year's book selections. So far, Amy's suggestion of the twelve books all being set in different countries had an edge over Josie's idea of novels published in every decade from the beginning of the twentieth century. Frankly, she wasn't passionate either way. The company and friendship meant far more.

Her gaze strayed to Gage and she studied the back of his head. His black hair was longer and thicker these days, but she wouldn't be able to enjoy it that way for much longer. Yesterday he complained that relaxing into civilian life was one thing, but looking like a yeti — his words, not hers — was a step too far. The floppy-haired Hugh Grant look was never going to be an option.

She couldn't help worrying about Gage. He'd been far more deeply affected by his unsatisfactory conversation with Wally Harris than he wanted to admit and she wasn't sure how to help him.

'Get ready to mark the last answer sheet and find out this month's champion,' Pixie yelled.

'I'm going to be so furious with myself when I hear the answer to that Latin one.' Evelyn shook her head and frowned.

215

'You can't know everything, dear sister.' Ophelia's teasing earned a sharp look from Evelyn, before a wry smile took over and she made a joke about always being able to rely on family to put you in your place.

'I'm some sorry my dad was worse than useless with poor Gage,' Becky whispered. 'He's a thoughtless old bugger sometimes.'

'You've spoken to him?'

'Rang me, didn't he? Thought I'd be sympathetic.'

'I take it you weren't?'

'Not bloody likely.' Becky bristled. She'd torn her father off a strip and told him he'd better try to make amends next week or he wouldn't be welcome at her house again.

Tamara grimaced. It would tear Gage up if he felt responsible for driving a wedge between a family who'd rubbed along fine before his reappearance in their lives.

'Don't you worry, love. Dad will come around. Anything for a peaceful life is his motto.' The mildly despairing remark sounded like a parent talking about a recalcitrant toddler. 'He's weak. No staying power. When things get tough, Dad throws in the towel, moves on and starts again.'

'But you still love him.'

Her friend turned bright red.

'I'm not criticising you. It's completely understandable.'

Becky patted her hand. 'I'm some glad Gage came to find me.' Her eyes twinkled. 'And met you while he was at it.'

'Me too.'

'Are you pair ever going to stop nattering?' Laura shushed them.

'You're worse than Evelyn,' Tamara groused.

Pixie started to read the last set of answers, but stopped when she reached the final question to do a mock drumroll on the bar. 'I'll ask Gage to tell us the answer because no one else got it right.'

Evelyn's groan resonated around the pub, and there were a few smirks and satisfied mutters from their fellow contestants.

216

'The bugger were in the marines, so the rest of us didn't stand a chance,' Vernon Bull complained.

Gage would be deeply embarrassed if Tamara had a go at the shopkeeper and ordered him to watch his words. She would love to remind Vernon how much he'd given for his country with very little thanks. But her hero would say, and quite correctly even if that irked her in the moment, that Vernon's right to free speech was worth fighting for.

Pixie patiently explained how she got all the questions from a pub-quiz group online, so there had been no fixing and never would be. She wrapped up with the tart comment that they could take up any complaints with the new owners in January. 'Put them out of their misery, Gage.'

'*Per Mare, Per Terram*,' he said firmly and proudly. 'By Sea, By Land.'

'Well done. That clinches the trophy for Proper Choughed tonight, so I think it's only right you come up.'

A lump lodged in Tamara's throat as he straightened his stance and walked over to the bar, his awkward gait barely visible over the few short steps. The usual round of applause, cheers and jeers continued for several minutes.

'Time to go home?' Gage's deep voice by her shoulder surprised Tamara and she lifted her face for a kiss.

'As long as you can let go of the trophy long enough to come to bed.'

Gage grinned and passed the trophy over to Paul with a flourish. 'Take care of that, mate. Some of us have things to do and places to be.'

Tamara said a swift goodnight to her friends and gave Melissa an extra hug to wish her safe travels.

'It's time we started celebrating Christmas.' His right arm snaked around her waist.

'That's the best idea you've had all week, Mr Bennet.'

'I thought so too.'

217

CHAPTER TWENTY-SEVEN

'Honestly, it's fine. You go do your shopping. We're all good here, aren't we, Ems?'

His niece stopped tweaking the window display and turned around. She'd been working full time since college had finished for the Christmas holidays last week. The festive rush had slowed to a trickle, and today there were just a few last-minute customers who'd left their present shopping until Christmas Eve.

'Yep.' She tossed her head. 'If I'm here I don't have to be stuck at home listening to Ollie and Lily getting all childish and excited about Father Christmas. Then there's Granddad keeping on about Scotland and how it's the best place on earth.' Emily scoffed. 'If it's so great, why did he scuttle off down here for Christmas instead of spending it with his partner and her kids? They're little, so wouldn't they want their dad there?'

Gage noticed Tamara wince and he wished he could reassure her that he wasn't bothered. The fact his father had been in Penworthal for three days but hadn't come anywhere near the shop said it all.

'If you're both sure, I'll brave the crowds in Truro. I won't be long. I've no interest in dawdling around the shops

218

and don't want to get drowned when the bloody rain starts again this afternoon.'

Last week's crisp, snowy weather had melted away, leaving behind milder temperatures but almost constant rain. Today's grey, dry morning was a much-needed break, but the forecast was lousy with gale-force winds blowing in tonight on top of even more rain.

'Anything you need?'

Gage shook his head. 'No, thanks. My shopping's all done.'

Apart from Tamara, his gift list only consisted of Becky and her family. Instead of buying everyone books, which would strike them as a cop-out, he'd done some sleuthing and begged his sister for ideas. Four pairs of fashionable trainers were wrapped and ready for the kids, along with new seat covers for Paul's van. Becky had been the real challenge, but that's where Tamara had come in. She'd remembered hearing her friend talking wistfully about never having been to London or being able to afford to take their large family on holiday. It had seemed ideal to combine the two and so she would be getting a gift card for an all-expenses-paid long weekend in the capital.

'I'll leave you to it, then.' She popped a kiss on his cheek and headed towards the door. It flew open in her hand and almost knocked her off balance.

'I'm sorry, miss, I should've looked to make sure no one was on the way out.' The deep, cheerful male voice made Gage freeze on the spot.

'Have you come to check up on me, Granddad?' Emily's cheery voice penetrated the mist swirling around his brain.

A ghost from his childhood stood less than a metre away, wearing a tentative smile as if unsure of his welcome. As well he might.

The years hadn't been kind to his father. There was little sign of the fit, jovial man with a head of thick dark hair, twinkling eyes and ready laugh that Gage remembered so well.

219

'Do you want me to stay?' Tamara asked.

'No, it's okay. I'll see you later.'

She didn't look convinced but complied, and the door closed behind her. There was only one customer left lingering in the travel section.

'Ems, can you keep an eye on things here while I take your grandfather back to the kitchen?'

His niece's sharp gaze, eerily reminiscent of Becky's, shot between them. For a change she didn't toss out a smart remark, but simply nodded.

'Tea or coffee?' Gage stationed himself by the kettle.

'Tea's fine. Milk and two sugars.' Wally settled on one of the stools with his elbows on the counter. 'Quite some place you've got here, boy. You've done well for yourself.'

'No thanks to you.' The blunt reply exploded out of him before Gage could stop it. 'Sorry, I shouldn't have said that. It's in the past and—'

'No, you're bloody right. Young Becky's had a go at me already and I don't blame either of you. Feel free to thump me if it makes you feel better. I'd do it myself if I had the strength.' An attempt at laughing turned into a hacking cough and it was a while before Wally caught his breath.

'Drink your tea.' Gage hitched his hip on the other stool and set down two mugs emblazoned with the green-and-gold logo of The Mighty Pen.

'Ta. I don't s'pose Health and Safety would be too happy if I croaked in here?' Wally said with a wink.

'Not really. Hell of a lot of paperwork.'

That set them both laughing. The simple act of sharing a joke forced him to remember how much he used to love his wisecracking father. That brought Gage back to the past and he went deathly quiet, wrapped in his own thoughts. This was his chance. Maybe the only one he'd be offered. He needed to get it off his chest now. Wally had to know the effect his sudden abandonment had had on his second family.

220

'What's up, lad?' There was the slightest hint of a Scottish accent in his father's gruff voice.

Here goes.

* * *

The wind whipped her wet mac around her legs and Tamara kept her head down to battle along the street. Ever since she'd reluctantly left Gage this morning, he'd been on her mind. If he was able to draw a line under the unresolved relationship with his father, that would be the perfect Christmas present.

She wrangled her shopping bags into the boot and dragged off her coat to throw it on the back seat. Because of the community lunch at the pub, they'd agreed to wait until tomorrow evening to enjoy their own celebrations at her house. They'd have an abundance of their favourite things to snack on and a fancy bottle of champagne.

The roads out of Truro were rammed with everyone trying to beat the bad weather, which was due to arrive around teatime — that was, if you believed the weather forecasters.

She arrived back at the house and emptied the car, getting even wetter in the process. It was only a brisk five-minute walk down to the bookshop but she didn't fancy getting soaked yet again, so Tamara pulled on the seriously unsexy waterproof trousers, coat and boots she wore for coastal walking.

The strong, gusty wind buffeted her along and almost pushed her into the road when she turned the corner. Since they weren't directly on the coast, it was unusual for them to get it this bad. If the winds blew down power lines, that would be people's Christmas-dinner plans wrecked.

She was surprised to see the bookshop was in darkness except for the fairy lights illuminating the window display. A sign saying they'd closed early because of the weather was fixed prominently to the door. There was no sign of life in the flat

221

above either. After whipping out her phone, she sent Gage a text asking where he was.

At Becky's. Come and join us.

She backtracked down the road and turned onto Wesley Lane, walking past what used to be her sister's hairdresser's shop before stopping outside number nineteen. The tree in the front window with its sparkling lights should've cheered her up, but had the opposite effect. Things must've gone okay with his father, so maybe it'd be kinder to leave Gage with his family and let them spend some time together.

Her phone pinged again. Pixie.

Could do with another pair of hands peeling veg for tomorrow. Any chance?

Tamara tapped in a thumbs-up and smiley face, and hit send. Another text to Gage told him where she was going and she shoved her mobile back in her pocket without waiting for a response.

The warm fug generated by squashed-in bodies and high spirits swamped her as she stepped into the pub. First order of business was wriggling out of her heavy waterproofs before she sweated to death.

The pub closed at eleven o'clock tonight, but by then most customers would've left either to go home to play Father Christmas or cross the road to the church.

Her parents had started taking them to the Christmas Eve service as soon as she and Tracy had been old enough to stay awake, but she'd fallen out of the habit when Toby was young and somehow had never picked it back up. The idea of singing the familiar carols again was appealing.

After wriggling through the mass of people, she finally reached Pixie.

'You're a lifesaver.' Her friend's face lit up. 'Rocky's in the kitchen trying to juggle the regular orders with prepping

222

for tomorrow, so he'll probably kiss you for turning out. Gage didn't mind?'

Now wasn't the moment to explain her conflicted feelings. Peeling potatoes would be the perfect displacement activity to stop her fretting over something she couldn't yet put into words.

* * *

Gage's gut instinct told him something was off with Tamara. He could ignore it for now and plan to sort things out later, but he'd learned from his time in combat to pay attention to what his senses told him.

'I'll be off now,' he announced and added a brief explanation about going to help Tamara.

No one could complain about him wanting to do his bit for the community. It wouldn't be ideal to talk while they peeled a mountain of spuds, but he'd make it work. His military training had left Gage hyper-aware of his surroundings, so it'd been childishly easy to spot her lurking on the other side of Becky's garden hedge. What he wanted to find out was why she hadn't at least popped in to say hello.

'We're all going to church later. Are you and Tamara coming?' Becky asked.

'I don't know. She hasn't mentioned it. If we aren't there, have a happy Christmas and we'll see you on Boxing Day.'

Hopefully Tamara wouldn't mind that he'd accepted an invitation for them to join the family for a buffet lunch before his father returned to Scotland. After his long, soul-baring conversation with Wally, he was able to accept that loving and trusting his father so completely, the way he'd done as a young boy, was never going to happen. They'd inched towards a sort of benign, caring friendship where Gage wouldn't ask more of Wally than he was capable of giving.

'Go and make your girlfriend happy,' Wally said and clapped a beefy hand on his shoulder. 'If I'd done more of that and less of being selfish—'

223

'We can't change the past, only the way we deal with it going forward.' Gage noticed his family's startled looks. 'That's the sort of counsellor speak I learned after my knee injury did my head in.'

'You're a good boy.' His father swiped at his eyes. 'Now clear off before I start blubbing like a wee bairn.'

After a round of hugs, kisses and farewells, Gage trudged off down the road, slipping down the alleyway beside the pub. He tapped on the kitchen door and Rocky came out.

'You can't take her away, mate. The pub is packed and I'll never be ready for tomorrow without help.'

'Relax. I came to offer another pair of these.' Gage waggled his hands.

Rocky tugged him inside and he came face to face with a stunned Tamara.

'Surprise.'

'It certainly is.' A thread of uncertainty ran through her voice. Had he made the wrong choice by coming? But her eyes softened with relief. 'Come with me. I'll put you on carrots and parsnips. There's a stool you can perch on.' She steered him away from the chef, who headed straight back to the fryer to pull out a sizzling batch of chips.

Gage took the black apron she offered and slipped it over his head before knotting the ties around his waist.

'I'm almost done with the potatoes and then I'll tackle the sprouts. Here's your task.'

A massive orange mesh bag of carrots sat on the floor by another just like it, packed with parsnips.

She found him a chopping board, peeler and sharp knife. 'Cut them about finger size if you can. They'll be glazed with honey and roasted together tomorrow.'

For a while they worked in companionable silence and as the piles of cut-up vegetables grew, Gage sensed time slipping away.

'Dad and I cleared the air.' He noticed her surprise when he called Wally that. Keeping his voice low, he gave her a

224

shortened version of what had happened after she'd left that morning. 'I didn't plan to close early, but he really wanted me to head over to Becky's and I thought—'

'You don't need to apologise for wanting to spend time with your family.'

That was the rub. His family. He'd been so caught up in the surprising turn of events that she'd ended up feeling left out.

'I'm sorry I didn't call and that I let you worry about how it went.' Gage set the knife down and touched her arm. 'Sharing is new to me. Any chance you'll cut me a little slack?'

'Of course. If you'll do the same for me?' She sounded timid and unsure. 'I've relied on myself so long it's hard to give up that independence.'

'I would never ask you to do that, or want you to,' he said fiercely. 'Your independence and strength caught my eye that first day. It's a huge part of what makes you "you".'

'It was childish of me not to come to Becky's. I almost did. I — bloody hell, you saw me, didn't you?' Her face flared a bright pillar-box red owing little to the steamy kitchen. 'Dodging outside the house and sneaking away?'

'Guilty as charged. I couldn't help it.'

'So, this is your way of telling me not to become a spy.'

'Stick to cakes and crumbles.' Kissing her was inevitable and Gage made the most of it.

A 'Fuck me!' from Rocky pulled them out of things, reminding Gage exactly where he was. Rocky had grabbed a plastic bucket from under the counter and positioned it on top of a puddle of water beside the walk-in fridge. 'This roof leaks like a bloody sieve.'

'It's been a problem for a while,' Tamara said. 'Pixie's complained to the brewery a million times, but they keep putting off doing the repairs.'

'I'm surprised Health and Safety haven't picked them up for it,' Gage said.

Rocky scoffed. 'That's because it's always been dry when we've had inspections,'

225

'Are you playing Father Christmas tonight?' Gage asked.

'Yeah, course I am.' The chef's face was wreathed in smiles. 'I even bought a costume. All part of it, innit?'

'Of course it is. Make sure you get lots of pictures with little Jamie tomorrow so you won't forget his first Christmas,' Tamara said.

They all went back to work, and Gage started on the parsnips.

'Did you measure those with a ruler?' Tamara giggled at the carrots he'd cut and placed in a bucket of cold water. 'Talk about military precision. By the way, do you fancy going to the carol service?'

'What made you ask? Not that it's a really weird question with it being Christmas Eve, but we've never talked about it and . . .' Her embarrassed voice trailed away. 'Funny enough I thought about it earlier, but I wasn't sure if you'd be interested.'

It reminded him just how little time they'd known each other. There was a huge range of subjects they'd not touched on yet. 'It really excites me we've got so much more to find out about each other.'

'That's an awesome way to look at it. Let's go. Most of our friends will be there and perhaps we can turn it into our first Christmas tradition together.'

'I love the sound of that.'

226

CHAPTER TWENTY-EIGHT

Tamara didn't usually find it hard to control her emotions in public, but tonight was a different story. She blamed the film of tears glazing her eyes, and her inability to speak, let alone join in 'O Little Town of Bethlehem', on a whole host of things. Gage's strong, warm hand wrapped around hers, the twinkling strings of Christmas lights illuminating the ancient granite church, the wheezing of the old organ and being surrounded by so many of her dearest friends. They all combined to affect her in a totally unexpected way. She tried focusing on the colourful Victorian stained-glass windows behind the altar. But that didn't help because it brought her back to a long-ago Christmas Eve when her mother had patiently explained the bible stories behind the designs to Tamara, while her dad had fed Tracy sweets to keep her imp of a sister quiet. If she started thinking about Tracy too much now, she really would start crying.

Early this afternoon she'd ignored the nine-hour time difference with Australia and phoned her sister, hoping against hope that she hadn't gone to bed already. After they'd exchanged the usual Christmas greetings, Tamara had blurted out how worried she'd been and begged Tracy to say if she'd done anything to upset her. Tracy had burst into tears and confessed that she'd been so dreadfully homesick that talking to Tamara made her worse. Although it tore her to hear Tracy so unhappy, at least she knew the truth now. Gage had been wonderfully supportive and they were trying to work out how to afford a trip to Australia in the not-too-distant future.

'I'm really glad we came.' Gage snaked his arm around her shoulder. 'I'd forgotten.'

'Me too.' She snuggled into him and savoured the brush of his hair against her skin. How different her life was to a year ago, when it hadn't bothered her to work until closing time in the pub because there was nothing and nobody to rush home for.

The church clock struck midnight as they sang the traditional final carol, 'Silent Night'. To avoid lingering outside in the miserable weather, everyone started milling around to swap Christmas greetings.

'Come and meet my dad properly.'

Tamara choked up again. Talk about the true power of forgiveness. It was nothing short of a miracle that he could speak fondly of the father who'd turned his back on his son for all those years.

It amused her to hear Becky chide her children and warn them not to be rude and run off. Despite the fact they were all teenagers, all four did as they were told.

'Dad, this is Tamara.'

'Of course it is.'

Wally Harris's brilliant smile bore such an uncanny resemblance to Gage's, she was momentarily taken aback.

'You were a young girl last time I saw you. You've grown into a right bonny lass. I was sorry to hear about your mum and dad. They were good people.'

'They certainly were and I miss them every day.'

'You've taken on a big job keeping this one in line.' He gave Gage a light punch on the shoulder.

'He might say it's the other way around.'

228

That made everyone laugh.

'It's good to see you again, Mr Harris, and I hope you'll come back again soon.' Tamara hoped it didn't come across as a dig.

'It's Wally. None of this Mr Harris nonsense. And I'll definitely be back. Can't lose track of my boy again. The two of you should make a trip up to Scotland and see us. You'd be very welcome.'

'Thanks. I've never been any further than London, and that was only one time on a school trip.'

'Happy Christmas, lass, and we'll see you both on Boxing Day before I head back north again.'

'We'd better go.' Becky interrupted them with a wry smile. 'They're getting restless.' She nodded at her kids, who were all looking at their phones and exuding an air of boredom.

Outside it was all they could do to stay upright in the strong wind. They battled across the road and headed as quickly as they could to her house, where the very first order of business was getting rid of their wet shoes and coats.

'I'm sorry I don't have a Father Christmas costume.' Gage's husky voice was laced with innuendo. 'But I did put something under the tree earlier that you could go ahead and open now.'

'Would that be for my enjoyment or yours?'

The arch question made him chuckle. 'Hopefully both.'

'I was about to offer tea and warm mince pies, but I suppose they can wait.'

In the living room, she switched on the tree lights. He crouched to pick up a box and handed it over with a wicked grin. Tamara was about to rip off the wrapping paper when she studied it more closely.

'Father Christmas pigs? Seriously?' She opened the box and the first item she lifted out was a pink satin thong. Next came a matching bra, but when Tamara opened it out she laughed so hard tears rolled down her face. Gage's eyes sparkled, lit like a little boy who'd pulled the most magnificent prank, because two tiny curls of pink silk hung from the

229

nipple area to mimic pigs' tails. There was also a pair of pink silk ballet slippers with toes shaped like pigs' feet.

'There's something else.' He whipped out the last thing from the bottom of the box. A pink satin headband with a pink-and-white piggy ear fixed to each side. Gage stood in front of her and carefully slid it into place. 'There we go.'

'Do I even want to know where you found all this?'

'Let's just say the internet caters to every taste.' Gage wrapped her in his arms. 'I wish I could carry you—'

'Don't spoil it. We've had this out before, so put that nonsense to bed.' She tried to look stern. 'Which is where I want to be right now — with you. And if you don't take me there soon, there'll be no good tidings of comfort and joy in this house.'

'I'll shut up.'

Men who listened were worth their weight in gold. Happy Christmas to them.

* * *

Gage lifted a hank of Tamara's hair to kiss the back of her neck. After coming to bed late and christening the saucy pig lingerie, she was exhausted and fell straight asleep, but he only managed to doze off and on for what was left of the night. It was still dark outside and a glance at the clock told him it wasn't quite seven o'clock yet. On the nightstand, her phone started buzzing and he was in two minds whether or not to silence it.

'Who is it?' Tamara's voice was thick with sleep.

'I'll see.' Gage leaned across and checked the screen. 'Pixie. She can't need more veg peeled because we did enough to feed an army. You want me to get it?'

'Hand it over. I'll see what she wants.' Tamara yawned and pushed a bunch of tangled-up hair from her face. 'Happy Christmas, what can we—'

Pixie broke in and sounded worried from the little he could catch.

230

'We'll throw some clothes on and be right down.' She hung up.

'What's happened?'

'Vernon rang a few minutes ago to tell her to get to The Rusty Anchor pronto. He'd popped into the shop to fetch a packet of stuffing mix for his wife and was locking up when he heard a loud noise coming from the pub. He looked up and saw large parts of the roof caving in. It wasn't in good shape as you know, and all the rain and wind must've finished it off.'

'Hell. No one's inside, right?' Thankfully the flat over the pub had been standing empty for a while, ever since the last tenant moved out.

'She isn't sure.' Tamara's breath hitched. 'But she can't get hold of Rocky and is terrified he might've come in early to start cooking the turkeys.'

A picture of the puckish little chef's face yesterday, excited about playing Father Christmas to his baby son, filled Gage's brain. They silently dragged on clothes before taking turns in the bathroom.

This really wasn't how Christmas Day was supposed to go. He'd planned to spoil Tamara with a lavish breakfast in bed before they went to help with the Spirit of Christmas preparations.

Luckily the wind and rain had died down and by the time they turned onto Church Street, people were starting to emerge from their homes, many wearing coats over their night clothes.

Pixie came out of nowhere and flung herself at Tamara. 'Rocky's in there. I've talked to him on the phone and he's trapped under that heavy metal table we use for the prep work. The police and fire brigade are on the way and they've ordered us to stay out.'

'They'll be running a skeleton staff on Christmas Day, so it could be a while.' Gage frowned. 'You might want to call the doc if she's home and get her down here. I'll see if it's possible to go in.'

'Me too,' Tamara said.

He knew that tone. Arguing would be pointless. Depending on the situation they found, they might need her strength and agility.

They skirted the crowd and picked their way around piles of roof shingles to reach the back of the building. Gage yelled at Rocky through the broken kitchen door.

'About bloody time. Come and give us a hand, mate. The missus will wonder where I've got to. I promised I'd be home after I stuck the turkeys in the oven.'

'Hang on a minute while we see what's what.' He pulled one of the broken boards away to make the hole larger. 'Are you hurt?'

'Me right ankle isn't too good and I've had a bit of a bash on the head. Apart from that I'm good. It's a bugger, though, 'cause I'm stuck under the table and the thing's too bloody heavy to lift. If I had a few more muscles, it'd be useful.'

At least the young man's sense of humour was still intact. 'Don't move. I'm coming in.'

'You want me to try first?' Tamara said.

'I think I'll be okay.'

The tendon around his bad knee protested when he bent his body in half to clamber in. He stopped to assess the situation. The roof was almost completely gone, so the kitchen was covered with roof slates, insulation and broken rafters. The thick dust filling the air made it hard to see. In his mind he mapped out a path and started edging closer to Rocky. He spotted the young chef's head and could see his red hair was grey with dust.

'We need to shift the table off you, but I'm not sure if we should try to move you out of here. Might be best to wait for the paramedics.'

'Don't be daft, mate.'

'You could end up paralysed if we're too hasty.' He shouted back over his shoulder. 'Tamara, we need you in here too. Sorry.'

In the old days, he could've lifted the stainless-steel table by himself.

'No problem.'

A touch of envy sneaked in as she picked her way nimbly through the debris, but it was wiped away by admiration for this wonderful woman.

'We need to lift the table off Rocky and put it over there.' He pointed to the front wall and the shattered window.

They each grabbed one end and on a count of three, hefted the table into the air. Tamara took an unfair share of the weight, but Gage wasn't in a position to argue. This was no place for pride.

'Stay still, Rocky,' he said firmly. 'Answer a few questions for me first.'

It was clear Rocky knew who he was, where they were and what'd happened, so concussion shouldn't be an issue. Gage rattled off some standard questions about whether Rocky had any numbness or tingling in his limbs, any trouble breathing and if he could move his arms and legs. All the answers were negative, and the chef's only real pain came from the ankle that had caught the brunt of his fall.

'What do you think?' Tamara asked.

'He's probably fine but—'

With an ominous groan, another rafter crashed inches away from Gage.

'We need to get out of here now,' he said decisively.

'I need a hand up.' Rocky sounded worried now.

'I'll get you.' Tamara reached across and stuck her hands under the chef's armpits before heaving him out. 'I'll carry him.' She threw them both a firm look. 'No offence, Rocky, but you're hardly a muscle-bound hunk. I've single-handedly carried boats that are heavier than you.'

As if the chef weighed no more than a sack of potatoes, she hauled him up in her arms and left Gage to follow behind.

'Couldn't you at least let me have a quiet Christmas Day without any patients?' Judy's cheerful voice and wide smile

233

were a welcome sight when they reached the door. 'Next time you can call the emergency GP service. Joke! If you could put Rocky down, I'll take a look at him.' She gestured to an old wooden chair Gage recognised from Vernon's shop.

Tamara did the honours.

'Mum! Are you hurt?' Toby ran towards them, his eyes bulging with panic.

Tamara said firmly. 'I'm fine, Toby, honestly.' She reached for her son with one hand, and Gage with the other. 'We're going to leave Rocky in Judy's tender care and get on with Christmas. Toby, love, you should head back home to sleep because I know you've only just got off work. We'll put our brains together and see how to still pull off the Spirit of Christmas meal.'

Gage wasn't daft enough to tell her that was ridiculous. If she could wave a magic wand over a crusty ex-serviceman like him and transform his life, rustling up a festive meal for thirty people from the wreckage of the pub should be child's play. He met her gaze and nodded. His way of saying he was all in.

'Sleep's overrated,' Toby said with a shrug. 'I'll text Chloe and get her down here too. She'll want in on this.' He angled a faint smile at Gage. 'My partner is like yours. Stubborn. Hates to miss out on anything.'

Gage seized the olive branch and grinned back. Maybe Tamara was right and they could pull off a Christmas miracle.

234

CHAPTER TWENTY-NINE

If she'd eaten breakfast, it would've been splattered over her shoes by now. It was only after she'd finished playing Superwoman and put on a blasé act in front of her son and Gage that she realised how reckless they'd been. But would she do it again? Hell, yes. Seeing Rocky's white-faced wife, clutching their baby son in his elf pyjamas and hovering over her husband while Judy checked him over, confirmed they'd done the right thing.

'It always hits afterwards,' Gage murmured in her ear. 'Sometimes it's right away, but it can be days or weeks later. Something triggers it and there you are again. I still have nightmares and probably always will.' His voice broke. 'I would never have forgiven myself if—'

'That's enough, okay?' She blinked back tears. 'The lunch.' Tamara begged Gage to go along with her. 'The venue is obvious. The—'

'Bookshop.' He chipped in to finish her sentence. 'We need to borrow a few more tables and chairs to go with the ones we've got for the café. That's the easy part.'

Her mind raced. There was no hope of salvaging any food from the pub. Would it be the end of the world if they celebrated with sandwiches and crisps rather than turkey? Wasn't the companionship of gathering together the important part?

235

'Is this the village-lunch-rescue committee?' Chloe joined them, her blonde ponytail swinging. She looked stunning in a sparkly red jumpsuit.

'I suppose it might be.'

'What can we do to help?' Evelyn appeared, followed closely by Quinten and Ophelia, who looked worryingly frail. 'The rest of the girls who are free are on the way.'

'I'll open up the shop and we can gather there to make plans,' Gage offered. 'Toby, do you want to come shift furniture with me?'

'No problem. Lead the way.'

It warmed her heart to see the two go off together.

'We need to start spreading the word and asking for contributions,' Evelyn suggested. 'Everyone overbuys food. The only challenge might be the meat, but we'll make do with whatever we can get.'

'We heard the news.' Paul arrived now. 'We're all here to help. Except Daniel. We left him home to keep an eye on the turkey and he'll bring it down for you when it's cooked. The kids fussed a bit when Becky told them, but taking care of neighbours who'd be on their own or whatever — that's Christmas, isn't it?'

Paul would be mortified if she hugged him, so Tamara made do with a smile and a nod.

Half an hour later, the bookshop kitchen was organised chaos, and Chloe and Evelyn had taken charge of coordinating the donations that were pouring in. They certainly wouldn't be short of mince pies, Christmas puddings, fancy biscuits and chocolates because Vernon had arrived, with his wife in tow, having stripped his shop of everything he'd planned to put on sale tomorrow at half-price.

The hum of conversation grew louder as the piles of cut-up vegetables grew. Gage had laughingly rolled his eyes at the sight of yet more carrots and parsnips that needed peeling. The mouth-watering spicy aroma of Christmas puddings steaming away filled the kitchen.

236

'How does that look?' Emily held out the chalkboard they normally used to highlight their bestselling books, adapted to display today's menu.

They were up to four turkeys now, along with a spectacular joint of beef brought in a few minutes ago by Monica, who'd heard about the news from Wilf Buckingham. Wilf and Karen had been among the first to turn up, bringing with them their seven-kilo turkey. They insisted that, on their own, they would've been eating turkey until they were sick of it. Tamara persuaded Monica to ring her husband to tell him to get down here and join the party. All the helpers were intent on staying, in addition to the original list of people who had signed up.

'That's awesome, Ems.' Gage beamed at his niece. 'Are the tables—'

'All done and decorated. Ollie and Lily didn't do a bad job on them.' High praise for the siblings she usually referred to as useless wastes of space.

Evelyn poked her head around the kitchen door. 'Our first guests have arrived.'

'The buffet is ready for people to come through and serve themselves,' Monica said proudly. The woman was someone who could be relied on to do a job well and was an asset to the village. They needed more like her.

'I'll tell them.' Tamara stepped back into the shop, but couldn't make her announcement straight away because the sight of everyone happily gathered took her breath away. In addition to the tables in what would soon be her café, others were squeezed between the bookshelves. People weren't necessarily sitting with their own families or friends, either, but had fitted in wherever there was space. Wilf and Pixie were taking orders at the impromptu bar they'd set up, and it was a relief to see her friend looking less stressed now that she had something to focus on, other than her wrecked pub. The Spirit of Christmas name couldn't be more appropriate today.

Quinten's precise, professorial tones silenced the room. 'Before we eat, I think a round of applause is in order for the

237

wonderful people who stepped in to pull off this meal under challenging circumstances. As Tiny Tim said in *A Christmas Carol*, "God bless us every one."'

'This is all down to you,' Gage whispered.

'Don't be daft. I'm stubborn, that's all, and don't like to be told I can't do something.'

'Do you think we should aim for a similar turnout next year?'

She met his glittering dark-blue eyes and nodded. The promise of more Christmases together was the only gift she needed today.

* * *

'To us.' Gage clinked his champagne glass against Tamara's and revelled in her glorious smile.

They'd been exhausted by the time the bookshop had been shipshape again, and although the nap they'd decided to take should've helped, had they napped? Had they hell. Not that he was complaining. He'd celebrated the festive season in many parts of the world and in a variety of ways, but none equalled today. To be with this special woman and surrounded by family and friends, in a community that had embraced him and his new venture, was perfect.

'Are you ready for your proper present now?'

'You mean my piggy lingerie was improper?'

'Absolutely.' He chuckled. 'Fetch the pink envelope from under the tree, then snuggle back here with me and open it.'

Gage studied her face as she pulled out the card inside and read it once, then read it again.

'You sneaky thing. This is awesome.' Her face glowed. 'I've always wanted to see the Griselda Hill pottery in Ceres where they make the Wemyss pigs.'

'And while we're there, you get to choose a personalised commission that they'll make specially for you.'

238

She flung her arms around his neck and kissed him on the mouth. 'You are absolutely the best.'

'I picked those dates in late June for our trip because they coincide with the Ceres Highland Games. They're the oldest in Scotland, according to my research. Our hotel is only about an hour or so from Edinburgh, so I thought we could visit my dad as well while we're that close.'

'I'd love to.' A tiny frown marred her smile. 'But what about the shop and café?'

'All organised,' he said boastfully. 'Melissa and Emily volunteered to run the shop, and Becky's excited about taking on the café. I'm sure they'll have help from our other friends too.'

'You've been plotting behind my back.' She sounded anything but cross. 'It's your turn now.' Pink blotches flared on her skin. 'We must be more alike than we realised because I've gone down the same road with your gift.' Tamara whipped out a gold envelope from behind her back. 'It's not for the two of us, but you'll understand why when you take a look. You're not the only one who pays attention.'

A minute later, Gage held two tickets in his hand and couldn't stop smiling.

'Taff's going with you.'

She'd arranged for them to join a four-day tour of the Normandy beaches with a group of military-history buffs. Anything connected to the D-Day landings, and particularly the important role played by the Royal Marines, was a longtime obsession of his. The opportunity to follow in their footsteps was a dream come true.

'I won't ask how you'll run the shop as well as the café in my absence because I'm sure you've got that sewn up.'

'I might have.' A teasing smirk pulled at her lush mouth. 'I'd say we know each other pretty well, considering the short time we've been together.'

'Yep, we've got this.' It hovered on the edge of his consciousness to say more.

239

'You must be starved. I know I am.' With a bright smile, she sprang off him. 'We passed on food earlier for excellent reasons, but I need something to soak up all this champagne. I was far too busy to eat a lot at lunchtime and I doubt you had much either.'

He squashed a flare of disappointment. Maybe she'd saved him from making a fool of himself.

'And since then your thoughtless boyfriend has kept you otherwise occupied.'

'Not thoughtless at all. He's my super-sexy, favourite hunk.'

Gage wasn't arguing. He'd take whatever compliments she threw his way and be grateful. Very grateful. 'Let's go fix some snacks.'

Tamara popped a couple of baking trays in the oven, loaded with miniature spring rolls, tiny pork pies and chipolata sausages. Following her instructions he put together a platter of cheeses, cold meats and pickles, along with crackers and grapes. It was the kind of thing he would've made himself as a single guy when he couldn't be arsed to cook. But according to her, variations on this were incredibly popular these days and laughingly called charcuterie boards. Tamara started fixing the slightly retro prawn cocktails they both had a weakness for in two antique, blue glass goblets she'd picked up at a flea market.

'Is there any chance Sandy might come out to play later?' he asked.

'Ah, now we find out what you *really* asked Father Christmas for.'

'I've been a very good boy this year,' he said huskily. 'I could nip back to the flat and get my white suit if you like?'

She turned her head to pop a kiss on his mouth. 'I knew I'd been a good girl for a reason.'

240

CHAPTER THIRTY

Gage didn't usually find it hard to keep secrets, but Tamara was making this one almost impossible. She had been baking in every free moment to perfect her recipes, and he'd dutifully eaten more cakes and pies in the last couple of months than in his entire life. When pressed on which was his favourite, he'd muttered that he'd happily eat the sharp-cheddar-cheese-and-chive scone with a touch of cayenne pepper every day. That'd made her laugh.

Alongside that she'd worked all hours to get the café exactly as she wanted for the grand opening in four days and must be exhausted. Only this morning she'd mentioned wishing they could celebrate together quietly at home rather than go to a New Year's Eve party at Nathan and Melissa's house. The impromptu gathering was all Quinten's doing, and Gage wasn't convinced it was a good idea. Evelyn didn't strike him as a woman who would enjoy being surprised, but there was a very genuine and poignant reason behind the plan so she'd hopefully play along.

'Is that what you're wearing?'

'What's wrong with it?' She tugged a baggy grey jumper over her black leggings.

241

'Don't people usually dress up for New Year's parties? I thought I might put a suit on.' He grinned. 'Not the white one.'

'It's not a fancy do at some posh hotel, so I don't think we need to worry.'

Gage racked his brains for another way to persuade her to change. Were the others having as much trouble with their better halves? 'I thought you might wear your new dress.'

After their Boxing Day lunch at Becky's, he'd been dragged along to the sales in Truro. He'd talked Tamara into letting him buy her a stunning deep-red silk dress that clung to all his favourite places.

'I'd love to show you off in it. Shallow, I know, but that's me. I promise I'll make it a very happy start to the new year when we get back.'

'Fine.' She sounded slightly exasperated, but he could live with that. 'Actually I'd quite fancy seeing you in a proper suit.'

'You mean you don't fancy me out of one?'

'Begging for compliments again?' Her finger trailed down his chest. 'Wear it and see what happens.'

'It might not fit.' Gage patted his stomach. 'All those Cornish pasties have taken a toll on my six-pack.'

Tamara's husky laugh stirred him. 'Let's put it this way — if you can't squeeze into yours, I'm not wearing mine either.'

He conceded with a weak smile. 'It's at the flat. I'll go change.'

'You do that. I'll walk down and pick you up en route.'

'In heels?'

She snorted. 'Ye of little faith.'

Deceiving Tamara still felt wrong, but he couldn't break the promise he'd made to Quinten. Evelyn's original plan for a small spring wedding might've worked if Ophelia hadn't deteriorated so obviously over the past month, despite her stalwart efforts to appear bright and engaged during the Christmas festivities. Quinten's idea to pull off a surprise New Year's Eve wedding had faltered when he'd discovered both partners needed to sign the necessary documents at the register office

242

for their intention to marry. Then there was a mandatory minimum twenty-eight-day wait. Twenty-eight days they might not have.

They also couldn't marry anywhere other than at a legally approved venue and Nathan's house wouldn't count. Quinten had decided the lift it would give Ophelia to see her sister happily remarried was worth a little deception, which was when he'd enlisted Melissa and Nathan's help. Ophelia need never find out this 'wedding' wasn't actually legal, and later the couple could pay a quiet visit to a register office to make it official.

Gage had just finished knotting his tie when a message popped in from Tamara. It instructed him to come down to join her because she didn't intend to risk her ankles by climbing up to meet him. He checked his appearance in the mirror and smoothed down his newly shorn hair. She'd grumbled after their shopping expedition when he'd insisted on getting a haircut, and had been only slightly mollified when he'd instructed the stylist not to go too short. Compromise. A learning curve for them both. He locked up the flat and headed down.

'Right, are we ready to . . .' His throat turned drier than the Sahara Desert.

'I knew the dress was too much. I should've put a proper coat on too instead of this silly thing.' Tamara tugged at the gossamer-fine gold wrap that partially covered the creamy skin exposed by the daring dress underneath.

'Too much? You're gorgeous. So out of my league, I can't imagine why you're with me, but I'm not arguing the toss now.'

'Wise man. You're pretty hot yourself.' She eyed him hungrily, and it wouldn't have taken much to change his mind and whisk her off to bed. 'That isn't an off-the-peg suit. Let me guess, it's a designer number from your days as Tori G's arm candy?'

Gage turned the same deep crimson as her dress. Neither of them accepted compliments well. 'Let's go see in the new year in style.'

'Good idea. Hopefully I'll get to find out what you've been so devious about these last few days with the surreptitious

243

texts and abruptly ended phone calls. With all your training, I thought you'd be a better liar.' The corners of her lush berry-stained, glossy mouth turned up in a wicked smile.

Silence seemed his best option. They both glanced across at the empty pub, which was all in darkness. Yellow-and-white caution tape was strung all around the front, and large blue tarps covered the holes in the roof.

'Sad, isn't it?' he mused. 'Tonight should've been Pixie's big send-off.'

They arrived outside Nathan's house alongside Josie and Harry.

'Do you know what these men of ours are up to?' Josie pounced on Tamara. 'It's a good thing Harry never went in for undercover work because he couldn't fool anyone to save his life. And voluntarily putting on a suit outside of work? Pull the other one.'

'I don't have a clue either and mine's the same. Useless.'

Gage and Harry exchanged wry smiles, but said nothing.

The front door was wide open and they could see the house was heaving with people.

'Melissa and Nathan are really pushing the boat out.' Tamara's eyes narrowed on him again. 'A little get-together to see in the new year? Right.' She shook her head.

'Hurry up.' Nathan beckoned them from the doorway. 'We want everyone in place before they arrive. I'm afraid some of the guests will have to stand, but we've saved seats at the front for the book-club group and partners.'

'Seats? And who arrives?' Tamara asked, but Nathan ignored the question.

Gage took her hand and started walking. 'For once just go with the flow.'

* * *

She made a quick head count of their group and the only people she couldn't spot were Evelyn, Quinten and Ophelia.

244

That must mean something, but what was it? Nathan was talking intently with someone she didn't recognise, an older grey-haired woman wearing a sombre black dress, its severity softened by a lacy white collar. Melissa, on the other hand, kept rushing around shushing people. This wasn't normal New Year's Eve party behaviour.

As the doorbell rang again, Melissa raced out to the hall and muffled conversations drifted through. Evelyn gave a loud squawk and Ophelia gasped before letting loose a torrent of French. Melissa popped her head back around the door and gave her husband a triumphant nod.

Nathan cleared his throat. 'Some of you have been brought here under slightly false pretences, but I hope you'll forgive us when you discover the reason.'

'Get on with it, or it'll be next year before you're done!' Paul called out.

'Right.' Nathan touched the unknown woman's arm. 'This is Sade Collins. She's a Unitarian minister and is here to marry our dear friends Evelyn and Quinten.' His impish smile broke out. 'I'm afraid we kept it from her closest friends, because—'

'You knew we'd tell her.' Josie spoke up. 'The Back of Beyond Book Club sticks together, through thick and thin. We'll let you off for once, but you'll pay for it later.'

'Abso-bloody-lutely.' Tamara gave Gage a sharp poke in the ribs when his only reaction was a smug grin. Something sneaked into her head and she picked at it, struggling to remember the details. 'This isn't legal, is it?'

He shook his head and her hand flew to her mouth.

'Quinten's organised this for Ophelia, hasn't he?'

His serious expression was the only answer she needed.

'In that case you're forgiven.'

Quinten nodded nervously around as he scurried up to the front. Always a smart, rather eccentric dresser, he'd excelled himself tonight.

'The local fancy-dress shop must be missing an outfit,' Gage muttered.

245

She couldn't blame him for sounding bemused. The plum velvet suit was startling enough, but combined with a cream silk shirt fronted with a froth of cream lace and finished with a flamboyant plum satin cravat, the effect was eye-catching.

The room hushed as the 'The Blue Danube' waltz started playing.

'That's Evelyn's favourite.' Tamara pulled out a hanky and dabbed her eyes.

The sisters walked in, arm in arm, wreathed in smiles. No one would think that the bride-to-be had had her wedding sprung on her five minutes ago and that the other was living on borrowed time. *Aren't we all, though?* She gazed at Gage through tear-soaked eyes. *I want every minute I can wring out of it with him.*

Evelyn wore the same lilac sheath she'd chosen for Josie's wedding when she'd been part of the girlfriend posse, a fun term they'd come up with for themselves instead of bridesmaids. But tonight, her mass of silvery hair fell around her shoulders and perfectly set off the diamond necklace glittering around her throat. Ophelia was in dark-navy lace and appeared even more slender, as if she were disappearing before their eyes.

Gage pressed a small piece of paper into her hand. 'From Josie,' he whispered.

This was like being back at school again. Tamara read it, smiled and nodded at her friend.

At the end of the brief service, the minister announced that Evelyn and Quinten were husband and wife. That was their cue. Tamara and the rest of the book-club members all hurried to the back of the room where Melissa was waiting with a pile of Daphne du Maurier books. She doled out one to each of them and they paired off to raise the books in the air. Louis Armstrong's deep, unmistakable voice filled the room singing 'What a Wonderful World'.

Over everyone's heads she saw Gage watching her and the intensity of his gaze rocked her to the core. Tamara hoped he wasn't getting any ideas. Or did she? That was the conundrum.

246

If anyone had asked three months ago if she'd consider getting married again, or even be in a long-term relationship, she would've laughed in their face. That was before meeting Gage. The world as she knew it had tilted and twirled like a fairground ride. The question was whether she wanted to plant her feet on solid, reliable ground again, or keep flying higher.

Evelyn and Quinten ducked under the impromptu guard of honour and the joy on their faces brought tears to everyone's eyes. *Whoever said love was for the young was a fool. The young take it for granted and believe they're the only ones who can feel this deeply and passionately. Love that comes later in life, when it's less expected, can be far more treasured.*

'We need everyone to gather in the hall for photos, please.' Nathan clapped his hands. 'It'll be a squeeze, but we'll be quick. Then it's time to party.'

Once she found Gage again, she'd do exactly that.

* * *

Gage watched Tamara as she huddled in a group with her friends. The women dipped their heads to listen to something Melissa was saying, and next thing they were all hugging her. They let go to link hands and broke into a raucous impromptu version of 'I'm Gonna Be' by The Proclaimers. The lyrics talked about walking five hundred miles to reach the person you love. He would happily do that, and more, for her. Bad knee or no bad knee.

'They've done all this for me, haven't they?' Ophelia spoke close by and he met her sad expression. 'It takes a lot to pull the wool over my eyes.'

'But you won't point that out to them.'

'Of course not. You know me better than that.'

'I do indeed.' Gage glanced around. 'Shall I find you a chair?'

'*Non, merci.*' Ophelia slipped back into French. A sure sign she needed to put the barriers back up. 'I will soon tell my

247

new brother-in-law that I'm tired and am going home. If he insists on tearing Evelyn away to join me, I shall be very cross.'

'If I can stop them, I will.'

In that moment he had the eerie sensation he wouldn't see Ophelia again. She shook her head with a silent plea for him not to say anything more. Gage squeezed her frail hand gently before letting go. There were many different sorts of bravery, but this tiny woman epitomised the best.

She pulled out a vivid smile and braced her thin shoulders before walking briskly across to Quinten. Gage watched her take him aside and speak a few brief words before she turned around and left.

'Whatever's wrong with you?' Tamara draped herself over him and pressed her warm body against his. At a guess, he'd say more than a few glasses of celebratory champagne were behind her effervescence, along with very little in the way of food. He hadn't eaten either. The crush to get near the buffet laid out in the kitchen had put him off.

'Just wishing I could dance with you.'

'Then don't be a misery guts.' Tamara pouted. 'I'll ask Nathan to put on a slow song so we can have a proper kiss.' A playful giggle bubbled out of her. 'My oh-so-serious son might be watching, but so what?'

Toby had the New Year's holiday off, so he and Chloe were also in attendance. The four of them had managed to have a quick chat when the photos were being taken.

'I've got some amazing news, but you can't tell anyone else, okay?'

He pretended to zip his mouth shut.

'Josie noticed Melissa was drinking orange juice instead of champagne but didn't want to risk upsetting her by saying anything. The next thing Melissa went all shy and admitted she took a pregnancy test last week and it was positive.' Tamara beamed. 'It's very early days, so she's afraid to say too much yet.'

'I assume Nathan knows?'

248

'Absolutely and he's over the moon.'

'That's wonderful.' Gage wrapped his arms around her and lowered his mouth to hers. 'In case you were wondering, I don't need a dance floor to kiss.' It was a while before they came up for air. 'As soon as it's the new year, I'm taking you home.'

'That sounds wonderful,' she said breathily.

A few guests had left early, making more space for those hanging on. He noticed Evelyn and Quinten having a serious talk at one point, and crossed his fingers that the new bridegroom could fulfil Ophelia's request.

'Everyone needs to grab a glass of champagne because you can never have enough bubbly,' Melissa said gleefully as she made her way around the room carrying a loaded silver tray.

He and Tamara exchanged secretive smiles as they each took a glass. They found a spot by the bay window where they could nestle together. The television showed the thousands of people crammed into Trafalgar Square where it must have been raining because most were wearing waterproof ponchos or huddled under umbrellas.

The countdown began and at the stroke of twelve, everyone started cheering and kissing. Of course someone started singing 'Auld Lang Syne'.

Gage tightened his arms around Tamara and as she gazed up at him with sparkling eyes, he finally got the nerve to say the words he'd been holding back long enough. 'I love you. So much. I was afraid I'd scare you off if I said it too soon, and if you still think I'm jumping—'

'I love you too. I've been the same.'

'A new year, a new us. Right?'

'Right.'

'How would you feel about moving in with me?' he asked cautiously.

'I'd like that very much,' she said with a broad smile and kissed him.

'It's time for our newlyweds to go,' Nathan announced. 'Let's give them a rousing send-off.'

Outside they all took one of the sparklers Melissa and Nathan were passing around. The bright colours fizzed in the air as Quinten led his glowing bride.

'He was so right to do this. I don't think Ophelia ever guessed, do you?' Tamara's bright eyes fixed on him. Gage smiled back, lied, and agreed they'd pulled off a wonderful surprise.

They were told that hot drinks and mince pies were ready in the kitchen, but Tamara gave a tiny shake of her head when he raised his eyebrows at her in question. Time for their own New Year's celebration.

CHAPTER THIRTY-ONE

Tamara bounced up and down on her feet and wondered if it was possible to burst with excitement. The sixth of January would always be etched on her brain. Rather like falling in love, she was convinced that dreams you waited a long time to achieve were all the sweeter.

'I still can't believe it. My own café!'

The pride in Gage's eyes was unmistakable. 'You deserve it. You've worked hard for this. We'll be the "it couple" of Penworthal now,' he said teasingly. 'Looks good, doesn't it?' The sign over the shop front had been altered and now had an extra line that said: *and The Pig Pen Café*.

'We'd better go in. They're all waiting for us.'

The shop was packed for the official opening and smelled wonderfully of freshly baked cakes. Emily was now trusted to man, or rather woman, the till and was guarding it with her life. Luckily, the new year had come in like a lamb, so they were making the most of the mild, dry day to leave the front door wide open.

Inside, Tamara stood still for a moment to admire how well the design she'd settled on for the café blended with the bookshop. The pale-green-and-white paintwork was the same,

251

and Georgie had used the identical rich maple wood for her serving counter and the awesome shelves that displayed her pig collection.

To fit in with the retro pale-pink tables and chairs, she'd gone vintage for the café's china too. It'd been easy to find a selection of mismatched floral tea sets because they sold for very little at the flea markets these days.

The one extravagance was the pink glass pig-shaped vases she'd tracked down online and filled today with pink rosebuds. But in pride of place, on its own special shelf, stood Moccus, the large Wemyss pig Gage had bought at the auction. Instead of going for a literary connection, she'd chosen to name it after the Celtic god associated with boars and pigs. With such a beautiful lucky mascot, how could the café do anything but succeed?

The sight of her book-club friends, gathered near the pink ribbon they'd tied across the café portion of the shop, made her eyes prickle. They were all there except Evelyn, the woman who in many ways had shaped Tamara's mind and been a continuing source of strength and guidance.

Early on New Year's Day, they'd heard a siren disappearing down the street and soon her phone had started ringing. Her friends had started passing around the sad news that Ophelia had slipped away quietly in the night. Next week Ophelia would be buried in the Penworthal churchyard, a surprising request she'd made of Evelyn and Quinten in her final days. Understandably, Evelyn wasn't able to face them all today, but she sent Tamara a beautiful handwritten note saying how proud she was of her achievement.

Perhaps a small café, in a bookshop, seating no more than twenty people and selling homemade cakes, wasn't a huge dream in the scheme of things, but this was her village. Her people. Her community. Being an integral part of that mattered.

'Speech. Speech,' Paul yelled. 'Some of us took off work for this and we want cake.' His rumbling laugh set off a round of claps and cheers.

252

'I couldn't—'

'Of course you can,' Gage said, urging her on. 'All you need to do is thank them and cut the ribbon.'

'I'll keep this short and as sweet as my cakes.' That brought more laughter. Thanking everyone for coming was easy, and it raised a few more titters when she ran through a few of the crazier names they'd thought of before settling on The Pig Pen.

'You've got hungry customers waiting for a slice of your famous lime-drizzle cake.' Gage's boast touched her. Tamara's take on the ubiquitous lemon drizzle that was found in every café in the land these days was pretty exceptional.

'I almost forgot. Sorry, everyone,' she shouted. 'Becky has the kettle on, so I think it's about time to do this.' The small pair of scissors she had ready finally came into play and with a flourish she snipped the ribbon. 'To celebrate the café opening, I want you to enjoy whatever you like as my gift.' Tamara grabbed Gage for one swift kiss and a tight hug. That was the ration for now. 'With all this captive audience you should sell a load of books too.'

'Tyrant.' Gage's fake grumble made her smile.

* * *

'Are you ever going to stop grinning?' Paul slammed a brimming pint in front of Gage. 'You would think no one else ever fell in love with a pretty maid before. I know you're over the moon Tamara's moved in, but just wait till she gets you up the aisle. It'll all change then.'

Gage laughed and shook his head. 'Give us a chance.'

Although it was February already, this was the year's inaugural meeting of the Book Club Refugees as they'd decided to postpone the January meeting because of Evelyn's loss.

The pub kitchen was still out of commission, but the brewery had pushed to get the roof repairs done quickly so the new licensees could at least reopen the bar. It was odd not to see Pixie presiding over things, but she'd made the move to Cardiff over the holidays and life moved on.

'Leave him be.' Nathan clapped a hand on Gage's shoulder. 'Don't take any notice of this old misery guts.'

'I think it's great,' Tessa said. 'I've got a bit of news as well.' Her face flushed. 'Amy and I have been together five years, so we thought we'd make it official and tie the knot.'

'That's bloody terrific.' Gage spoke first and was followed swiftly by all the others. 'When's the big day?'

'Probably in the summer. We're thinking a destination wedding somewhere warm, Jamaica maybe. We don't have to consider our families because I doubt any of them will come wherever it is.' Her careless shrug didn't match the flicker of sadness in her eyes. It was common knowledge that Amy's parents had cut her off when she and Tessa had become a couple, but the younger woman's background was more of a mystery.

'We'll have a party here when you've done the deed,' Barry said stoutly. 'Nothing like a wedding for a good old knees-up.'

'My wife's already informed me that she expects a second party after we do the official thing at the register office. Apparently, fake ones don't count.' Quinten's plump cheeks turned pink. 'Not that she didn't appreciate the New Year's Eve one, especially knowing I'd thought of it for Ophelia's sake . . .' He didn't drop his head fast enough to hide his emotions.

Nathan chimed in. 'You and Tamara certainly haven't wasted any time moving in together.'

'Good on you, I say.' Quinten's voice was unsteady. 'I know it's not the same, but Evelyn and Ophelia almost left it too late to reconcile. None of us know how long we've got, so make the most of every second, young man.'

'On that note, I'll get another round in before we go our separate ways.' Harry levered off the chair. 'We'll need the strength to hear the gossip from tonight, and, as a distant afterthought, what books we'll be forced to hear about this year.' He chuckled. 'From what I'm hearing, you've joined

254

the saintly Nathan who reads and discusses the books with his good lady wife.'

Gage didn't try to deny it.

'That's going too far for me but it's all good for business, right?' Harry joked.

'You hit the nail on the head there!'

* * *

'So, are we all agreed on books set in different countries for this year's theme?' Evelyn said briskly. 'It's an excellent idea and should broaden our outlooks on the world.'

The clear implication was that living in rural Cornwall was no excuse for becoming isolated and ignorant. That was something she'd pounded into their heads for years at school. She'd reinforced the idea that even if they didn't get the opportunity to travel in the physical sense, the world was still their oyster if they made a point of exploring it through books and other media.

If Tamara dared look at Laura, they'd start giggling and send their indomitable leader back into headteacher mode.

'Tamara, we know your mind is elsewhere, but could we have your attention for a minute? Amy has a clever idea and we want your opinion.'

'Sorry, I was—'

'Daydreaming? I know,' Evelyn's voice softened. Her frown lines smoothed and a new sense of empathy poured out of her. 'I'm finding it a little hard to focus tonight as well.'

Of course, her distractedness wasn't for joyful reasons. She hadn't mentioned Ophelia so they'd followed her lead, guessing she needed a mental break from her grief for a couple of hours.

'Amy, why don't you explain it again for the benefit of those who missed it the first time,' said Evelyn.

'Don't worry, lovey. I was mentally planning my meals for the week,' Becky whispered.

255

Amy ran a hand over her sleek black hair. She was such a contrast to the ebullient Tess, with her shaggy blonde mop and happy-go-lucky manner. 'I know we all enjoy hosting book club, but perhaps we might make a change this year?' She aimed her next words at Tamara. 'I've heard Gage wants to expand events at the bookshop, and I wondered if he might be open to the idea of staying open late once a month so we could meet there?' A rare impish smile changed her whole appearance. 'It needn't put a stop to him joining the Book Club Refugees booze-up because you could make sure we didn't vandalise the place.'

Seeing her friends gathered together was a highlight of the month and when it was her turn to host, that did add another layer of stress to her busy life. Everyone insisted they didn't care if the house was untidy, or if there was nothing more exciting to snack on than a packet of Vernon's special-offer biscuits, but no one followed the mantra. It was true that holding the meeting at the bookshop would boost Gage's business, and free everyone to enjoy the evening more, at least all except for her. With the café being there, how could she not offer to handle the refreshments? After a long day on her feet, that was the last thing she wanted. How mean was she?

'But only under one condition.' Amy put on what they secretly called her scary lawyer face. 'We all take turns doing the snacks. If people want to team up, that's fine. But we do it all and leave the café as we find it, so Tamara doesn't have extra work in the morning before opening. We can even make it BYOB and bring our own wine. It's perfectly legal.'

Tamara wasn't sure how she felt about having her mind read by someone other than Gage. 'I'm happy with that and if we vote to give it a try, I'll put it to Gage.'

'Just stick on your pink piggy lingerie and he'll be pouty.' Becky chortled.

She was about to ask how her friend knew about that when mortification swept through her. She recalled foolishly blabbing about Gage's sexy present after a few too many glasses of champagne on New Year's Eve.

256

Everyone fell into fits of giggles. Amid all the laughter, Evelyn managed to winkle out of people whether they approved or disapproved of Amy's idea, and it was no surprise when everyone voted yes.

'Right, that's settled. Tamara will ask Gage if he'll agree to give us a try. And now, I suggest abandoning the facade of talking about books and moving on to weddings instead. The Back of Beyond Book Club will keep the bridal industry in business this year. I wondered if we might consider the possibility of a group holiday to Jamaica.'

She happened to be watching Amy, whose reaction was priceless. A gasp burst out and Amy's hand flew to her mouth as tears leaked out from under her dark-rimmed glasses. This was what true, deep friendship was all about.

257

EPILOGUE

If it wasn't for the tempting spicy scent of mince pies filling the air, Gage would find it hard to believe it was Christmas Day again and time for another Spirit of Christmas dinner. The venue had moved back to the pub because of its added space. Forty people had signed up, but they would feed closer to sixty because last year's helpers had all volunteered to pitch in again.

Tamara had volunteered to make the desserts other than the Christmas puddings, so in between baking for the busy café she'd whipped up endless batches of mince pies, several extravagant sherry trifles and bowls of fresh fruit salad. Rocky was steaming his homemade puddings in the pub kitchen while he oversaw the rest of the meal, with help from Becky and Monica. His own family would join them later to eat.

'You haven't got time to muse on what a wonderful life you have.' Tamara had sneaked up behind him. 'I'm not referring to that awful, sappy Christmas film it's almost impossible to avoid on the telly over the holidays either.'

'Do I have time for this?' Gage whipped a sprig of mistletoe from behind his back and held it over her head.

258

'Always.' Her floury hands wrapped around his neck and drew him into a lingering kiss. 'I'm glad we decided to close for the week and reopen after New Year.'

'We need a break and it's not like we'll lose much business because everyone's skint.'

They generally did a good job of balancing running two businesses with their private life. The successful café had brought more business to the bookshop, and vice versa. It helped that he'd taken Emily on full time at the bookshop after she'd finished college. His niece had done brilliantly in her A levels and she'd decided to take a gap year before going to uni. She wanted to work and save as much money as she could to avoid taking out any big loans.

Emily had cleverly used social media to offer artists and craftspeople display space at the shop and café. They chose a new one every month to showcase and keep things fresh, and they took a small cut of the sales. A military-history group met on the first Monday of every month, traditionally the quietest day of the week, which was another big success. The newest experiment, set to start in January, was opening at six o'clock twice a month to host local writers who needed a quiet space to work. And then of course, there was the book club. That experiment had gone well and they'd decided to continue meeting there.

'I was thinking about everything that's happened since last Christmas,' Tamara mused. 'At Easter there was Evelyn and Quinten's second wedding party. Amy and Tessa's beach wedding in Jamaica was awesome too and definitely gave me the travel bug. Scotland was fab as well.'

He'd been touched when she'd chosen to have her specially designed Wemyss pig wear a green beret and Royal Marines insignia. Embarrassingly she christened it Gorgeous Gage and now it sat pride of place on her dressing table.

'You didn't think much of your time in Normandy, I know.' Her gentle teasing didn't diminish what had been a poignant trip for Gage and Taff, and one he would never

259

forget. 'I'm so glad you took me to meet Grandmama Louise before she passed away.'

'She thought a lot of you.' Gage's smile was tinged with sadness. It had hit him hard when the old lady had died, but at least he'd had the consolation of knowing they had reconnected before it had been too late.

'Don't forget little Freddie's arrival,' Gage added.

'How could I? He's such a darling.'

Everyone had been thrilled when Melissa and Nathan's dream had come true with the arrival of Frederick William Kellow in late August. Named after Daphne du Maurier's husband, Frederick Browning (something Nathan strenuously denied, but no one really believed) and Melissa's father, the little boy had Nathan's auburn hair and his mum's grey-green eyes.

'Do you think next year will be any quieter? It will, surely?'

'Quiet? I don't think so, Mum.' Toby breezed in, clutching Chloe's hand. 'We've got some news. We're pregnant. Due in early July. We'd planned to wait a bit longer because Chloe takes her finals in late May, but she says it'll be fine and I'm sure it will. She's a trooper.' Pride radiated off her son.

'Oh, my God, that's wonderful!' Tamara's grin couldn't be wider. 'Am I old enough to be a granny? And that'll make you a granddad. How does that sound?' She beamed at Gage.

'I'd love to be able to say that, but I'm not really entitled and—'

'You certainly are,' Chloe said firmly and Toby nodded, backing her up. 'Our child will be incredibly lucky to have you in his or her corner.'

Gage lowered his head, overcome with emotion.

'You might not be quite so thrilled about our other news.' Toby's expression turned serious. 'Chloe's accepted an incredible job offer after she graduates, but the company is in York so we'll be moving. I've applied to do a geriatric-care course at one of the hospitals and if I'm accepted, they have a nursery on site for the baby.'

260

'It's a great opportunity for you both. Congratulations.' Gage surreptitiously squeezed Tamara's hand and she collected herself enough to sound equally enthusiastic.

'We'll obviously have to give up Gwartha-an-Dre, and Melissa's decided now is a good time to sell the house.' Toby looked unsure. 'We've heard you say that living over the shop has its drawbacks, so might it suit you?'

'In what way?'

Gage suppressed a smile in case Tamara thought he was laughing at her. 'They're suggesting we might consider buying it.'

'Us?'

'Why not? You've always said, apart from Nathan's house, it's your favourite. You could have the kitchen you've always dreamed of. The renters are moving out of your house soon, so you could sell it and we could pool our money. It should be easy enough to get a mortgage.'

She looked shell-shocked.

'It's a lovely old place and walking distance from the shop.' Gage turned to Toby. 'We'll talk about this properly after Christmas when we've got time to sit and think it through.'

'I'll have a word with Melissa and let her know there's a possibility we might be interested,' Tamara said. 'How are you feeling, Chloe? I didn't think to ask.'

'Incredible. I haven't been sick at all, have I?' Chloe grinned at Toby. 'My nurse here is very happy about that. He cleans up enough puke at work, don't you, dear?'

Toby nodded, but his adoring look said otherwise. A brief wave of regret washed through Gage for the baby that Victoria never had.

'It's time we started carrying stuff over to the pub,' Tamara said briskly. No doubt she'd read the way his mind was going. Although he'd carry it in his heart always, they were in complete agreement that expanding their family wasn't something they wanted to pursue. Their lives were already wonderfully full.

261

After they'd packed off the young couple, he caught hold of Tamara's arm. 'You okay?'

'I will be.' She blinked hard. 'I would never hold Toby back and I'll support them a hundred per cent. I've never clung on to Toby and I'm not starting now. Let's go and celebrate Christmas and all it means with the friends, neighbours and family we're fortunate enough to have around.'

* * *

'Pixie? Oh my God, what an awesome surprise!' Tamara set down the two heavy glass bowls of trifle on the nearest table and flung her arms around her old friend. 'When did you arrive? Why didn't you tell me you were coming for Christmas? How long—'

'She still talks just as much, doesn't she, Gage?' Pixie laughed.

'I did try to warn you.'

Tamara swung around to face him. 'You knew Pixie was here.'

'Maybe.' He tweaked a smile.

'Bob and Maria wanted a week off to visit their daughter back in Liverpool before she emigrates to Canada, so I agreed to run the pub for them while they're away. I've got a fortnight off college, so it's all good.'

'You sneaky thing. Fancy not telling us.' Tamara glowered at Gage. 'Well, most of us anyway.'

'I only found out because Pixie happened to ring Bob while I was getting a drink one night and the man's a bit chatty, so he ended up telling me.' He looked shamefaced. 'Bob said she wanted to surprise people and asked me not to say a word.' Gage nodded at the boxes of mince pies he was carrying. 'I'll take these into the kitchen while you chat a bit more.'

After he'd disappeared, Pixie beamed at Tamara. 'You look amazing. Love suits you. And Gage seems a different man. That's your doing.'

262

A flush crept up her neck. 'We're both different. In the best sort of way. He's a lot more relaxed and able to socialise far easier with people. He's settled. Content.'

'No wedding bells yet?'

She shook her head firmly. 'We're fine as we are.' She'd only shared her plan with one other person and needed to keep it that way a little longer. 'I must get on. There's lots to do and people will start arriving soon.'

The next hour was a whirlwind of activity, but somehow by noon everything was in place. The first diners started to trickle in and soon every seat was taken. Christmas music played quietly in the background and the hum of lively conversations filled the pub.

Monica popped her head around the kitchen door. 'We're ready when you are.'

Tamara had been designated to give this year's welcoming words. 'Happy Christmas, everyone. It's wonderful to see you all here and I know we have a feast ready for us. I'll follow Quinten's example from last year and quote Charles Dickens from *A Christmas Carol*, "God bless us every one."'

There was good-natured jostling as people queued for the buffet and soon everyone was tucking in. Gage had saved her a seat, so she squeezed in by him.

'What's up? You aren't eating.'

Tamara put on a smile, and picked up her knife and fork. 'Just catching my breath, that's all.' She stabbed a bite of turkey and popped it in her mouth. 'Mmm, it's lovely and moist.' It took some determination but she ploughed through the whole lot, all the way down to the last sprout. 'I'm off to help with the desserts.' She put a hand on Gage's shoulder before he could stand up to join her. 'You stay there. You've done enough and there are plenty of people in the kitchen already.'

The only person she'd confided in was Monica, because she couldn't sneak the extra-special dessert she had made past her eagle eyes. Tamara retrieved it from the fridge now and set it on the counter to add the last decorative touches.

263

Rocky, Laura and Karen stopped what they were doing to give her curious looks, but she ignored them and picked up the platter with its gorgeous vintage Royal Worcester 'Village Christmas' design, another of her Etsy bargains, and pushed out through the swing door. Tamara set the platter carefully down on the end of the bar and tapped a knife on a glass to get everyone's attention.

'I hope no one will mind if I hijack things for just a few minutes.' She beckoned Gage over. 'Will you come and join me?'

His reluctance was obvious, but he did as she asked.

'Everyone knows we're business partners, and the other kind too as well.' Her cheeks heated. 'This is my way of asking you to take it a step further. I created this Mistletoe Promise dessert specially for us. You'll see there are two different sides. Mine is a cinnamon-spiced vanilla cheesecake with a sweet biscuit base, topped with glazed cranberries and pistachios. Your side has a tortilla-chip base and a savoury cheesecake filling made with grated Gruyere, green chillis and green onions, garnished with chopped red and green peppers. But see how it comes together in the middle — just like we have. Even the sprigs of imitation mistletoe in the centre are a combination of sweet green fondant and fresh parsley.' She giggled. 'I wouldn't actually recommend eating those.'

'What are you asking?' Gage said huskily.

'I know I told you once that I didn't want to get married again and you've never really said one way or the other . . . Sorry, I'm rambling.' *Here goes.* 'Life's too short not to seize every moment and every bit of love we're offered — so marry me, Gage, because you're all I want, for always.'

The stunned expression washing across his face wasn't how she'd imagined this might go. Agonisingly slowly, it was replaced by a smile. A glorious, heart-stopping smile she couldn't resist and never wanted to. Tamara's heart thumped, her breath came in short puffs and she thought she might faint if he didn't answer soon.

264

'You've got more courage than me because I've been carrying this around for weeks, waiting for the right moment.' Gage pulled a small red box from his pocket. 'I even had a word with Toby and he's on board.' He nodded towards her son, standing at the back of the room.

Toby smiled broadly and gave a big thumbs-up.

'I told him my plan too!' Tamara couldn't believe her son managed to keep both of their secrets. 'So, is that a yes?' she said playfully.

'Of course it is.' Finally he kissed her, and the pub erupted in celebration. 'I'm thinking of a honeymoon in Oz maybe?'

Emotion gripped her throat and for a moment all she could do was nod. 'Haven't you forgotten something?' She waggled her left hand in the air.

Gage turned the vivid scarlet of someone who'd fallen asleep sunbathing and was paying the price.

'If you don't like it, we can get something different.' He flipped open the lid. 'It's a pink diamond.' Another blush. 'A bit of a nod to your pig fetish.'

It was as if the deep-pink, square-cut diamond in a simple platinum band winked at her. 'OMG, it's perfect.' Tamara beamed. 'Like you.'

'I hope you never find out how untrue that is,' Gage joked and slipped it on her finger.

They were swamped with people all rushing to congratulate them and over the crowd she caught sight of Pixie's satisfied smile.

'Happy Christmas, Mr Bennet.' Tamara draped her arms around his neck and kissed him.

'Happy Christmas, soon-to-be Mrs Bennet.' Gage returned the kiss. 'I believe I need some of that Mistletoe Promise cheesecake. A slice from both sides.'

'Me too.'

THE END

265

THE CHOC LIT STORY

Established in 2009, Choc Lit is an independent, award-winning publisher dedicated to creating a delicious selection of quality women's fiction.

We have won 18 awards, including Publisher of the Year and the Romantic Novel of the Year, and have been shortlisted for countless others. In 2023, we were shortlisted for Publisher of the Year by the Romantic Novelists' Association.

All our novels are selected by genuine readers. We are proud to publish talented first-time authors, as well as established writers whose books we love introducing to a new generation of readers.

In 2023, we became a Joffe Books company. Best known for publishing a wide range of commercial fiction, Joffe Books has its roots in women's fiction. Today it is one of the largest independent publishers in the UK.

We love to hear from you, so please email us about absolutely anything bookish at choc-lit@joffebooks.com.

If you want to receive free books every Friday and hear about all our new releases, join our mailing list here: www.joffebooks.com/freebooks.